# *Falling*
## *into*
# *Glory*

*Also by Robert Westall*

Gulf
The Kingdom by the Sea
A Walk on the Wild Side

*for younger readers*

The Christmas Cat
The Christmas Ghost
If Cats Could Fly...

# ROBERT WESTALL

# *Falling*
## *into*
# *Glory*

MAMMOTH

## Author's Note

Because I have had to use my old home
town, and my old school, as background for
this book, it is doubly important to stress
that all conversations, actions, thoughts and
hopes expressed in it are but the purest
fiction. Such stuff as dreams are made of . . .

For Alick Rowe and Michael Morpurgo.
One old dog to two more.

First published in Great Britain 1993
by Methuen Children's Books Ltd
Published 1995 by Mammoth
an imprint of Reed International Books Ltd
Michelin House, 81 Fulham Road, London SW3 6RB
and Auckland, Melbourne, Singapore and Toronto

ISBN 0 7497 1755 6

A CIP catalogue record for this title
is available from the British Library

Printed in Great Britain
BPC Paperbacks Ltd
A member of The British Printing Company Ltd

# Contents

**Part Four**

**Part Five**

# Part One

## 1: Playground Delights

I first saw Emma Harris when I was ten.

In the war.

Our junior school had just been flattened by a landmine. We rejoiced, for it had been a soot-black Victorian prison. With dark-brown classrooms, iron desks and windows too high up to look out of. The reek of ammonia in the urinal made your eyes water, so you could hardly see the struggles of the black-beetles drowning in the gutter, peed back by crowds of laughing boys, however they struggled to save themselves.

The hall floor put splinters in your bum whenever you were forced to sit on it. Which was often; with our hands on our heads, till our arms nearly dropped off. This was not a punishment; merely a way of keeping us tidied away when they couldn't think of anything else to do with us.

We didn't grieve for our school. Nor for the head and the senior mistress who'd been firewatching inside. She was a blonde beast with massive calves and hair coiled German-fashion each side of her head. She caned us for spelling mistakes, and we suspected her of being a German spy. He was a red-faced devil with Brylcreemed black hair and a brown pinstripe suit, who caned us for everything; talking, lateness, running in the corridor or torturing stray cats were all grist to his mill and his tireless right arm.

We deeply regretted the later news that they'd been dug out not merely alive, but unharmed and ready to carry on business as usual. Whereas the manager of the Rex Cinema next door, the nervously jovial patron of our Saturday morning cinema riot, had been killed outright. I thought darkly then that God did not know his business . . .

Typically, the cinema stayed closed till the end of the war. Whereas we were back in school the following Monday morning. Six classes, huddled together, in the hall of neighbouring Spring Gardens. Sitting in circles, with no desks to write on. Carrying all our worldly goods home every night, in little attaché cases borrowed from our mothers. My nana found me an old unspillable glass inkwell, with a deep inner glass lip, that would not drop ink no matter which way you held it up. It made me quite famous for a couple of days, until everyone had turned it upside down, shaken it like mad, and still not been able to spill a drop. The ink inside was a weird green, all my mother had been able to get. When you wrote with it, on the cheap paper, the word sent out thin roots and branches across the paper's rough surface, until your word looked like a fuzzy little bush, and was quite unreadable. This distressed me deeply, for I was a neat child at heart.

Spring Gardens was a posher school than ours had been. Trees in the playground; and the windows came down nearly to the ground. The kids came from the private estate. They watched us curiously, through the windows of the hall, as if we were wild animals in a zoo. But there were advantages. They were not caned, and

8

now, being so public, we were no longer caned either.

In those days, at the start of school, and at playtime, a teacher would emerge and blow a whistle. You were supposed to freeze instantly. In the bad old days, our head had frequently walked among us, clouting or twisting the ears of those who hadn't frozen quickly enough, or who wobbled where they stood. But now we were brought in by the Spring Gardens teachers, who simply blew their whistle a second time, to make us run into neat little rows, two deep; to be ordered to march in with a curt flick of the wrist.

Two Spring Gardens teachers did playground duty alternately. One was a veteran of World War I, who always drilled us while standing himself in army fashion, legs braced apart, chest thrust out, hands clasped behind his back. He had white hair and was incredibly thin. Whenever the breeze blew, the legs of his baggy trousers wrapped round his thin limbs like flags round a pair of slender flagpoles. I had a wild fantasy that he was purely a skeleton under his clothes as he had been gassed in World War I.

The other teacher who drilled us was Emma Harris. She was young. She stood exactly as her senior colleague stood; perhaps she copied him, thinking it the stance of authority. But the effect was altogether different. Her breasts stuck out magnificently and, when the wind blew, it pressed her light summer frock against shapely thighs.

I was utterly enthralled. I dashed frantically for the nearest end of our front rank, and exchanged sharp digs of elbows with any who disputed that point of vantage. I longed for stronger winds to blow . . .

And yet I was a sexual innocent. The previous year, a

friend returning from three years in London had explained the facts of life. I had dismissed them as his own personal fantasy, and a fantasy so revolting that I never spoke to him again, for fear such madness might be infectious. It also put me off London for many years.

I had not the remotest idea what breasts were *for*. I only knew I liked to look at them. I would have liked to stroke them, as I liked to stroke dogs and rabbits and the fat shiny worn leather of our settee at home. I was famous in the family for my stroking.

But, even beyond her breasts and thighs, Miss Harris was pleasing. She had spring and bounce. Her forehead was high and smooth and creamy; her cheeks would have put roses to shame. Her hair flowed back, deep red and silky, under a red bandeau. Her nose turned up, right at the end, her eyes were large, dark and sparkling, and her lips rounded and shapely. She looked about her with eagerness, as if she was waiting for the start of the Christmas pantomime.

Did she guess the effect she was having? I doubt it. And I never knew if she had the same effect on my classmates. I would rather have died than ask any of them. They would have mocked and torn me to pieces, if they'd known how I felt. I just wanted her to take our class for any lesson she wished. But she only ever marched us in.

But it was her breasts that fascinated me. I had never even seen a photograph of a naked female breast; though I hoarded photographs from *Picture Post* of Windmill girls, whose feathery fans showed the merest edges of breasts. These I kept stuffed into one of my father's round tobacco tins, shoved down the darkest cranny of our flooded and disused air-raid shelter,

10

where my mother would never find them. How, if I was so innocent, did I know my mother would disapprove? Because, if she got to the photographs first, they'd be torn out and crumpled up and thrown on the fire, with a wary glance in my direction. Of such actions are forbidden fruits made . . .

Eventually I passed the eleven-plus exams for grammar school, and was kitted up with a grand new yellow-striped uniform, and passed into a new world of oak panelling, where teachers wore long swirling black gowns, and there was a huge library, nearly as big as the public library in town. And, up to my eyebrows in the problems of being clever and too fat to play games, I forgot Miss Harris, I thought for ever.

## 2: Falling into Glory

What tricks nature plays on us, through our bodies. I was a weedy child, tallish but not at all nimble, and with no taste for rough games. My face was thought pleasant, in a chubby way; I smiled a lot, and charmed most people.

And then war broke out. My mother, who had gone very hungry during the U-boat campaign of World War I, and who frequently remembered queuing all day for a piece of suet, and being turned away empty-handed, became terrified that I, her only chick, would be starved to death by Hitler. By hook or by crook, by charm at the butcher's and friends at the grocer's, and often by going hungry herself, she fed me up like a prize pig. And I, biddable and greedy child, ate all she gave me, and grew truly enormous. The first words I heard, when entering the oak-lined heaven of my grammar school were: 'God, look at that fat slug.'

It was a very trying time. Our form captain, between lessons, addressed the form on what marital efforts my father must have put in, to procreate an elephant as enormous as me. I attended those sessions in the school hall, near-naked, in which extra-tall boys, and extra-fat ones, were solemnly weighed and measured before being given extra clothing coupons; that our bulk might be decently covered, in spite of clothes rationing. Crowds gathered to watch. Remarks were passed, just below the teachers' level of hearing (or so the teachers pretended, though they often sniggered themselves) which have left scars to this day.

I might have become the form butt and buffoon, except I was the cleverest. And took great and ruthless care to remain so. No one got help with their work from me. And it was sweet revenge to see their crestfallen faces, when they got bad marks or came bottom.

But it was not enough for me. I had the fat boy's pathetic desire to be good at soccer. I was always first on to the field, and last to be picked for a team. I had no nimbleness, no eye for a ball that might have saved me. My over-eagerness just made me more clumsy. I missed open goals at one-yard range. An endless source of hilarity, and yet I kept on. My quick mind could see what needed doing; my lumbering body simply could not do it.

Oh, what rage and hate will pack into a fat frame! Most of all, hate for those little quick clever boys, who could almost make the ball stick to their feet, make it sit up and beg. One of them kept the ball away from my cumbrous dashes for five whole minutes, like a bullfighter goading a bull, while the rest of the class, and even the teacher, fell about in helpless laughter.

And there was unpleasantness in the changing-rooms afterwards. It was alleged that *I* had breasts like a woman. Most of them just played it for laughs, but there were nastier boys who would drive me into a corner and ask for a 'quick feel'.

This went on for five years and then, when I was about sixteen, a quiet miracle happened. All my fat

13

secretly turned into heavy bone and heavier muscle. I did not notice it myself at first, so conditioned was I to being called 'Fatty'. But we built a rockery at our Scout hut, and somebody noticed that I could lift stones nobody else could lift, not even the Scoutmaster. We went on long hikes, and I came striding home when the rest could hardly walk.

Then came the day, in the changing-room in the lower sixth, when a cheeky third-year dared to call me 'Fatty' in front of his mates.

Something snapped. I reached out and picked him up by the shoulders and just held him there, kicking and dangling. Glaring into his face at a distance of six inches. I wanted to tear him in half, and he knew I could do it. Then inspiration dawned, and I just hung him by the collar from the highest coat peg and left him yelling.

The story was round the school in half an hour, and no junior ever called me 'Fatty' again. Just 'Akker' because my name was Atkinson.

The day of 'Fatty' had gone. It gave me the courage to admit I'd never be any good at soccer.

But there was another game some played. Rugger. One lunchtime, I went out to inspect the first fifteen practising. There seemed little room in it for clever footwork. But there was a lot of pushing and shoving, and throwing people to the ground, or heading for the line with three other people clinging to your back. Brute strength seemed all; and size. When small clever boys got the ball, they were often flattened and got up winded.

This was the game for me.

I volunteered and fell into glory. It was the spring

term, and the ground was soft and muddy, so I lost all fear of falling. I still had a poor eye for the ball, so I aimed for the man with the ball instead. I threw people around with wild abandon. The other players grew a little afraid, which made them make mistakes. I came off plastered with mud from head to foot, immensely pleased with myself. The master in charge, Bill Fosdyke, said I might make a front-row forward, when I calmed down a bit.

I learned the basics of rugby. That there are packs of forwards, who wrestle and hack in the mud, trying to win the ball off each other. And when they do, it goes to a little bloke called a scrum half, whose job it is to pass it to a line of backs, who run with the ball, passing it from one to the other. And at the very back, is a fullback, who has the unfortunate task of clearing up other people's mistakes.

I cheerfully slugged it out with the packs; but my main speciality became the quick clever opposing backs. They have to keep their eye on the ball while they're passing it, and it is very difficult to keep your eye on the ball when twelve stone of bone and muscle is bearing down on you, with the sole purpose of crashing your face in the mud. With an awful expression on its face . . . for I have to admit that by that time, I had also become as ugly as sin. My face had turned into slabs of bone and muscle too. I frightened myself when I looked in the mirror. And if I was becoming a hard man, I would *look* like a hard man. Smiles were out, scowls were in. A hairy ape who smiles is a pitiable character. I became Caliban, full of hate, and God help the Ariels of the three-quarter line if I caught them . . .

15

In three weeks of practice, I demoralised the first fifteen backs, so they were dropping the ball all over the place.

So Bill Fosdyke, somewhat disgruntled (for he was an old back himself, a handling man), said I might as well demoralise the backs of other schools, and put me on the first fifteen. He did it with ill grace, saying I *might* be useful. Rather, I suppose, as hyenas are useful in cleansing the earth.

Ours wasn't a very *good* first fifteen. It usually lost most of its matches. Now, it wasn't so much that it began to win, as the other sides began to lose. I created shambles in which we scored mean, scruffy, scrambled tries. While dear Bill Fosdyke stood on the touchline with the opposing masters, apologising for the way I was ruining a decent handling game . . . a gentleman's game.

But I could swagger now. I was on a school team, however crummy. I was one of the boys.

## 3: Miss Harris Again

It was then I began to notice, in bus queues and on buses, that I was having a strange effect on women. Most just looked at me and looked away again quickly; some might have shuddered. As if I *was* the original hairy ape. But some, and those among the prettiest, I would catch staring at me again and again. They would look away if I caught their eye; but when I shot them another surreptitious glance, they would be staring at me again. As if transfixed. As if I was causing some inner tremor in them, which they could not tear themselves away from.

Of course, lost in my deep shyness of women, which I still had, I would have died rather than do anything about it. Still, it puzzled me, this mixture of fascination and repulsion. Until, in A-level English, I had to do an essay comparing the uses of landscape in the books by Emily and Charlotte Brontë. So I read *Jane Eyre* and *Wuthering Heights*. And discovered the ugly hero: Rochester and Heathcliff. I much admired Rochester; but Heathcliff was the man for me. He had power, magic power, and he never cared what the pretty privileged people thought about him.

It was now that Miss Harris joined the staff of the

grammar school. I would hardly have recognised her.

We never thought of our female staff as women at all. Mostly they were elderly, all over forty. Their hair was piled up on top of their heads by the use of a multitude of hairpins, rather as our grandmothers' was. Disclosing scrawny necks. On their feet, they wore sensible black flat-heeled shoes. Between, they were enveloped in academic gowns, which gave them the general bulk and outline of penguins. Their skirts were shapeless, colourless and long; their ivory blouses so laden with frills and furbelows that no hint of bosom was visible; the effect was more of an ancient snow slope about to collapse into an avalanche. Most wore spectacles, over mottled cheeks. True, there were observable variations. Miss Summers was very tall and thin; her friend Miss Rawcastle who lived with her, was very short and stout . . .

That's not to say they weren't good earnest teachers, and most of them kindly, and a few might laugh at a joke, once in a blue moon. But the overall impression was that they were dusty; rather like museum exhibits. We never thought of them as women; we seldom even thought of them as people who had lives of their own.

It showed in the matter of nicknames. The masters all had nicknames. Conk Shaw, Slasher Liddell, Puggy Winterbottom. And all the wonderful legends that grew round them. The giant Conk Shaw, appearing at the head's door with a naughty boy tucked wriggling under each arm . . . We mimicked them, told over and over again the old stories about them, rejoiced in their oddity.

But no woman had a nickname. Just 'Ma'. Ma Freeman, Ma Antrobus, Ma Summers. All spinsters, and yet, in their way, quite motherly.

Of course, there were exceptions. The glamorous Mrs Brown and Mrs White, wartime emergency teachers in their bright-coloured suits, high heels, nylon stockings with seams up the back. Their glamour gave them a quite unearned popularity. But with the coming of peace, Mr Brown and Mr White returned from active service and reclaimed their beauties back to domestic bliss, narking us lads very much.

The other exception to the general dustiness was the deputy headmistress, Katherine Merry, MA Cantab. Six feet tall, with snow-white hair piled up high and the coldest blue eyes I had ever seen, she sailed like a galleon through the dull herring-fleet of her sisters. Her diction was precise; her voice very quiet. You had to strain to hear her, and in her lessons you could hear a pin drop. She never threatened, and never punished. But to risk offending her was unthinkable; for beyond lay a landscape of pure ice, a North Pole none of us would dare to enter. In her Latin class, in the second year, I had lucky breaks in the summer exam and scored an unheard-of nincty-two per cent. She did not praise me or smile at me. (She never smiled.) Instead, she took my mark as the norm, and for half an hour she froze the rest of the class for falling below it. My normality exposed their utter worthlessness. It made me very popular with the rest, I can tell you.

This was the female staff Miss Harris joined. Dressed like all the others. Of course, you could tell she was younger. But is a young penguin more sexy than an elderly penguin? Except to another penguin, of course . . . But it was more than that. Some light had gone out inside her; the spring was gone from her step;

she no longer looked round the world expectantly, waiting for the pantomime to begin.

Besides, I knew all about breasts and thighs and bottoms by this time. I dwelt among an abundant supply of them. Whereas the practices of our all-conquering rugger team were lucky to draw three spectators, and one of them a black labrador that kept on joining in the game, the girls' netball practice was attended by nearly every lad in the school. They could nearly have charged admission . . .

And yet we sixth-formers paid some tribute to the remains of Ma Harris's youth and beauty. The girls somehow discovered she was called 'Emma' and 'Emma' she became to us all. In private, in secrecy.

And the rumour started that she was trying to catch Fred Wrigley, head of history, in a last desperate attempt to land a husband before she withered like all the rest.

The girls, when challenged, could produce no evidence, except that she was in Fred's history department, and was sometimes seen talking to him round school. But what we lacked in facts, we made up in fantasy.

Myself, I thought she would have to be desperate indeed to want Fred Wrigley. A bachelor and a bore. He had been both before the war; then had joined up and somehow made the rank of captain.

He had gained a sort of glamour by winning the MC at El Alamein. But rumour had it that Fred had been wandering around no man's land, having carelessly mislaid all his men in the smoke of war. Hearing a stray shell coming, he had dived into the nearest trench. Which happened to be full of about five hundred

Italians, desperate to find someone to surrender to. Fred had been able to lead the Italians back to the British lines because the Italians knew the way . . .

His A-level history lessons were known as the Twilight Hour. He was said not to notice if you were asleep or even doing other teachers' homework, and that he cared even less.

On the other hand, he seemed to have a deep-seated unease about being unpopular. Which drove him to confide in sixth-formers in the saloon bar of the Gibraltar Rock on Friday, Saturday and Sunday nights, when, in his patched sports coat and beer-stained cavalry-twill trousers, he was invariably found to be propping up the bar. It was a sad mistake. For one thing, the sixth-formers shouldn't have been there. And for a second, his confidences were nearly as boring as his history lessons, being mainly concerned with the awfulness of women, the horror of matrimony, the niggardliness of teachers' pay, and his hopes of landing a job at university.

Alone of the male staff he had no nickname. He was an old joke; but he survived as an old joke because sixth-formers quite like old jokes, when there are no new jokes to laugh at. And the fictional pursuit of him by Ma Harris occupied us for many happy hours. Sometimes we had her frontally assaulting his two-room flat in Linskill Terrace, scaling the ivy in the middle of the night. And Fred surrendering to her, like his Italians had once surrendered to him, and lying back on the bed not knowing what to do and just saying, 'Carry on, Emma.'

At other times, we had her ambushing him as he was carrying his washing home to his mother in two

Woolworths' carrier bags (a common sight on Sunday afternoons). It was admitted that Ma Harris was more of a man than Fred would ever be, and some even said she had more hairs on her chest . . .

Anyway, in a brief spurt of energy and initiative (and probably meant to feature in his latest hopeless application for a university lecturer's post) Fred organised a three-day trip for the history sets, to the Roman Wall; in the Easter holiday of my lower-sixth year.

It says much about the quality of his teaching that even in that early Easter holiday, when the public tennis courts were not yet open, the weather cold and wet, and most of the sixth bored out of their minds, half of them refused to go.

So he had to throw the course open to the rest of the sixth, and I signed up. I went because I like walking, and some of the history girls were very pretty, and in the pub in the evenings there might be a chance to get to know them better. Or they might fall off the Wall and give us a glimpse of their knickers.

The course was at the Once Brewed youth hostel, at the very end of the holiday. And what a miserable holiday it was. Cold belting rain on Good Friday is bad enough; but sleet on Easter Monday? And all the other days . . . nothing to do but reread old books I'd loved in the second year, while my mother fell over my outstretched legs and nagged me. I even fell out with our dog. A desert. But that's how life is in the sixth; a riot followed by a desert. So full one minute of matches, girls, laughs, homework and yard-football. Then, suddenly, nothing, and you begin to wonder whether, if you don't get away from home soon, nothing will ever happen again; and the very air of your bedroom chokes you because, unlike the bed, it hasn't been changed for months.

In the end, on Easter Tuesday morning, I was driven through the rain to the public library to change my books. Having scrounged two of my mam's tickets as well.

I was just having my books stamped when a thought hit me. I said to the librarian, 'You haven't got a little book on the Roman Wall?'

That librarian was a real character. We called him Tommy Trodden though his real name was Smurthwaite. He was called Tommy Trodden because he was supposed to have a huge wife at home whom he was utterly terrified of though no one had ever seen her. So, people said that if he couldn't be boss in his own house, he made sure he was boss of his own library. He only hired girls as assistants; very pretty girls. But since he was only five feet four himself, they also had to be very *small* girls. People said he had the finest collection of miniature beauties in the whole of England.

But he took it no further. His only bad habit was gambling on the horses. Every hour, on the dot, you'd see him trotting along Prudhoe Street to place his bet at the newsagent's that was a cover for an illegal bookie. People said he made a small but steady profit, and that got him a lot of respect.

His only other vice was that he loved books too much to lend them out to the public. His office was lined from floor to ceiling with great luscious new books the mere public never saw. He was a dapper little bloke, with a red waistcoat over a comfy little paunch, and a beard like the late King George the Fifth.

'A *little* book on the Roman Wall,' he said with fierce contempt. 'You might as well ask for a *little* book on the history of the world.'

Under his fierce blue-eyed gaze I shuffled and mumbled. Then he led me, humiliatingly, to the children's section, and passed me down a very small book, with a bad painting of a woman in hiking clothes, carrying an easel and paints, on the cover.

'I think this will fit your requirements!'

I gave it five minutes; I didn't even bother to sit down. It was sentimental rubbish, full of encounters with handsome young shepherds and bunny rabbits, and Deep Thoughts about Antiquity. I took it back to him and banged it down on the counter in a rage.

'Haven't you got anything better?'

'Oh, yes,' he said with a slightly malicious grin, not batting an eyelid. 'Dr R.G. Collingwood Bruce. Three volumes.'

'I'll have them.'

He went into his holy of holies, and came staggering back with three volumes about as big as tombstones, bound in red leather with gold titles that glittered richly. He watched my face, but this time it was me that didn't bat an eyelid.

'I'll put you in the reference library.'

I'd never been in there before; I didn't even know it existed. I liked the highly polished floor, the huge oak tables with leather tops. It felt like an empty church. It *was* empty, barring one old bloke who had covered his table with tattered documents and was combing his straggly beard with his fingers and muttering to himself in a thoughtful, learned way.

I felt I was among scholars. It was a solemn moment.

24

Then I opened the Collingwood Bruce and, just as with the rugger, fell into glory. It was like finding a new home you never knew you had; that had been waiting for you all these years. The ancient cross-hatched maps; the precise, detailed steel engravings of weapons and mile-castles. And, as I devoured the masses of print, a sense of a whole great way of life lying hidden underground, under our feet, under the modern roads and factories. The wonder was, it was all *still there*; and I was going to look for it.

He had to throw me out, at half-past five; I stared at him, dazed with the effort of coming back to the twentieth century. I got to my feet and almost fell down with stiffness, cold and hunger.

He seemed to approve of me, for the first time.

'You'll want these tomorrow, then? I'll put them on one side for you. What's your name?' And he wrote my name on a torn piece of paper and slipped it into the first volume; and it seemed like a blessing. More than that. A baptism, as in church. I was a scholar. Just like my old friend with the straggling grey beard.

My mother nagged me something cruel for not coming home for lunch. She said she'd had me dead under a bus. She showed me my egg and chips, glazed and fossilised to the browned plate with the heat of the oven. I was so hungry I levered them off with a knife and ate them anyway. But when I told her what I'd been doing, an awe seemed to fall on her too.

'Your grandfather was a great one for his books,' she said. 'I wish he'd lived. You two would have had such talks.' And that was the greatest praise of which she was capable.

For the next week, from opening to closing time, I

lived with those books. I even crossed the road to avoid schoolfriends I met while going through town. How would I know what to say to them, when my mind was full of vexillae and cohorts, cist burials and urn burials? When all they would want to talk about was how Newcastle United had done against Manchester City? Besides, it would be a waste of fifteen precious minutes, when I might have learnt something of the military tactics of the Emperor Hadrian . . .

I became a willing pariah, a furtive secret man. Months later, I would look back and shake my head in amazement, and wonder what had possessed me. I'd never liked history much. Packed it in after O-level, fed up with the Corn Laws and the Speenhamland System. I suppose it was because I had found the Wall for myself.

# 4: The Wall

Anyway, I went to Once Brewed stuffed to the gills with facts, with what to me was Holy Writ.

And on that first evening, after we'd had supper and made up our bunks, old Fred got us together for a lecture on the Roman Wall. And of course, being old Fred, he'd done most of his preparation in the saloon bar of the Gibraltar Rock.

There is an earlier defensive earthwork, that runs behind the Wall. Consisting of an earth wall, called the 'fosse' and a ditch called the 'vallum' which he pronounced 'wall-um' in his old fashioned way. And Fred began getting it wrong, and calling the earth wall the 'wall-um' . . .

'The *ditch* is the vallum,' I hissed to Jack Dowson. 'The wall's the *fosse*.' I was outraged. But the outrage made my whisper loud, and I never had a quiet voice anyway. I think everybody heard; they all looked across at me. And Ma Harris, who had come along for the trip and was sitting across the circle, gave an emphatic confirmatory nod.

Fred gave me a very dirty look. It seemed to unsettle him. I could see he wasn't in very good nick; he'd probably had a skinful the previous night.

He blundered on, getting half the things he said

wrong, and starting to lose their attention, and I just felt so *angry* that my lovely Wall was being so messed up.

But it might have passed off harmlessly, if he hadn't got 'Vindolanda' and 'Vindobala' mixed up. They were both big Roman forts, but Vindolanda is on the Wall itself and Vindobala is a base supply camp about four miles south. By now we were getting all kinds of sheer rubbish. And I just couldn't *bear* it.

'Vindolanda,' Fred would say.

'Vindobala,' I would mutter, in my great booming whisper.

The third time it happened, Fred, who was pale and sweating by this time, played the teachers' favourite trump card, normally capable of flattening anybody.

'Perhaps you would like to give this lecture, Atkinson,' he said with heavy sarcasm. 'You seem to know so much more about it than I do.'

I don't know what got into me. But before I knew it, I'd said, 'Yes,' decisively, and stepped out of the circle to the blackboard, and taken the pointer from his nerveless fingers.

I think he went and sat down; I think he was still thinking I'd make a total idiot of myself. But I didn't. With that pointer in my hand, I seemed to become a different person. I really socked it to them; using our slang expressions as well to get their shaky attention, and making little academic jokes; even saying, 'As Dr Collingwood Bruce has pointed out . . .'

I think it was Ma Harris who gave me the strength. Because I taught straight at her; hers was the only face I saw in the crowd. And her face was lit up, her huge eyes shining, her lips slightly parted, as I got point after point right, and she gravely nodded and nodded and nodded.

It was as if the Ma Harris of my childhood had come back; the girl who was waiting for something wonderful to happen, and I was actually making it happen for her. But at the same time, she was supporting, approving of me, as if she was my teacher and I her brightest pupil, doing her real credit.

And I got all their attention in the end; even Jack Dowson's. They laughed at my little jokes; they forgot I was just a fellow pupil.

Then finally I ran out of things to say.

And the realisation of what I'd done descended on me . . . I just stood, waiting, hoping, for a merciful death.

But in the silence, Ma Harris smiled, and put up her hand as high as her face, with one finger upraised. I think that's the way they ask questions at university.

'May I ask one question?'

'Fire away,' I said, with exhausted grandeur.

'I'm not quite clear on the different purposes of a mile-castle and a turret.'

I answered, and she thanked me gravely. Then somebody else asked a question . . .

At the end, Fred Wrigley got up and said to Ma Freeman, who was sitting next to him, 'I need a drink.'

I think he was just trying to get away from us; but it was a sad mistake. All the usual drinking lads from the Gibraltar Rock put on their waterproofs and followed him up to the Twice Brewed Inn.

I walked up with our mob, and they were all crowing, and saying I was brilliant, and how I'd shown old Fred where he got off, and what a wet he was. And I just felt all shaky and sick, and wasn't saying anything.

Anyway, we got our half-pints, mainly of cider and

shandy, and went and stood by the door. The room was so ill-lit and full of fag smoke that you could hardly see a thing. Except that Ma Harris was standing in the middle of a crowd of girls. You could tell she was popular; they were standing really close to her, and still yakking on telling her how marvellous my talk had been. And she was nodding and smiling. And she didn't look any older than they were, and yet she did. And I began to try to work out why. I mean her dark red hair was just as shiny as theirs, and her cheeks were just as pink and curvy . . . It was the little lines between the curves. A little thin thought line up her smooth brow; soft bruised lines below her eyes. Little hooky lines at the corners of her mouth, which came when she set her mouth determinedly. And then I looked back at the girls' faces, and by comparison with hers I didn't like them so much. She made them look too smooth, unfinished, pudding-ish; even though one or two were really pretty. Because there were no lines on their faces, you couldn't tell what kind of people they were, or what they'd do next. It made them dangerous; they might start giggling at you at any moment.

Perhaps she felt my eyes on her face. I know she turned and saw me, then made up her mind and came across to where I stood among the lads. And a little silence fell; you could tell every ear was flapping. But she knew every ear would be flapping, so she didn't say anything embarrassing, just, 'Congratulations,' which was OK. Then she asked me something else, about the Roman bridge foundations at Corbridge, which can only be seen in dry weather, when the river is low. And my lot faded away to seek fun elsewhere, having had as much of Rome as their tiny brains could take for one night. But we went on talking about Corbridge.

Then Fred Wrigley came across, with half a pint in each hand, and said to her, 'I've got you another one.' You could tell he was as jealous as hell.

But she said, 'I couldn't possibly drink another one. I'd be up half the night. Thanks, just the same.' That little frown mark came on her forehead. I could tell she was narked with him.

Then she asked me another question about the bridge, and after standing like a fool for five minutes, he just went away and I saw him drink both halves himself, in the end.

My soul sort of soared, and floated up next to the smoky ceiling. She had given old Fred the heave-ho for *me*.

Then the landlord called time and we all straggled back to the hostel. The wind was getting up, with rain on it, and in the dark she and I got separated from the rest and left behind. I thought perhaps she meant it to happen, and again my soul soared in drunken loops.

But when she broke the silence, what she said was ordinary enough.

'Why did you give up history?'

'The Black Fan,' I said. 'I couldn't get away fast enough.'

She sighed. The Black Fan was the deputy head, Gordon Fanshaw BA. The worst that I can say of him is that he never hit a boy, never laid a finger on one; and yet we were all insanely afraid of him.

He would say, 'Do you think I'm an idiot, boy?' and wait for an answer; and whatever you answered, he'd have another clever question waiting to trip you up. And the endless silences while he waited for you to answer, and you felt he was like a little black boiler with top steam pressure up, just waiting to explode. Though he never did. But it was always there, the mad black hate of boys in him.

So when I said, 'The Black Fan,' I meant it. I had partly chosen my A-level subjects so as never to have to suffer the Black Fan again.

Ma Harris sighed. 'That man,' she said, then checked herself. The old unbroken rule; teachers never discuss other teachers. Then she said, 'You didn't have to be in his group; you could have been in mine.'

'And suppose you left, and then we got *him*.'

'I'm not going anywhere,' she said, and her voice suddenly went low and depressed.

We had stopped and turned to face each other; we were that intense. Suddenly a gust of wind stronger than the rest hit us, and we moved closer in to the shelter of a wall.

'You're a born historian,' she said. 'You understand how things fit together. I've never heard anything like that talk you gave. Not from a seventeen-year-old. You never put a foot wrong.'

'Wasn't me. Good old Collingwood Bruce.'

'Can you imagine any other sixth-former doing it?'

I thought of them; and laughed. 'It's just me. I get *things*. Last year I was crazy about old ships and Old North Shields. In the war, it was the American Air Force. I get something into my head and I can think of nothing else. My parents say I've got a bee in my bonnet. And then I just lose interest, just like *that*.' I snapped my fingers together; perilously close to her nose.

'Yes, but can't you see – they're all *historical* things – bodies of knowledge. That's why I say you're an

32

historian.' In her urgency, she reached up and grabbed my arm.

I looked around the dark nervously. If anyone passed now, they would surely think we were lovers . . . but no one passed, on that windy night.

She noticed my nervous glance, but she did not let go.

'It's not too late to change your course. You've only missed two terms. With your brain you could catch up. I'm not fooling you. You've got a *gift*. I've heard lectures at Cambridge that were worse than yours. You can *excite* people. Don't bury your talent in the earth. You'll regret it for the rest of your life.'

Again I could hear in her voice that she'd done things she'd regret for the rest of her life.

'Look,' I said, 'I'm trying to catch up in Latin already. My Latin's a shambles. I can't do extra work in history as well. It'd kill me.'

She just went on holding my arm and looking up at me with those great big earnest eyes, though I could only see them as pools of darkness in the pale blur of her face. She *wanted* me; as nobody else had ever wanted me, not even my mam and dad. All right, it was innocent; she only wanted me in her history class. But wanting is wanting, isn't it?

I don't know what came over me. Maybe it was being alone in the dark. I'd never stood that close to a woman before, except my mother. And my cousin Gordon's pretty young wife, who, because she was safe in her marriage and fond of me, had teased me into kissing her at a New Year's Eve party. It had got a great family laugh; but I'd *liked* it. The smell of her perfume and hair, the warm softness of her shoulders . . .

Now I could smell Ma Harris's hair. I suddenly

wondered what she'd do if I kissed her. I mean, I could do it easily, before she knew what was coming. Before she could stop me, it would be done. And there'd be some kind of unforseeable explosion, because I would have broken all the rules. What kind of explosion? I hadn't the faintest idea. That was half the attraction . . .

Strange; at that moment she let go of my arm. Almost as if she'd sensed what I was thinking.

She said, in a dead, flat, voice, 'Oh well. I'm just being self-indulgent, I suppose. It'd be nice to teach somebody who really cares for once.'

'Your girls care.'

'They care about getting good marks; passing exams. They haven't got an original thought in their heads.'

She turned away, and we walked on. Suddenly everything was flat and dead.

As we reached the gate of the hostel I said, 'I'll let you go in first. Otherwise there'll be talk. You know what they're like.'

'*Really?*' She sounded quite shocked. Then she said, in a low voice, 'Thank you. For thinking about me.' And went in.

I stood for five minutes in the dark, thinking about that moment I'd nearly kissed her, and wondering what she would have done. I'd nearly done something silly and mean and ungrateful; then I hadn't. I should have been feeling virtuous; so why did I feel so flat and bored?

Only one more memory stands out from that trip. The day we made Ma Harris into a human sacrifice on top of the hill overlooking Vindobala. There's a stone pillar on top, about twelve feet high. A landmark. And we had

34

lunch up there, lying in the weak sunshine, eating sandwiches. It was the last day.

All that trip, Ma Harris had gone from strength to strength. Really mixed in with us, laughing and making jokes. Not in a sucking-up sort of way; just being a free person among free persons. And she'd told us a lot about what it was like at university. I mean, she didn't demean herself by acting like a kid; she sort of pulled us up into being fellow-undergraduates. The boys were liking her a lot, as well as the girls; whereas old Fred went off and ate his sandwiches on his own, and got darkly muttered about, as he still kept on ballsing things up.

She said now, idly, 'I wonder who put this pillar up. I wonder what it's for.'

And I said, 'I'll bet the Romans tied people to it, and made them into human sacrifices.'

'Rubbish,' she said, her eyes full of laughter. 'It's no older than the eighteenth century. You couldn't tie anybody to *that*.'

'Bet you we could,' I said.

'Go on, *show* me!' I think she expected us to do it to one of the girls. There had been a bit of cheerful wrestling and screaming with them, already. Over bags of crisps and things.

So she was pretty amazed when two of our lads grabbed her and hauled her to her feet. She was very dignified about it; didn't struggle or scream or anything, as the girls would have done. Just let herself be hoisted up on the plinth, and have her hands tied round the pillar behind her back. And then we all got out our cameras, while Jack Dowson posed with his arm upraised, as if to plunge his clasp knife between her magnificently prominent breasts, which really made her blouse buttons strain, in the approved Hollywood fashion.

When all the cameras had clicked, we quickly untied her, amid a lot of laughter; even the staff were laughing, all except Fred, who scowled like a fiend.

That was a pretty popular photo; a lot of people asked for prints.

I have mine still. It's so innocent I could cry.

# 5: At Nana's

'There's some spring cabbage for your nana,' said my
mother. 'Just nip down on your bike with it, there's a
good lad.'

I went blithely. I never went down to Nana's unless I
was sent with something. But I was sent often, and glad
to be sent. It made it right between us, that I'd been sent
with something; we both knew what we were about. If
I'd come off my own bat, there'd have been a question
hanging in the air between us, that would have made us
both uneasy. Why had I come? What did I want?

As it was, she opened the newspaper wrapping the
cabbage; said, as always, 'Very nice.' Shoved it on one
side and asked the inevitable question, 'D'you want a
mug of cocoa?'

And as always I said yes, and lay back in my dead
book-loving grandfather's chair, shut my eyes and drew
in the smell of her house. A smell I'd been smelling all
my life. Dust, slight damp, the smell of old carpets rolled
up tight and shoved in a cupboard to moulder for years.
Never thrown away, because one day they might come
in useful.

She never threw anything away. As a child I was
always coming across boxes, under beds, in sideboards,
full of the strangest things. Lumps of miniature steam

engines, made by my father when he was an apprentice. A knobkerrie that had belonged to a Zulu warrior. Photographs of my father, dressed as a Western outlaw, in a big stetson hat with a spotted neckerchief tied across his nose. Or of my mother as an Indian squaw in fringed buckskin with a solitary gaudy feather sticking upright from her usual neat bun. For months when I was little Nana fooled me that they really had met on the prairie, and that I was a child of the Old West. Photographs of my grandfather in full Highland dress, though I had long since established that he was no more Scots than I was, and had not marched south with Bonnie Prince Charlie . . . the whole house was like the British Museum run by the best liar in the world.

She plonked the cocoa on the bamboo table beside me. Full of condensed milk, three spoonfuls of sugar, it was nearly as thick as treacle. Lovely. All her cooking was forceful. Her rice pudding could have been sliced. When I was little, and hungry, she would forage from the larder a huge piece of cold Yorkshire pudding, leathery and gravy-soaked, that I would eat with my fingers, dripping gravy on my jumper. I approved of my mother's cooking, but eating at Nana's was as exciting as dining out in Cairo or Bombay.

She sat down, with a satisfied grunt, in the chair opposite, across the clippie rug she'd made herself. A small, very solid figure you could never have called fat. When I was a baby, ten and a half pounds in weight, my mother had been too weak from her confinement to carry me. Nana had carried me easily, till I was nearly three. Silver hair tight back in a bun, cheekbones worthy of a Russian countess, eyes small but far apart and the most amazing blue that leapt right across the room at you. Rosy cheeks, lightly veined.

She had . . . simplicity. What she thought, she said. Whether it was mischief that made her eyes sparkle, or a drat and damnation when one of her gas mantles collapsed in a sudden flare of yellow flame. She was as warm and simple to cuddle as a teddy bear. In her was utter safety.

I had long ago coaxed out of her a photograph of herself when she was just married, my age, seventeen. Before she had had her eight babies, and lost seven of them. Before she had become so ill, they thought she would die, and all they could do for her was carry out her couch into the back yard on sunny days. In that photograph she had the same fearless get-at-it look she had today. Life was something to be tackled, and no shilly-shallying.

Sometimes, alone, I would get out that photograph and stare at it, go back in time and ask her, 'Sarah, will you marry me?' And wonder what answer she would have given.

I had my doubts, because she sometimes said wistfully, 'Your granda was a bonnie lad, a very bonnie lad when he was young.' She said the same of my father; she never said it of me. Would she have married this ugly bugger, full of thoughts that terrified even himself? I glanced across at a tilting mirror on her sideboard, that showed me my own face, peering out of darkness. Looking, not handsome, never handsome. But mysterious. Her house was full of tilting mirrors, giving you your own face mysterious, out of darkness.

Certainly I would have married *her*; any man in his senses would; if she would have had him . . . But I was safe home and dry: her only beloved grandchild.

Now her eyes lit up with mischief.

'I expect your ears have been burning,' she said.

'Oh, aye?' I said, very offhand. She would have her pound of flesh out of me, before she told me who she'd been talking to. She was a proper torment.

'A lady,' she teased. Her face squeezed tight to hold in the laughter, which made her suddenly look about eight years old.

'I don't *know* any ladies.'

'You know this one well enough.'

'Me mam,' I said, with a sigh of mock-weariness.

'No, not your mam. Nor your Aunt Rosie.'

I surveyed her mantelpiece, with its red velvet pelmet with the bobbles, that I'd spent hours playing with as a child. The brass candlesticks, the Staffordshire figure of Nelson, much chipped, that had been my father's doll as a baby. As if I couldn't have cared less.

'Very impressed with you, she was. You've really clicked there.'

I was tickled pink with curiosity, though my face in the mirror didn't show it.

'Our Gordon's wife? Young Vera?' That would explain the warmth that was coming out of Nana.

'Noooooooooh,' she said, really loving it. 'Somebody at your school.'

'Oh God, *not* Connie Fisher?' Connie Fisher was an embarrassing fat girl who lived three doors down from us.

'No, not Connie Fisher, whoever she is when she's at home.'

Which was a blatant lie. Not only would she know Connie Fisher, she'd know Connie Fisher's mam, grandma, uncles and even the posh cousin who lived down Whitley Bay. She knew everybody in town. I looked at her, exasperated.

'I said a *lady*.' Absolutely busting to tell.

'Not Katie Merry.' I was into fantasy now, joking.

'No, not *Miss* Merry. Somebody young. Somebody very pretty. Somebody who thinks you're *wonderful*.'

'I give up,' I said. Did I have a wild crazy hope?

'Miss Harris,' she said.

'I don't believe it. How do you know *her*?'

'I don't. But I was at school with her mother. Her mother had her late. Miss Harris thinks you're a bobby-dazzler. The bee's knees. She says you could be a great scholar when you grow up. A *teacher*, even. A public speaker. Mebbe an MP!'

I glanced in the mirror, checking my cool cynical smile was in place.

'You look as smug as a cat with butter on its paws.' She piled fuel on my fire. 'Mrs Harris says she's never heard Miss Harris talk so much about anybody. Said you knew more about the Roman Wall than the top man himself.'

'That wouldn't be hard,' I said, and told her about Fred Wrigley. She sat, absorbing every word, storing it away. Then I sensed she wanted something more. She wanted something to tell her friend Mrs Harris in return. I said, after long careful thought, 'She is very pretty. And very popular with the kids. I think she's the best teacher they've got. But she looks so sad, sometimes. Like a bird in a cage.'

That satisfied her; her eyes misted over a little. She cried as easily as she laughed.

'You've got a feeling heart,' she said, 'a very feeling heart. Just like your granda, God rest his soul.'

Then she moved on to grumble about the smell of the guano works, which was always bad in the warm weather, when the wind was in the south-east.

I cycled home with my heart full of . . . what? Something precious, but also something safely dead. Something merely to take out and look at sometimes when times were rough; like a photograph, or a pressed wild flower. Nice. Not at all dangerous. Not after being passed through the teatime chat of two elderly sentimental ladies.

# 6: Friends

Very pleasant, summer term after exams. That lunchtime we gathered in our usual place, a windowsill at the back of the hall. The best vantage point. The amphitheatre of hall seats stretched away beneath us, right to the head's study door. We could see everybody who came and went. Katie Merry, her lips pursed tightly over an armful of reports; a kid skulking hangdog by the radiator, trying not to look as if he was waiting to be caned.

Through the window, we could watch the girls playing tennis. Pamela Travis, bending over the net to retrieve tennis balls, was wearing blue frilly knickers. Beyond, a milling mass of boys was playing cricket in two dozen tightly interlocking games and squabbling over whose ball it was. Beyond, the field ended at a big ugly asbestos garage and the disused pit heap of Preston Colliery.

We'd been made prefects that morning; belting down the amphitheatre steps two at a time, which was *de rigueur*; coming to a skidding stop by the head's massive hall table, having our hands warmly shaken and having the shining red and gold badges pinned to our lapels. One by one, to a very variable amount of clapping; which foretold the amount of trouble we'd have with the little swine next term. Robin Bulmer, for instance, swot and non-games-player, got a slow clap from a single pair of hands more insulting than silence. Jack Dowson, on the other hand, already captain of cricket, got a riot of clapping, as well as cheering and even a bit of whistling (which the head instantly silenced with a look).

I'd got something in between. More than Tony Apple, anyway.

'That Pamela Travis is not bad,' said Tony lasciviously, now.

'Tripe,' said Jack. 'Her backhand's bloody awful.'

Tony had gone too far again. And Jack had put him down. Jack didn't like sexy talk; none of the rest of us did, either. But Tony was always going too far. Flashy, we thought him, with his big conk and never a Brylcreemed hair out of place. His father was a businessman, and gave him far too much pocket money, so he always had the latest jazz records. A good winger for the rugger team; but when he wasn't playing rugger he sneaked away to play soccer for the YMCA team down the town; with the yobs. He tanned a bit too quickly and easily. When we were being nasty to him we called him Antonio, and alleged his father made his money from ice-cream. There were suspicions that he might lack guts when the chips were down, like the Italians in the war. We were a cruel lot, and he was the cruellest of us.

Whatever held us together, it was not love. Or trust. Or faithfulness. I think we rather hated each other.

I often wondered bitterly, on the way home in the evenings, just what did hold us together. We were nearly all on the Arts side, and held that scientists were not quite human. Science was a mere *trick*, like waggling your ears, or seals balancing on balls in a circus. You didn't have to have brains to be a scientist. If you told scientists jokes, they just said, 'Yewhat?' But Teddy was a scientist, and he was one of us. Two things gave him his place. One was that he couldn't spell for toffee, which confirmed all our prejudices. He had gone in for the Scripture essay prize, and began his essay: 'In the beginning was the Word – Holy Bibel.'

His other trick was giving people what he called 'horse bites'. That meant creeping up behind them and twisting their leg muscles in a way that gave them lasting and excruciating cramp, so they couldn't move for about twenty minutes, and then only with agony.

He had taken the part of a spear carrier in the school production of *Hamlet* just to give Apple, who was playing the Gloomy Dane, a horse bite right at the start of one of his long soliloquies. Which he had had to deliver motionless, even standing on one leg, instead of prancing about flashily, as he usually did. What was even better was that the head of English went mad at him afterwards, and, bound by schoolboy honour, he had not been able to say a word in his own defence. And so the English stage lost another Olivier . . .

What held us together was Jack Dowson. Everybody in our group wanted to be Jack's special friend, and he got a lot of fun playing one of us off against another. Just for laughs. Everything in his life was angled for laughs, and he never cared how much the laugh cost anybody else. He was totally ruthless.

Why did we want his friendship so? He wasn't very tall, and he was frail. He was, I suppose, even uglier than me, with a real disfigurement, a drooping eyelid, what they called a lazy eye. But on Jack, it had the glamour of a duelling scar. His was a fine-boned aristocratic ugliness.

He had a wonderful eye for a ball, and an amazing bodily cleverness. He once beat Apple at tennis, playing every shot between his own legs. For laughs. Fielding at cricket, he had once caught a swallow on the wing. At rugger, in spite of his frailty, he was fearless, and often injured. I could have killed the people who hurt him. On the other hand, when he did do something badly, he always faked a limp afterwards, to get sympathy.

He was a creature of legend. He was called in at the last moment, to play for the local rugby club on the wing, when their regular winger was injured. And scored a try, among the grown men. He could play 'Les Patineuses' on the piano; in his darker moods he would refuse to come out with us, instead lying on the couch for hours, with his eyes shut, listening to classical music. His dislike of girls was legendary. He had read all the works of P.G. Wodehouse so often he knew them off by heart. Above all, he was a wit, who could make remarks that would convulse a whole class.

Oh, how can you explain love? Endless snubbed, mocked, unrequited love? The kind that Watson felt for Sherlock Holmes? That is what Jack inspired.

As for Wilf Kimber: he wasn't as bright as the rest of us, but he was the best fighter in the school when he was younger, and was still called upon to deal with people who got a bit much. A sadly divided lad, and yet the teachers had just made him head boy, so they must have seen in him something we never had.

Why did we include Bunty Pickles, the giant redfaced Yorkshireman who wore pinstriped suits to go out to

46

the cinema in the evening, and smoked big cigars and had naïve bourgeois ideas that we endlessly mocked?

What makes the top group? The fact that others lingered round us, hoping to be noticed, even with mockery? Waiting to be summoned into the charmed circle? The circle had no charm, for those in it. Only insult and pain. How often, glowering and brooding home, I vowed never to speak to them again, to cut them out of my life, to find some decent friends who wouldn't let me down. But somehow I was always back with them in the morning. Somehow the decent blokes were a howling desert of boredom.

Thus we sat, on the second last morning of my last term of innocence, waiting for something interesting to turn up that was worth taking the mickey out of, and drearily discussing the prospects for next rugger season, when so many were leaving.

'Who we going to have for scrum half, now Graham's going?'

'Stevie Prentice.'

'The second-team fullback? You must be mad.'

'Look, he's a tough kid. If they come round the scrum wanting to flatten him, he'll just stand and wait for them, and flatten them instead. *Then* pass the ball out.'

'You're *mad*.'

'Just you wait and see. I've had a word with him . . . he'll do it.'

'Who are you, to have a word with him? Who made you captain?'

It was at this point that a lad called Shelley came up and said casually, 'They're running a trip to Clatterburn Hall in the summer holidays. A week. Sleeping on mattresses. Working in the woods. Lot of the girls are going.'

That last was enough to cause a rustle of excitement.

'Who's *they*?' asked Jack.

'Fred Wrigley and Emma Harris. And some others, but Fred is organising it.'

'God help us all.'

'Into the woods . . .'

'I can just see old Fred, swinging from branch to branch, with Emma under one arm, like Tarzan.'

'You mean Emma swinging from branch to branch, with Fred under one arm.'

'It'll be a laugh,' said Jack. And that was enough.

# 7: Stout Cortez

That week at Clatterburn Hall was a sort of heavenly gift. It went right; right from the start. Tony Apple announced he couldn't go, because his parents were taking him abroad on one of his father's 'business trips'. Teddy announced he wasn't chopping down anybody's sodden trees in anybody's sodden wood and sleeping on a sodden mattress for no pay. Bunty Wilson, after much pressure, confessed he had to go back to Yorkshire because his grannie was getting married again. We had a lot of fun mocking Bunty's sexy grannie; people reckoned her stage name was Diana Dors.

That left me and Jack and Wilf. And Wilf, as next year's head boy, had had several meetings with Lorna Thompson, next year's head girl, and it had bloomed into a romance, or at least they'd been seen together in the back row of the Carlton.

The way was open to spend a week with Jack alone, without any competition. I hardly gave Emma a thought. She was no more than a faded picture postcard in the back of my wallet.

My one problem was getting there. Clatterburn was forty miles away. Of course the staff were laying on a bus for us. But what an ignominious thing, to travel on the bus with everybody else, like a schoolkid. I wanted to make an *entrance*. Which meant going on my bike. I had this vision of the rest of them spilling out of the bus, wretchedly sorting out suitcases, and me swooping down on flying wheels . . .

But of course there were snags. The road to Clatterburn, near the Scottish border at Carter Bar, was across high and lonely moors. And my bike was not what it had been; and I was not the cyclist I had been when I could do seventy miles a day, even if it meant driving myself sick and hardly being able to walk for three days afterwards, my bum was so sore. These days, I never cycled further than Nana's. But I told myself one had to suffer to be famous; oiled my bike and had three missing spokes replaced, and went for a couple of short rides that left me totally knackered.

I hardly slept, the night before. Dreadful visions of getting a puncture, halfway across the moors. Or a busful of jeering mates overtaking me on a hill I was having to *walk* up. Or, worst of all, having to cravenly cadge a lift off them, because my legs had given out.

At five, I heard my parents stirring; Dad was on the six till two shift. I got up and dressed and announced I was going *now*. God, that caused a flap. Mam tried to thrust a cooked breakfast on to me; I couldn't eat a thing. I finally jammed down half a slice of toast to shut her up. Then I was out to my heavily laden bike and away like the clappers. I just had this mad urge to get there, before disaster struck. I pedalled so hard I kept on having to stop for a stitch in my side. Sleepless, hungry and already exhausted, I was an accident waiting to happen.

And then the sun rose at my back, unseen, and threw as a greeting gift before me my skimming blue shadow on the golden road; somehow a superhuman shadow, long and slim, hurling itself forwards towards Clatterburn. And encouraged by my superhuman companion, I dared to look about me, and it was a very beautiful August morning, with just a hint of frost in the air, and the sky blue from horizon to horizon. A morning so early it all belonged to me. Even the birds still seemed to be asleep. And I realised I had done ten miles, and only had three times as much to do, and my legs, my temperamental legs, weren't aching at all.

The kiss of my tyres on the dew-damp road; the friendly unceasing whirr of the gears; the open-cast coal workings, empty and solitary as the highest Himalayas, the bulldozers sleeping, quaintly Martian. Then a string of colliery villages, to be passed with speed and stealth, lest they waken and swallow me again into a world of smoke. Four colliers, going on the morning shift, black iron men on black iron bikes, their heads bowed to where the road was grey, their breath steaming like carthouses on a frosty morning.

A wrong turning, an anxious burst of speed, a moment's panic, then a blessed signpost, the first signpost that mentioned Clatterburn, a grimy rusty signpost near a grimy rusty garage in a grimy rusty little mining village, and on it the name that banished all the grime and rust. Then only the smell of young heather and running water, and the rush of the wind on the open moors. The road turning north-west, where the hills were clouds, and the clouds were the open sky, and over the hills and under the clouds lay Clatterburn.

The long hills, that were only friendly rivals now, greeted joyously, combatted fiercely and remembered with satisfaction. The merry little milestones with their jolly white wink, that now seemed to come with increasing frequency. The quiet pleasure of munching a chocolate biscuit in time with my pedalling.

Knowesgate Bridge, a vaguely preposterous triumphal arch of red brick and cast iron, an urban joke in faint but excusable bad taste, then, at last, my lady of the high moors, in purple silk and the grey gauze of mist, embroidered with the classical austerity of wall and stream and wire fence. Double telegraph poles leading up into the sky . . .

And then the last hill crest, and the shock of the earth's sudden surrender, the dawning realisation that the telegraph wires were leading down in front, all the way to Clatterburn.

The savage crash of gears, the mighty kick of the pedals across the summit, then faster, faster, faster, with the becalmed mist writhing and eddying in my slipstream.

The morning spell was drawing to a close; the sun gathering everyday warmth, smoke from cottage chimneys, the rattle of milking pails from a roadside farm, the spell nearly over in time and space and yet a vague feeling of expectancy, the vague feeling of the best yet to come. If I could finish my journey before the morning spell broke . . .

The last wink of a milestone; a signpost saying Clatterburn Hall, a dark tunnel through woods, and then the old front, glowing gently in the sun.

And someone waiting for me. She waved. She waved again, more emphatically. She stood alone at the open door of the Hall, shading her eyes against the low sun, and I skidded to a stop in front of her.

'Atkinson!' she said, her eyes wide with amazement.

'You were supposed to come for lunch! You've come for breakfast!'

How can I describe that moment? I was Columbus, returned with all the wonders of the Indies. I was stout Cortez, silent upon a peak in Darien. All the adventurers and explorers who ever lived. This was my New Found Land, and she was its queen. At that moment there was nowhere else in the world. And she didn't break the spell; she stood caught up in the same wonder.

That's what they never understand. They think us lascivious little devils, only wanting to grope and fumble in the dark. They don't realise love is about kings and queens and New Found Lands.

She showed me from sun-glowing room to sun-glowing room. This is the great hall, this is the ballroom where we shall dance, this is the great dining room. All the more fantastic for being totally empty of furniture.

And then she said, almost sadly, like a queen abdicating a throne, 'We'd better get you some breakfast. You won't mind eating with us staff?' We walked towards the kitchen sound of cutlery and the smell of bacon and eggs.

Why didn't I say, 'I don't want bacon and eggs. I want hunger and you'?

But the greedy animal in me suddenly realised it was terribly hungry, and said, 'Yes please!'

We walked into the kitchen full of teachers and strangers, and she said, full of excitement, 'Here's Atkinson. He's cycled all the way and got here for breakfast. Isn't he clever?'

And they all stared at me with less than approval, and Fred said to me, fork halfway to his mouth, 'You look like Mahatma Ghandi in those shorts. Bandy Ghandi.

They're not *decent*.'

And my whole marvellous kingdom collapsed into ruins, and I sat at their table, an unwelcome visitor with my eyes down on my plate all the time, and ate bacon and eggs that nearly choked me.

# 8: Pairing Off

What makes happiness? Miseries build up like storm clouds, but when you try to list happinesses, they seem so trivial.

By day we worked in the woods. Cutting down weakly thin trees that the grim grey woodsman pointed out to us. He was not impressed with us; he'd rather have had real workers so he could pay and slave-drive them.

The boys cut the trees down; we tried doing it the Boy Scout way, but it didn't impress him. Then other boys chopped the tops and branches off, to make poles. This was called 'snedding' and we had a running sexy joke about snedding, which the girls didn't find funny. The girls were only allowed to gather up the cut branches and feed them on the fire. They hung about and grumbled in groups, while we tried to impress them with our fearless manhood by such things as stripping to the waist, hurling big tree trunks around, hurling each other around. Some tried hurling the girls around, or tickling them under the chin with branches, or threatening to throw them on the fire. Nothing seemed to work. They just grumbled.

The girls made *their* move between finishing work and supper. We had settled down scruffily to playing pontoon on our mattresses, amidst a clutter of shandy bottles from the Hall shop, when gentle knocks came on our bedroom doors, and there were invitations to tea. Careful precise invitations to named people. They had obviously carved us up among themselves, after some discussion. First we jeered at the idea; then we hurried off to get washed and comb our hair flat with water; and then we presented ourselves. Telling each other we'd only come for the grub; supper was a long way off and we were hungry . . .

The girls had achieved minor miracles. Tablecloths had appeared, to spread on the bare boards. Teapots and cups had been scrounged from the kitchen; large cakes brought from home in tins.

And having quelled us with a display of manners, they insisted on becoming real people. Proper introductions were made, to girls we'd been yelling rudely at, across the yard, for years. Hands were taken and shaken. And, between our efforts to eat cake without making crumbs on the beds, we learnt that they had their jokes, their clowns, their leaders and heroines and undying friendships just like us. They were uncannily like us, and quite unlike the bleating flocks of sheep we'd bashed our way through heedlessly in the school corridors; and even less like the complaisant houris of our daydreams. To our own amazement, we found ourselves becoming friends.

People began to pair off in the most alarming fashion; girls had a way of cutting a bloke out of the pack. Suddenly, somebody's lifelong best mate belonged to some girl, and was going down to supper with her.

All but me and Jack. There was a girl after Jack, a leggy redhead called Leila Sampson, but she might as well have saved her breath to cool her porridge. Jack just spent his time talking to the whole room, making them laugh with his father's stories of fish-merchant skulduggery. She didn't get within a mile of him, clever swine that he was. And there was a girl who had her eye on me. Joyce Adamson. I was annoyed they'd allocated me to Joyce Adamson; she was a rank outsider, a laughing-stock. That showed how *I* ranked in the girls' listings.

Mind you, considered with a cool eye, Joyce Adamson wasn't bad. She had nice long shining brown hair, and a straight nose, and large and beautiful blue eyes. But she was five feet ten, and well built. Not fat, just well built. We'd often, in our more hilarious discussions, considered her for the front row of the school rugger pack.

But, much worse, she was practically a deaf mute. She had never been known to say anything in class beyond 'Yes, Miss Freeman' or 'No, Miss Antrobus'. We knew she was no fool, because she always got high marks; but that was by taking copious notes every time the teachers opened their mouths, and learning them off by heart, at exam time.

She gave me several tentative smiles. I returned them with unfeeling stares, and got on with making jokes with Jack.

I consoled my bitter heart by remembering that Emma thought I was stout Cortez.

The best times were after dinner, when we gathered round the big wind-up gramophone in the ballroom, and listened to Danny Kaye. Emma had brought the records, and we played them till we nearly wore them out; till we knew them all by heart, and sang along with them,

57

mimicking every cockeyed note and pause for breath.

Emma would linger at the back, and enjoy our enjoyment. She was like a little sun, that week, radiating pleasure wherever she went. If she poked her head round a bedroom door, with some essential message, while we were having tea, she'd be asked straight in for a cup by the girls, and made the fun even more fast and furious.

Whereas we listened with shudders for Fred's brothel-creeper footsteps to squeak past the door. Fred was full of grumbles that week. Every evening after dinner, he passed on a succession of complaints from the woodsman, the cook, the secretary. He worked so hard making sure our lights were out by ten o'clock that we frequently prolonged our card-playing sessions till midnight, when we would much rather have been asleep. But it was rather a lark to watch old Fred snooping around the outside of the Hall, counting the lighted windows, and then hearing him come belting upstairs like an Olympic athlete, and burst into a room where all the lights had just magically gone out, and the air was filled with artistic snores, or Jack's querulous complaint, 'What's the *matter*, sir? You woke me up. Can't you sleep or something?'

Then the thumping furious footsteps would recede, and out would come the cards again . . .

How did I feel about Emma, in all that happy time? My feelings had gone oddly quiet again. She had become simply a splendid bonus, that was all. When she came into a room, I felt deliciously *safe*. The world was going my way, the light was brighter. And something quite marvellous was in the offing, just below the horizon of the world. Something quite unspecified . . .

## 9: Finest Hour

I must now come to my Finest Hour. It was the last night. I was in the kitchen, with five of the girls, finishing washing up supper and making them laugh. All the more attractive girls had paired up with their blokes and were playing some mad game of hide-and-seek, out there in the dark. We could hear their shrieks of excitement through the open window, from time to time. I intoned solemnly:

'There was a young lady of Hyde
Ate too many green apples and died.
The apples fermented
Inside the lamented
And made cider insider inside.'

It got a giggle. Even unattractive girls like to think about their insides fermenting, I suppose. I considered the other items of my dwindling repertoire of limericks. The one about the good old Bishop of Buckingham was definitely out.

At this point Wilf Kimber and Lorna Thompson burst into the room. Head boy and head girl. A long-established and near-celestial couple. But they didn't look celestial now. Wilf's face was a pale and sweating white. Lorna was practically carrying him. His left hand was clutched tight round his right elbow, and he winced with every step. Broken collar-bone, for sure. I'd seen that gesture on the rugby field.

'We were running,' gasped Lorna, nearly as pale. 'We fell down the cellar steps. I fell on top of him. I heard something go snap.'

'Sit him down,' I said. 'Get a blanket. He's in shock. Strong sweet tea — three sugars.' Funny how the old habits stayed with us from the war.

To show how good my idea of strong sweet tea was, Wilf immediately threw it up on the stone slabs of the floor.

'Get that cleared up,' I said. 'I'll fetch the teachers.'

I ran upstairs and hammered on Fred's door, Ma Freeman's door, Puggy Winterbottom's door, and finally Emma's door. No answer anywhere. Infuriated, I opened Emma's door but she wasn't there. Just a bra and two pairs of nylon stockings hanging on her radiator to dry.

I was dismissing my thoughts as not only unworthy but irrelevant in an emergency when Jack Dowson came up behind me, had a good look at her room himself (how I hated him for looking at her bra) then said, 'They've all gone down to the pub in Fred's car. I met them in the lane.'

'Hell,' I said. 'I'll phone the Clatterburn Arms.' I ran to the office, where the only phone was.

The door was locked. And all the Hall staff went home at night. I ran back to the kitchen. They'd cleared up the mess and got a blanket around him, but he was being sick again, and gasping in between, and it seemed to me he must have broken more than his collar bone.

'I'll ring from the call box,' I shouted.

'It's two miles away,' said Donny Main. 'You'll be *hours*.'

'I'll go on me bike,' I said and then, 'Oh hell, it's got no lights.'

'You can borrow mine,' said Donny Main helpfully. I never wondered till afterwards why he didn't volunteer to go himself.

'You'll have to watch the gears,' he called after me. 'They're a bit tricky.'

I found his bike in the bike shed. It couldn't have been less like mine. Donny was a cycling enthusiast. It was a racer and, as I lifted it out, it seemed to weigh about six ounces. And it had deeply dropped handlebars. And toe-clips. I felt dreadfully uneasy trapping my feet in toe-clips. But that was just the start of it, as I discovered when I set off. The saddle was about two inches wide, and far too high. The brakes were in all the wrong places, and the whole thing twisted and wobbled, as if it was made of thin wire. And the gears kept leaping from one gear to the next without warning. So that one moment you'd hardly be pedalling, and going at tremendous speed, and the next you'd be pedalling like mad and getting nowhere. And the front light was hardly worth having; it illuminated two yards of tarmac in front of you, and the odd passing blade of long grass. And the road got steeper and steeper . . .

I remember thinking that, but for the grace of God, there was going to be more than one broken collar-bone that night. I knew I was in imminent peril of destruction; I felt rather like a mouse in charge of a racing car. And yet, oddly, all these fears were far far away. It was as if they were happening to somebody else. I kept thinking what a hilarious story I could make up about it for the girls, when, or if, I got back safe. If I didn't crash and lie in the road and Fred, returning from the pub, didn't run straight over me in a drunken haze . . .

After an endless time of swerving, fending off looming trees with my feet, panicky applications of brakes that nearly threw me over the handlebars, the lighted phone kiosk appeared suddenly as an utter but pleasant surprise. I got off, glad to be still alive, and dived into the kiosk.

'Put your two pennies in,' said the girl operator.

I hadn't got any money on me at all. But my wails convinced her. She put me through to the Clatterburn Arms, while she rang off in search of the nearest doctor. I asked for Emma. She was a long time coming, and her voice was giggly. But she snapped out of it straight away.

When I got out of the phone box, my legs went all wobbly. I decided to walk back. I'd been heroic enough for one night.

Fred's old Hillman overtook me first. He stopped with a screech of brakes, wound down the window and said in a very bad-tempered voice, 'Has the doctor passed you yet?'

'No. Nobody's passed.'

'Good,' he said, and revved the engine. There was just time for Emma to call out from the back seat, 'Well done, Atkinson,' and they were off like a cat out of hell.

By the time I got back, a bloke with a little bag was just coming out of the main entrance, accompanied by Fred, who was making a great fuss of him.

'The moment I saw the state the lad was in,' Fred said, 'I knew I'd better ring you straight away.'

'Good job you did,' said the doctor.

The lying hound, I thought, pinching all the credit. After I'd wobbled all that way.

They'd put Wilf, on a camp-bed, in a big empty room off the dining hall. After that, they'd all pushed off without a word, except Emma.

'Sit down,' she said, pushing me towards another camp-bed piled with blankets. When I had sat down, she sort of sat at my feet on the floor, about two yards away. She arranged herself artistically, her legs under her and her camel-hair coat over them. She was wearing her hair loose, with the bright red bandeau. She looked very pretty, though pale. She looked, somehow, like the heroine in a good British movie. And her great eyes were on me, in what looked suspiciously like utter adoration. It made me shift uncomfortably on the camp-bed. I wasn't used then to being adored; except by our dog. But I felt squirmingly that I could get used to it: given time.

'You saved our bacon tonight,' she said, in a low thrilling voice. 'We were totally in the wrong. We should never have gone off and left you all alone, with nobody in charge. If it had come out . . . if he had *died*, we'd all have been sacked. And never taught again. I told Fred we shouldn't all go to the pub, but he said it didn't matter for an hour. And it was the last night. And you were all nearly grown up. What could possibly go wrong?' She took a deep shuddering breath. 'Well, now we know. And you stepped in to fill the breach, and saved us.'

I felt profoundly uneasy at this vision of myself.

'It was just common sense,' I said.

'But it was you who *had* the common sense. What

were the rest of them doing?'

I laughed and said, 'Flapping around like wet hens.' Then I added, 'They'd have got around to it, given time.'

'I think you're going to be rather a special person, Atkinson. When you grow up.' She seemed to be in a dream, somehow. Or seeing a vision. Some vision of me on a pedestal.

'Hey, I'm just old me,' I said. I didn't like the responsibility of being her vision.

'You're even modest with it. So modest . . .'

Oh God, what was this? I'd seen this kind of thing before, but only as hate. People who would always make out I was a bastard, no matter what I said or did. Conk Shaw who'd tried for a year to turn me into the class buffoon in second-year chemistry. I could cope with it, when it was hating. But this . . .

'I want you to do one more thing for us tonight. I want you to sleep down here and look after Wilf, if he wakes. You're the only one I'd trust with him.' She went off into a string of instructions, that I tried to memorise, woozy between weariness and adulation. I just kept saying, 'Yeah, yeah.' I was far more terrified of being left alone with Wilf than I had been on the bike ride. I can't stand ill or hurt people. But I had a dim feeling that once you were up on a pedestal, you had to stay up there, or something terrible would happen.

She got up at last; she held out her hand so I could haul her to her feet. She stood very close.

'Goodnight, Atkinson,' she said. And she went up on to her toes, and her lips brushed my cheek. Then, with a smart clack of heels, she left me. As the door closed behind her, I thought how nice and curvy her legs were, in their high heels and nylon stockings with very straight seams.

I spent a lousy night. They'd turned up the central heating in that room, because Wilf would be in shock. He woke me up calling three times, and complained he was too hot, or felt sick. Then he was sick again, and I had to wander down through the darkened spooky hall, to rummage in the kitchen for something to clean up the spew with. I wasn't any too fussy what I used, I can tell you. They're probably still wondering where their best dishcloth went to . . .

I was not a good nurse. Wilf moaned a lot, and I can't stand people who moan. When they carted him off to hospital the next morning, to put him in plaster, I was glad to see the back of him, and he was probably just as glad to see the back of me.

And then it was time to pack up and go home. I was just waiting with my bike and my saddlebag packed, to wave the bus away, when Emma came over to me and asked whether I was in a hurry, or did I have time for a cup of coffee before I went?

I had time. I was quite willing to plav Mr Wonderful; after the night I'd had with Wilf, I felt I deserved it.

She left me in her room, while she went to fetch the coffee. She hadn't packed yet, and I nosed around. Looking at her books, to see what she was reading. Fingering the pair of nylon stockings she'd left to dry on the radiator, and yes, all right, sniffing a used blouse, to get the nice smell of her. I'd never been alone in a woman's room before, except my mother's.

Then she came bustling back, and gave me the coffee, and asked me questions. First, about how the week had gone. Had it been a success?

'Yeah, great,' I said. 'Smashing. But I'm not sure how much value the Hall people got out of us, clearing up the woods. There was a lot of horsing about, because the girls were with us. We'd have worked much harder on our own.'

'Oh, Atkinson, you're a puritan. Don't you *like* girls?'

'They're all right in their place.'

'And what *is* their place?' This morning, the paleness of weariness and near-disgrace were gone. Her cheeks were full of colour, her eyes shone, smiles came easily.

I was outfaced. 'Hitler said, "*Küche, Kirce, Kinder*",' I managed. 'Kitchen, church, children.'

'But what does Atkinson say?' Her lips slightly parted in eagerness, showing the white tips of her upper teeth, she was delicious. She silenced me utterly.

'Haven't you got a girlfriend?' she asked. 'I thought all the boys had girlfriends, in the sixth.' But when I said no, she didn't seem too disappointed.

And that was the way it went on. Her asking questions, and me giving my opinions at length, which she seemed to enjoy. And then she got up with a sigh, and said she must get on with her packing. I thought it was rather a deep sigh; but then I don't like packing to go home either.

Nana plonked the cup of cocoa down on the bamboo table next to me, and settled in her own chair, so smug you could almost expect her to purr like a cat.

'What you been doin' to Miss Harris?'

'Nothing!' I said, but my heart leapt within me strangely.

'Her mother says she does nothing but talk about you. She's sick to death of hearing it. She talks about you like you were Lord Nelson and Winston Churchill all rolled into one.'

I squashed a lot of feelings hard, and shrugged and said, 'A mate of mine broke his collar-bone. I went to phone for the doctor, that was all.'

'Not according to Miss Harris. She said you were the finest young man she'd ever met.'

It would have been ungracious not to say, 'I admire her a lot as well. She's the best teacher they've got. And ever so interesting to talk to. She talks to you like you were grown up, not some kid.' Not that I'd seen her since Clatterburn.

Nana sighed. 'It's a shame. She's had a hard life. Blighted, like so many. All the fault of that dratted war.'

'Oh?' Anything about Emma was fascinating now.

'She was engaged to a lad in the RAF. Reggie Montgomery, he lived down Tynemouth. He went to your school. He was shot down over Germany, a bomber pilot. Her mother says she's never got over it. Never looked at another man, since 1944. They were very much in love. They were going to be married on his next leave. Her mother thought she was going to die of it. They'd been . . . very close.'

So much in those two words. Very close. Things moved and rustled in the dark of my mind. I said, 'She deserves to be married. It's a shame. If she'd been ten years younger, I'd have chased her myself. She's far more interesting than our girls.'

'It's strange you should say that,' said Nana, a wistful and romantic expression clouding her face, her eyes far away. 'She said the same about you, you know. If she'd been ten years younger . . . Time's a funny thing. Ten years is nowt to an old beggar like me. Seems less than ten minutes. You see bairns in their prams, and the next time you turn round, they're courting.'

'There's hope for Miss Harris yet,' I said. 'She's still very pretty, when she's lit up. There's Fred Wrigley.'

'Oh, Mrs Harris told me about *him*. He's been round their house, off and on. Not good enough for her. A proper old bachelor. When they get to that age, and they're still tied to their mother's apron strings, a lass can't make anything of them. Miss Harris told her mother she wouldn't marry him if he was the last man on earth. She says you're three times the man he is, already.'

She got up, and stirred the fire with the poker. 'Aye, well, there's no point in "might have been". What is, is. How's your Aunt Rosie? I hear your Uncle Gordon's been off work with his back again.'

## 10: Wilf

At the end of the summer holiday, I decided to call on Wilf. He wasn't a special mate, but I was bored. And, if you do somebody some good, you want to see how your investment's getting on.

I knew where he lived; over the off-licence in Suez Street; but I'd never been. I knew it was a mistake, the moment his mother opened the door. Headscarf and wrinkled grey stockings and carpet slippers. She looked nearly old enough to be his granny. I immediately began to feel very sorry for Wilf.

'Yes?' she said suspiciously. Beady black eyes.

'I've come to see how Wilf is.'

'What's it to you?'

'I'm the one who looked after him, the night he hurt himself.'

'The one that let him be sick and didn't even wipe him down properly.' There was a meanness about her that sucked gladness out of the air.

She led me upstairs; there was a funny smell.

'He's been in a lot of pain. They let him out of the hospital too soon. He'll not be right for the start of term, and now they've put all that worry on him, being head boy.'

I wished to hell I hadn't come. I hate poverty. Wilf's uniform at school should have warned me. He wore his blazers till the sleeves were halfway up his wrists.

He wasn't pleased to see me. He looked bloody desperate. He started to slip his arm out of its black silk sling, to shake hands.

'Don't do that,' said his mother. 'You'll hurt your arm again.'

He looked pale and thin; nothing like the bloke who won the hundred yards last sports day.

'Sit down now you've come.' His mother moved some washing out of a chair. Underwear, with holes in it. I sat down gingerly.

'How you doin'?'

'He's not at all well. It's a disgrace. That doctor was nearly an hour gettin' to him. He was in agony for an hour. Then, does he rush him into hospital like he should have done? No, he just patches him up to wait till morning. Can't be bothered. He should be struck off. If he's not well, how can he pass his exams? And if he doesn't pass his exams, how's he goin' to get a good job? Then what we going to live on? I've scrimped and saved to send him to that grammar school, then all they can do is break his poor little arm.'

The look on Wilf's face . . . but his mother was running on.

'I'm a widow, you know. If the whole truth were known, them toffs at the grammar school wouldn't be looking so smug. They've never set foot through this door, to find out how he is. Ashamed they are, at what they've done. Ashamed to face *me*!'

'What have they done?' I was bewildered.

'It's not what they've done, it's what they didn't do. When he had his accident, they were down the pub boozin', the lot of them. He might have broken his poor little neck and they wouldn't care. That stuck-up Mr Wrigley and that high-and-mighty Miss Harris. What they did was against the law. Everyone says so. I'm goin' to the council about it. Councillor Pitney lives just round the corner. He's on your school governors. He'll get me my rights.'

A wave of pure panic swept through me; I didn't mind if Fred Wrigley got what was coming to him, but *Emma*! This was followed by an even stronger wave of rage and hate. How dare she, this scruffy old moaner? Set herself up against decent people? How quickly the lie formed in my mind.

'But they *left* somebody in charge at the Hall,' I said, full of well-faked bewilderment. 'Didn't Wilf tell you?'

'*Who?*' said Wilf, outraged in turn.

'Puggy Winterbottom.'

'So where was he?'

'In the woodsman's cottage in the stables, having a cup of tea.'

'How do you know?' Wilf's voice was now as full of grievance as his mother's. They were a proper pair.

'He told me he was going.'

'So why didn't you send for him?' An excellent question. But I had another excellent lie ready. 'Clean forgot, in the excitement. Anyway, what could he have done? He hasn't got a car . . . I can't see him riding Donny's bike. He'd have fallen off and broken his neck.'

'But he came in with the rest!'

'He heard their car coming back.'

Wilf looked doubtful now. Puggy was popular, a harmless little man. Wilf had no taste for getting him into trouble. I could tell he was losing interest in the whole business. But I couldn't stop there. I still felt fear

71

for my lovely Emma. I didn't want to lie awake and worry about her. I wanted to silence this horrible old cow once and for all. Put her back in her place at the bottom of the heap. Give *her* something to lie awake and worry about.

'I hope you haven't been saying these things to anyone else, Mrs Kimber? I wouldn't like to see *you* getting into trouble.'

'Trouble? What trouble?'

'Slander, Mrs Kimber. If you say nasty things about people that aren't true, you could end up in court.'

'Court, what court? I'm a God-fearing law-abiding woman! All I want is me rights.' But her beady eyes had lost their vindictiveness, became saucers of fear.

'The civil court,' I said. 'If you write wrong things about people, they can sue you for libel. But if you *say* wrong things, they can sue you for slander. The only defence you can make is that what you said was true, was not said out of spite, and was said for the public good.' I knew quite a lot about slander; I'd just been doing it in a boring compulsory lesson called civics.

So had Wilf. He grew alarmed. He turned on his mother. 'I *warned* you not to make trouble. I'm head boy next year. What they going to do to me if you start making trouble? They won't even give me a school-leaving reference. Then how can I get a good job?'

'He's quite right, Mrs Kimber,' I said. 'All sorts of trouble. Besides the money to pay your lawyers, to represent you in court.'

'Money?' she said in hushed tones. 'We ain't got no money.'

'No, but those teachers have. And the school. Pots of money.'

Tears brimmed up in her eyes. 'Aye, the likes o' them has plenty of money. And use it to grind the faces of the poor. I'm only a widow-woman, with nobody in the world to look after her.'

I decided it was time to stop. She'd be even more revolting as a snivelling wreck. I laid a friendly hand on her arm. 'There, don't worry too much about it. I dare say you've told nobody but Wilf and me, and I won't breathe a word.'

We worked a long time calming her down. Wilf gave me very unfriendly looks. If he'd ever been a friend of mine he wasn't any more. I got up and said heartily, 'Well, I'm glad that's all settled. See you next term, Wilf!'

I blundered down the dark smelly stair and let myself out, feeling I'd saved something young and beautiful from something old and ugly. If people like Mrs Kimber weren't kept in their place, where would we be?

The fresh air outside was great.

I went for a walk that night, and passed the end of Emma's road. It felt good, knowing she was just fifty yards away, reading a book or listening to the radio. At ease and safe, because of me. And she would never know, unless one day I decided to tell her, when it was all safely in the past. Then she would be grateful to me again; might even plant another brushing kiss on my cheek.

I felt, in a funny remote way, as if I owned her now. More than anybody else, anyway. Emma, Emma, Emma, I said to myself, and felt like I was kissing her.

# Part Two

## 11: William Wilson

I don't think Emma and I would ever have got together again, if it hadn't been for William Wilson. William Wilson was a disaster waiting to happen. He was in our year. A good-looking kid, in a frail girlish sort of way. He'd played Ophelia in the school play, and that hadn't done him much good. But our head of English was mad to do Shakespeare the Shakespearian way, with boys playing the part of girls, and he was a persuasive sort of bloke, and old William would do anything to get himself noticed.

William was simply a weed. No good at sport; five minutes on the rugger field and he'd have been torn to ribbons. Nothing great at schoolwork, either, though he was in no danger of being chucked out. No claim to fame whatever. But if he'd been content to sink down among the other anonymous weeds, no harm would ever have come to him.

The trouble was, he was not content to sink. He looked round to see who was famous, who were the school in-crowd, and he hung around us like a wasp buzzing round a jam jar. He had no wit, but he learnt our wit, and parrotted it.

And of course we made cruel personal remarks about each other; Jack Dowson's droopy eyelid, the size of

74

Tony Apple's conk, the creases in the back of my neck. But because we made them about each other, it didn't give *him* the right to make them. And he always accompanied his snide remarks with that high-pitched girlish giggle.

He buzzed around us a hell of a long time. And then he went too far, and he got swatted. It was just his hard luck that we were standing gassing, after lunch, by the coke chute.

By some incredible civic whim, one boilerhouse at our school was on the second floor. And to enable the caretaker to haul up coke, and let down ashes, there was this great galvanised tin tube running up the side of the school. About thirty feet high, and eighteen inches in diameter. And inside was a pulley and a rope and a hook for the coke-and-ash bucket. And one day, when William Wilson was waxing strong and would not go away even after three warnings and a punch in the kidneys, old Teddy simply unhooked the coke bucket, grabbed Wilson, shoved the hook under his belt . . . Wilson screamed and struggled, but two of us held him, and the rest pulled on the rope. Wilson vanished up the chute. It was so funny seeing his kicking legs vanish, and hearing his hollow howls echoing basso profundo from the depths of the tube. We laughed ourselves into quaking jellies, and then got on with our conversation, breaking out into renewed laughter every time Wilson's frantic howls boomed forth again.

It was not quite so funny when the bell went and they drifted away and left him dangling there. I started to follow them, then my conscience (or was it my sense of *real* trouble brewing) smote me, and I commandeered the help of John Bowes, and we undid the knot Teddy had tied in the rope, and lowered him down.

He was not grateful. He was a very funny colour, and his uniform was all ash, and he spat a flood of insults in my face. So we shrugged and left him.

I thought it would have cured him of hanging around us. But it didn't. He still hung around us; but whereas before he'd been trying to curry favour, now he was full of hate. And the whole thing turned really sour. It became their daily habit to haul Wilson up the coke chute. Even if they had to hunt round the school for him; which they had, towards the end. It had all the sick excitement of fox-hunting. The way they would capture him and lead him in a gentle and friendly manner towards that deserted and private corner of the school premises, damping his struggles with a firm grip on his wrists and elbows and covering his frantic cries with laughs, so it all still seemed a joke, to anyone who bothered to watch.

I lost all taste for it. I went and did something else. But it was always me that had to check the chute at the end of lunchtime, and even after school. It was always me and some passing stranger who let him down. Half-crazed and choking though he was, he seemed to grasp that I meant him no harm. He once put a hand on my arm, and tried to explain the horror of it, to me. The choking fumes from the boiler, the terror of the confined space; the terror of his belt giving way and letting him fall through the rusty scraping darkness.

He even showed me the thick new belt he'd had to buy, that wouldn't snap and let him fall. I thought him a fool, to spend good money on the instrument of his own torture. He revolted me by this time. I couldn't bear to have him touch me. I just turned away. He'd asked for it, and he'd got it . . .

And then came the day when I saw he'd wet himself in terror; the dark stain down both sides of his trouser legs. And I knew it had to be stopped. That somehow old Wilson wasn't quite right in the head any more.

That was when I went to see Emma.

I'd never been down Tennyson Terrace before. Just walked past the end. Nobody walked down Tennyson Terrace without good reason. A black notice said 'Private Road'.

Old-fashioned money; not at all like the flashy new-style money that lived down Whitley Bay, all dark blue pantiles and acres of crazy paving and boats on trailers in the drives, to make sure the neighbours noticed.

Tennyson Terrace kept itself to itself, like a maiden aunt. If Tennyson Terrace got its name in the papers, it was for opening a charity fête, or giving a talk to Rotary on 'The Dawn of Hymn Singing in Old Tynemouth'.

I passed between the pillars with sooty black balls on top that marked the entrance. The iron gates had gone for salvage in the war, after an incredible outcry from the inhabitants. But they were still there in spirit. My feeble soul cringed; my shoulders hunched against observant eyes behind lace curtains, as my feet quarrelled with the cobbles that the inhabitants of Tennyson Terrace insisted on keeping. To discourage bicycles, no doubt, and make difficulties for the smart delivery vans from butcher and grocer that kept them fed.

The front gardens were an unloved device for keeping the riff-raff at bay. Hardly anything grew. Black and white deserts. Sour black soil with white marble rockeries grinning sharp and serrated fangs. Rows of huge tropical sea shells bleached by the sun to the whiteness of skulls. In between, exhausted London Pride struggled for life. Huge dark monkey puzzle and holly trees darkened the windows. Privet clipped so hard there was hardly a leaf on it. The gardens of Tennyson Terrace made Preston Cemetery look cheerful.

The houses had portals, not doorways. Immense blocks of black stone that dwarfed Stonehenge. The same immense black slabs in the bay windows. The brickwork in between was a ghostly grey, with the green of algae on the north-facing sides. The doors were a sun-cracked white. The only glint of cheer was from the highly polished brass knockers, and the odd brass plate announcing a doctor, a chiropodist, a piano tuner.

I found Seventeen easily. The house number was picked out in gold leaf on the fanlight. The front step was holystoned as white as snow and very high and wide. I began to work out how I could step over it without leaving a mark. I pressed the white china bell-button that had 'Press' written on it. The surround was polished as bright as silver, and years of Brasso had left a dim halo on the blackened stone around.

Heavy female footsteps on the tiled floor of the hall inside. A female torso in a buttoned-up cardigan, so solid with corsets it would have made a good ship's figurehead. A face like Emma's, but heavier and turned to stone, under a rigid perm of iron-grey hair.

'Yes?' The face took in my uniform, but did not soften.

'Is Miss Harris in?'

'Miss Harris is having a cup of tea and getting on with

her marking. Can't it wait until tomorrow?'

I said, wondering if the magic would work, 'My name's Atkinson!'

The stone face crumbled into a smile of the most amazing warmth. 'Not *Robbie* Atkinson? Sarah's lad? Bye, I've heard so much about you! Come to that, I've known you since you were in your pram! I was at your christening! Come in, come in. Miss Harris will be tickled pink.'

I followed her solid back and hips along the polished tiles of the hall, and wondered if Emma would ever become that massive. Chrysanthemums bloomed in a polished brass Indian vase. The smell of polish and chrysants was like church. And there was an alarming crescendo of excited female voices and the rattle of teacups. If I'd been a horse, I'd have reared up in alarm.

But Mrs Harris, without turning her head, said, 'My Mothers' Union sewing circle,' and led the way up the gleaming stair-rods. I wondered whether she was the shop steward of the Mothers' Union.

'Our Emma could do with a break,' said the unturning head. 'She works so hard. She's done nothing but work since her daddy died. She was always her daddy's girl, especially since . . . the war. She's taken his death very hard. You'll do her good.'

It wasn't a hope; it was an order.

She tapped, curiously timidly, on the closed shining door.

'What *is* it, Mother?' Emma's voice came through the panels, querulous, irritated. I began to feel sorry I had come.

'A *lovely* surprise. A young man to see you.'

Quick, irritable footsteps. The door snatched open.

The cold light of a window caught the side of Emma's face cruelly. I'd never known she had so many lines . . . she looked tired to death. Her elaborate hair-do was escaping from its hairpins, as if she'd been running her fingers through it in exasperation. And she was wearing gold-rimmed spectacles, on a droopy golden chain that led down to her neck. They made her look scholarly but old. My visions of her, from Clatterburn, exploded like bubbles. I'd been having daydreams about a woman nearly as old as my mother, and I felt a stab of self-disgust. Then I comforted myself that I'd really come about William Wilson.

She glared at her mother, furious at the interruption. Then she looked over her shoulder and saw me.

I never saw a face change so quickly. Her hands flew to her hair, her spectacles. She smiled, but didn't know where to look. My heart gave a thump for her. I've never seen anyone look so vulnerable, and it made her young again.

'I'll fetch you up some fresh tea,' said her mother. 'And some nice little cakes. It isn't every day we have a gentleman visitor.' Then she was gone.

'Come in,' said Emma. She turned and walked away across the room. Her back and hips were like her mother's, only slim, miniaturised. She kept bending over, tidying up things and pushing them behind cushions as she went. She reached the huge black marble fireplace, put a hand on it for support, and turned to face me.

The spectacles had mysteriously vanished, though I could still see the cruel red mark on her nose where they'd been. And, maybe it was just the warm glow from the fire, but she suddenly looked about twenty years younger. Her smile was so shy. Her large green eyes could not quite stay on my face. She was all happy confusion. I'd never *quite* had that effect on anyone before. It made me feel like a magician.

Then I noticed she was wearing men's leather slippers, a bit too big for her. Somehow, I knew they must have been her dead father's. It seemed unbearably strange. She noticed me noticing.

'Oh,' she said. 'Sorry. It's just that they're so comfy. Teaching's very hard on the feet. You need strong feet and a strong throat, to be a teacher. Sometimes, at the start of term, my throat nearly packs up. Sit down, do.'

I sat in a big old-fashioned armchair, with shiny wooden arms. It was like my grandfather's old chair, but much bigger and grander. She bustled off somewhere behind me, while I ran my eyes over the tall bookshelves, each side of the fire. Some books were in bright jackets, and about history. But a lot were huge medical textbooks. This study had been her father's. I wondered if being there gave her the same feelings, half revolted, half exciting, that my grandfather's chair gave me.

Then she came back. Talk about being a quick-change artist! Her hair was down now, behind the bright red bandeau. She was wearing fresh lipstick and powder, and her feet were in high-heeled shoes. They made her legs look longer, curvier – I've noticed high heels always do that to women. They change a woman's whole shape . . . But she must have had to force the shoes on, her plump pretty feet looked painfully pinched.

She'd done all this for *me*. It made me feel fairly smug, I can tell you. And from her little tentative smile, she didn't seem to mind my smug look at all. A slight hint of perfume – I think it was 'Midnight in Paris', because that's what my mother wore – came floating across the hearthrug between us, as her mother came in with the tray of tea.

Emma poured out so neatly; silver teapot, china so thin you could see the tips of her fingers through it. I felt it was a very important ceremony, like the vicar doing communion in church. Then she passed me my cup and said, 'And to what do I owe the pleasure of this visit,' with one eyebrow deliciously cocked.

It was such a shame it had to be Wilson and the coke chute. As my voice ran on and on, I watched her age ten years again. Though her legs were still as good to look at as ever. Bloody old Wilson; he always could ruin anything.

She heard me out, then said, 'Can't *you* stop them?'

Why can't teachers, even the best, never understand how it is? I tried to explain the way things were. She said, 'But they'll listen to you. You're a *born* leader.'

She made it sound like Red Circle School, in the *Hotspur*. She made me sound like their head boy, Dead Wide Dick, who always solves every problem. I tried to explain the difference between comics, and real life.

'You're not *afraid* of them?' she asked, her face falling.

'They lay a finger on me, I'll smash their teeth in.' And I meant it. But I knew they never would lay a *finger* on me. They would just never speak to me again; except to jeer. But I would be out for the rest of my schooldays, something not quite human. Like that swot Robin Bulmer, whom all the kids catcalled after, on the way home. Everybody knows who's in and who's out. Even the first-years know. And our lot would do things like pouring water into my locker in the prefects' room, through the hole in the top; or one of my boots would get lost after a rugger match, while I was in the showers, and never found again. Or my homework would go missing from the homework shelf, or somebody would spill a plate of custard down my blazer, accidentally on purpose at school dinners. Oh, they have a thousand ways to make your life hell, if you *really* get across them. And once *they've* got you down, all the other wolves descend on you, that your friendship with the top crowd has been keeping off.

All this I tried to explain to her. But I felt that as a statue on her pedestal, I was growing feet of clay, and the clay was starting to dissolve.

'Look, they're my *mates*. It just started as a laugh. I was one of them, the first time. It was a joke. It's just that they won't stop . . . and if they go on, there's going to be *real* trouble.'

She said coldly, 'It can never have been a joke for William Wilson.' She might have been any old teacher, and me any old sixth-former, now. 'You're frightened of being an outsider. Wouldn't you rather be an honorable outsider, than a dishonorable insider?'

'No. Wilson isn't worth it.'

'Wilson – is – not – worth – it.' She shut her eyes in contempt. I couldn't stand it. I got up to go.

'Thanks for the tea.'

That got her eyes open quick enough.

'I thought you'd help,' I said bitterly.

'Oh, sit down. Let me think.' She thought. I waited, watching that single worry line grow up her creamy rounded forehead. The boot was on the other foot, now.

'Two of them are *prefects*,' she said. 'The head would

83

take away their prefects' badges. He'd suspend them; might even expel them. In their A-level year. There'd be a *hell* of a stink. Parents, governors . . . and so bad for the image of the school. It might get in the papers . . .'

'They're rotten prefects anyway. They don't do a stroke.'

'You're a pretty rotten prefect yourself. Standing by and watching it happen. Suppose Wilson tells the head about *you*?'

'Oh look,' I said. 'It doesn't have to go as far as the head. It doesn't have to be official. If *you* catch them, you can just give them a warning. That'd frighten the living daylights out of them. They'd never do it again. No names, no pack-drill.'

'And how am I supposed to catch them at it? I do have other things to do, you know!'

'Look, I've got a plan. There's one little window that overlooks the coke chute . . .'

'Yes, I know. It's in the corridor that goes beyond our women's staff room, up to the stock cupboard. Nobody goes there, except Miss Wilberforce when she's issuing new exercise books.'

I told her my plan. She found faults with it; suggested improvements. Finally, we had it perfect, and sat back and drank more near-cold tea, and she pushed the last pieces of cake on to me. She was flushed, pleased with me again; and herself. Everyone loves to be a conspirator, don't they?

Then her mother tapped on the door timidly, and came in to clear up the tea things.

'Hasn't this lad got a home to go to? It's gone half-past six.'

Emma laughed. 'Time goes so fast, when you're

enjoying yourself.'

'I suppose you've been putting the world to rights?' But her mother was pleased to see her like that. She gave me an approving look, and said, 'You must come to tea again, young man. You're as good as a holiday.'

We whispered on the front doorstep, like the conspirators we'd become. I'd put a cluddering great dirty footmark on the step, but Emma didn't seem to mind.

I walked home, thinking about how first she'd looked old, then she looked young. It was disturbing, and yet exciting. Women could change so much on the outside, because of what they were feeling inside. It made them seem vulnerable, like flowers that close up at night but re-open in the morning. Blokes always look the same, unless they're really ill, or get really mad.

I suppose that was the first time I thought of *exploring* Emma.

## 12: Disaster Averted

I nearly missed the next time they got old Wilson. I'd just come out of the showers, after a rugger practice, and was going for a late lunch of leftovers when I saw them laughing, dragging him across the yard. I strolled very casually into the back door of the school, then took to my heels along the bottom corridor, sending kids flying in all directions. Up the hall stairs three at a time, across the back and into the girls' half of the school, crashing into a soft cushiony mass of fifth-year girls, enjoying their indignant squeaks as well as the feeling.

Then I was at the door of the women's staff room, desperately trying to get my breath back before knocking. I nearly forgot to take the book out of my pocket that I'd had there for three days, I was that excited. The book Emma had loaned me; the key to the whole plan, idiot that I was.

I took three more huge breaths and knocked, trembling. The sound of chattering voices and tinkling teacups went on unabated. No one came. Time was running out. Once old Wilson was *up* the chute, it would be useless. I banged again, really hard.

Still no answer. Were they all *deaf*? I raised my hand a third time. The door opened with amazing suddenness, and left my raised fist within inches of the nose of

Katherine Merry MA. She regarded it as if it was a disgusting insect. I dropped it down and held it clenched in my pocket.

'Are you attempting to demolish the door, Atkinson?' She gave me a frosty stare that charged me with a crime, found me guilty and condemned me, all in about two seconds. I expected my prefect's badge to be taken away there and then.

I thrust the book at her. 'Miss Harris loaned me this.'

She took it and inspected it, as if it was incriminating evidence. I remembered Emma's care in choosing it for me. Her hand had hovered over D.H. Lawrence's *Kangaroo* but had moved on to a translation of Caesar's Gallic Wars.

'A sudden passion for Latin, Atkinson? It hasn't shown up in your marks yet.'

'In *war*, miss. The Roman Wall . . .'

'Oh, yes, I've heard all about your Roman *Wall*.'

The frost in her voice said hanging would be too good for me.

'Very well. I will see that she gets it. Shall I give her your *thanks*? Say you enjoyed *reading* it?'

All I could say was, 'Thank you, miss,' and go. What a flop!

But I had scarcely reached the bunch of fifth-year girls again (all of whom had flattened themselves against the wall at my approach, except one little cheeky one who was hoping for something or other) when Emma's voice came floating after me, as cold and formal as Katie Merry's had been.

'Atkinson? A moment!'

I almost *ran* back. She said, 'I wanted a word about chapter five,' voice still as cold as hell. I could almost hear the ears flapping in the common room behind her.

Solemnly we walked along the little corridor towards the stock cupboard.

'Caesar at this point is a little ambiguous . . .'

We reached the little window, stopped, turned and looked out, while she riffled the pages. It was like being on stage in the school play.

Below, the cut-off corner of the yard, by the coke chute, was desolately empty. Damn Katie Merry! They must have come and strung him up and gone. All for nothing.

And then, glory be, they haled into sight; Wilson must have struggled a bit harder than usual; he looked *awful*.

'What are those boys doing?'

'I don't know, miss.'

'Well, I shall certainly find out.' What play-acting!

The next second, she was gone, leaving Caesar on the windowsill as an alibi for me.

I went on watching Wilson's vain struggles; the ugly expression of glee on the faces of Apple and Teddy and their three lesser hangers-on.

Her small doughty begowned figure emerged from a door below; a door hardly anyone ever used. She got right up to them, before they saw her. By that time, they had Wilson up the chute, with only his kicking legs showing. He was yelling his head off.

I shall never until my dying day forget the look on Tony Apple's face when he saw her. It was worth a million quid.

A voice spoke in my ear, very close. A very cold voice.

'What are you grinning at, Atkinson? What is so *very* amusing?'

'Miss Harris . . . went to sort out some lads, Miss Merry.'

They were just lowering Wilson down the chute again. He fell on the ground in a blubbering heap. With the hook still in his belt.

'I think it will take more than Miss Harris to sort *this* out. I would advise you to get back to your prefect's duties, *if* you have any, Atkinson! I shall deal with this.'

She stalked away, making me feel the whole world had just opened up beneath my feet.

I was summoned to the head's study, shortly after the bell for afternoon school. There was nobody there, except the head and Wilson, for which I was grateful. Wilson was sitting in the chair parents normally sat in, with an empty teacup at his elbow. He gave me a desperate greasy-eyed glance that told me he'd blabbed the lot. Good old William!

The head didn't even try to put the usual frighteners on me. He was so pale and quiet, I could tell he was too angry for that.

'You knew all this was going on, Atkinson?' Every inch the major he had been in World War I. Somehow it made me stand to attention, like a bloke about to be shot.

'Yessir.'

'In fact, Wilson has told me you rescued him many times from the coke chute?'

'Yessir.' At least William seemed to be bearing me no malice.

'It did not occur to you, to tell a member of staff what was going on?'

'I don't tell tales, sir.'

'You would rather a helpless boy suffered?'

'I told them to lay off, sir. I *told* them there would be trouble.'

'But you never thought to tell them it was *wrong*?' The contempt, disgust in his voice was terrible. Then he said, 'Wait outside, Wilson!' And William slunk off like a whipped cur.

'I'd like the *truth*, Atkinson.'

'What *about*, sir?' I could hear that guilty wail coming into my voice.

'About your motives. About the fact that you were *with* Miss Harris, at the time that she noticed their behaviour. That is too great a coincidence for me to believe.'

'Don't know what you mean, sir!'

'Oh, but I think you do, very well. I think that, despairing of talking sense into those five boys, you deliberately *used* Miss Harris . . . a member of *my* staff . . . for your own ends.'

Suddenly, I sensed *she* was in danger. What danger, I couldn't quite figure. But from being a cringing rabbit, it sort of made me into a lion. I looked him straight in the eye (and it took a hell of an effort) and I said quite clearly and firmly, 'I don't know what you're talking about, sir.'

I think he knew then he wasn't going to win. Instead of pressing in on me, he went raging off round me, raging out at me in a hopeless sort of way, doing what damage to me he could.

'I have had to suspend five boys – two of them *prefects*, who will lose their prefects' badges. I shall have their parents to deal with now. I shall have the governors to deal with. If Wilson's parents turn nasty, I may have the police to deal with. Not to mention the press, and the good name of the school. If you'd spoken up in the first instance, as a good prefect should . . . If Wilson hadn't spoken up for you . . . and spoken up very warmly . . . I should have taken away *your* prefect's badge too.'

What else could I have done but slowly unpin my badge and throw it on his desk? Thinking, oh no, you don't blackmail me. You can stuff your little badge where it hurts most. I wouldn't be *your* prefect if you paid me.

He coolly handed me my badge back. 'Stop making melodramatic gestures. We're in enough serious trouble without you going hysterical on us. He was angrier than ever. But so was I now. And he was probing again.

'Is Miss Harris a *special* friend of yours?'

The danger to her was back . . .

'She doesn't even teach you, does she?'

'No, sir.'

'Then what's all this lending of books?'

'We talked a lot on the Roman Wall trip. She knew I was interested in the Roman Army.'

'Ah, yes,' he said, 'the Roman Wall trip.' Then added, 'You do seem very *close* with Miss Harris . . .'

'My grandmother's a friend of her mother. They were at school together. They help run the British Legion.'

I don't know why I said it; but for some reason, it worked. A certain light went out of his eye. I had retreated into some thicket of small-town alliances where, as a schoolmaster, he didn't dare to follow me. He was out of his depth, and we both knew it.

He said bitterly, 'Thugs, common or garden thugs, I can deal with. But you aren't a common or garden thug, are you, Atkinson? Nothing so simple. A good little *psychologist* . . .' He used the word with that special dislike, as schoolmasters always do. 'You're leaving this summer?'

'Yessir.'

'And you'll be expecting a good reference for university?'

I was silent.

'I think, Atkinson, you have a great deal of thinking to do. Send back Wilson as you go out, will you?'

I went without a word.

William came sidling and fawning up to me. 'I didn't *tell* him, Atkinson!'

'Tell him *what*?' I asked in disgust.

'That you helped string me up the first time. And I told him you tried to stop them . . . that you're a real *mate* of mine.'

I nearly threw up all over him. But I didn't. He could still go back and tell the head everything. So I just said, 'He wants to see you again.'

It was then that I looked up and saw Emma coming. She looked as pale as a ghost. I gave her the smallest perceptible grin and nod. As if to say, 'I haven't cracked. Our story still holds.'

The relief showed in her face.

Then I looked beyond her, and saw Katie Merry watching us, from the door of the school office.

I hurried straight round to her house, after school. She wasn't back yet, but her mother let me go up and wait for her. So I sat in the usual chair, and stared at her shelves of books, and fretted about the Head. Because I'd always thought the head a good bloke, till now. A bit like Mr Churchill, in a way; they were both short and stocky, with a good paunch under their waistcoats, and balding in front. All through the war, even in the darkest times, he'd addressed us every morning. Commenting on the war, lifting our spirits. He was always advocating that we took Dame Fortune as she came. He had a favourite wry story he never tired of telling:

'One morning in 1917, my colonel said to me, "You've done very well, Smedley. I'm going to recommend you for an MC and a fortnight's leave in Paris."

'I was cock-a-hoop. But by nightfall, the big German push had started, my colonel was dead, and I was in a German POW camp. Never count your chickens till they're hatched.'

He was never a sod; he always spoke to us man to man; he caned seldom; he expected us to be gentlemen, and most of the time we were. The words 'manly' and 'gentlemanly' were always on his lips. His favourite phrase for a leaving reference was 'a manly bearing and a gentlemanly disposition'.

Fat chance of that I had now. But worse than that, he didn't like me any more. I mean, you don't mind being hated by sods like Katie Merry MA and the Black Fan. That was a sort of medal. But to be disliked by a decent bloke . . . and what had I done to deserve it? Tried to save flipping Wilson. If I'd been a heartless sod, like some, I wouldn't be in trouble now.

I was still feeling sorry for myself when I heard her voice and her feet on the stair. I sprang up to greet her, tapping my prefect's badge and saying, 'I'm still alive.' I even managed a grin.

She did not respond. She threw herself down on the

sofa, wearily.

'You all right?' I asked, worried. 'I stuck to our story. He got nothing out of me.'

'So I gathered,' she said in a low voice. 'He warned me about you. He gave me a lecture on the undesirability of unsuitable friendships with boys your age . . . for a woman of my age and status. He made me feel like a *cradle snatcher*.'

I got up, very shocked. 'Shall I go?'

She levered her shoes off her feet, one after the other, by pressing the heels against the floor. I smelt the faint, not unpleasant smell of her nyloned feet, and saw where the shoes had cut into them.

'Damn him,' she said. 'I've done nothing wrong. I've got nothing to apologize for. He made me feel like a naughty schoolkid. No; stay! My mother's making us some tea. The *nerve* of that man. Of course, Katie Merry's been at him, poisoning his mind against me. That woman's *pure* poison. She's got a mind like a cesspit. And all those other old gossiping hens. I will not live my life to suit their book . . . no; stay!' She gave me the spark of a grin. 'We've got a bad name, now, so let's live up to it! One sugar or two!'

She said this as her mother came in with the tray. Then she added, 'The head's just told me, Mother, that my friendship with Robbie here is unsuitable. How d'you like that?'

'Pay no heed to him,' said her mother briskly. 'He's been listening to those spiteful old crows again. Mutter, mutter, mutter, they won't let you live. Dried-up old cows, there's not an ounce of juice left in them, to give any man. Pay no heed to them, chick. You and Robbie's not doing any harm. He's just a bit o' young life, that's all. Just what you need.'

And so, comforted, we sat and drank our tea and grinned at each other. In the end, she said, 'But scary . . '

'Yeah, scary. When Katie Merry caught me at that window, I could've died.'

'When she came up behind me in the yard, *I* could have died.'

'It'll be a nine-days' wonder!'

'Yes, we'd better be careful though. I think I'd better start coaching you at something. Give you an excuse to come here. Your Latin's pretty awful, isn't it? So I hear.'

I felt a look of alarm come on to my face. 'I don't think my dad'll pay for coaching. I don't think he can afford it.'

'I'll do it for love. After all,' she added with a roguish grin, 'my mother and your grandmother *are* great friends.'

## 13: Tricks with a Ball

I went every Tuesday, after that. And she wasn't mucking about. She said she was going to coach me in Latin, and she did coach me in Latin. For an hour, and I was sweating by the end. But she was a good teacher, and I was a good pupil and we made fast progress. I suppose all that was really the matter with my Latin was that I *had* to do it, to get into university, and it was fashionable among the boys to be bad at Latin, and I hated the teacher. But Emma was different, she made Latin seem precise and logical, like a ticking Swiss watch. With her, I began to enjoy it. And, at school, my marks began to go up pretty quickly, because she checked my work before I handed it in. We were a big quick success; I began to get the feeling that together we could beat the world . . .

And working so close at her desk. The smell of her hair; and I could tell what her every sigh and intake of breath meant; when I was going wrong, when I was going right.

But it was after the Latin that the best part came. She would yell down to her mother that we were ready for coffee and biscuits, then we would go and sit each side of the fire and talk. Mainly me at first; what was wrong with the world. Everything from the atomic bomb to our rugby team. I think I wanted to change everything then; I was convinced that *I* could do things better.

And she didn't fob me off, and shut me up, like my father and mother did, with old weary sayings like, 'You'll *learn*, as you get older' or 'It's all right in theory, but it won't work in practice' or a weary headshake and 'You can't put an old head on young shoulders'. I mean, in politics, well, my father would never discuss politics. He was a working man and a Socialist, and he said that anybody in the working classes who didn't vote Socialist was an idiot and worse than an idiot, and we usually ended up shouting at each other.

But she really listened as if I was an adult. And then when I'd finished grumbling, she would ask me what I intended doing about it.

'Well, there's nothing we can do about the rugby team. We've only got eight hundred in the school, and half of them are girls and another quarter are useless little kids, and most of the natural ball players are in the soccer team.'

'What do the soccer players do, when all the pitches are set up for rugger?'

'Hang about and grumble. Some of them play for town teams, like the YMCA, but a lot just hang around and grumble.'

'Why don't you invite *them* to play rugger?'

I gaped. I gabbled. 'Well . . . they're all . . . working class . . . I mean . . . the sort that leave school at sixteen . . . and go into the shipyards . . . they're the bottom classes . . . not our *sort* . . . rude lot . . . always spitting on the ground during a match . . . and the swearing . . .'

'In other words,' she said, 'no reason at all. D'you

think any of them would be any good at rugger?'

'Well . . .' I thought. 'They're no good with their hands.'

'What about the goalkeeper? Isn't he good with his hands?'

'Oh, John Bowes is brilliant . . . some of his saves . . . fantastic dives . . . taking the ball right off their feet.'

'Why don't you talk to John Bowes, then? He's a nice boy – I teach him. Not the world's brightest at schoolwork, but very respectable. He wants to be a policeman when he grows up.'

'Oh, I don't know. Our lot wouldn't like it much . . . and Bill Fosdyke, the master in charge . . .'

'You want to change the world, but you're frightened of what people will say about you. D'you think Hitler cared what people said about him? Or Jesus Christ? Or Karl Marx or Charles Darwin? You're beaten before you start, if you care what other people think.'

I could see that all too clearly. It landed on me like a ton of bricks. I stared at the hearthrug between us.

'Look,' she said, 'I'll tell you what'll happen to you, if you go on caring what people think. You'll go to university, and then you'll drift into teaching, then you'll meet a girl and marry her, and she will want kids and you'll go on teaching the same thing, year in, year out, till your kids grow up and give you grandchildren, and then you'll retire after forty years and fiddle around in your garden till they come to carry you away in a long box. And you'll look round when you're dying, and wonder where all the time has gone. I know. I've seen it happen to so many.'

'Oh God, *noooh*!'

'It's happening to me now. Oh, I go away for a

98

fortnight every summer: Salzburg, Oberammergau one year, Greece, the French cathedrals. Each year I think something wonderful is going to happen, something big is going to change. I come back raring to go ... and then it's back to the treadmill. And I know nothing is going to change for me now. I'm like a pet rat in a cage, running on its wheel to give it the illusion that it's going somewhere.'

We stared at each other in horror; because she had said too much. And then she said abruptly, 'Do you like music?' And dashed across to the huge wind-up gramophone that stood in the corner of her study, and put on the nearest record to hand. She sat down and listened with her eyes shut, hands clenched tight together.

The music boomed and soared. It got into my blood; it was wild. It made you feel that you were plunging on somewhere, out of control. And not caring one little bit. You knew there was going to be a hell of a crash, if it didn't stop soon, but you just didn't care. You *wanted* the crash to happen. Even when the music ended, to the clicking of the needle in the groove, the impending crash still hung in the air like smoke.

The gramophone went slower, and finally ground to a halt.

'God,' I said, 'what was that?'

' "The Ride of the Valkyrie", from *The Ring* cycle. Wagner. Wagner was Hitler's favourite.'

'What happened to the hero in the end?'

'He got the chop, as you would say.'

'Bet it was flippin' worth it.'

'I don't think he cared much, what respectable people thought.'

We were silent, again.

'All right,' I said, at last. 'I'll have a chat to John Bowes.'

I found it very hard to get near John Bowes; there was always a gang around him; he was a popular kid with the fifth year. Didn't seem to have much to say for himself; but the other kids hung around him, and I couldn't even speak to him, with them there.

I decided the only way was to follow him home one night.

So there was I, Friday afternoon, lurking along like a spy behind his gang, as they pushed each other into the gutter, snatched the bags off each other's shoulders and threw them in the middle of the road. They'd spotted me following, and were playing me up, because I was a prefect, and should have stopped such behaviour in public, in school uniform. The only one who wasn't messing about was John Bowes, who just strolled along in the middle of them, as if such behaviour was beneath his notice.

I nearly missed speaking to him altogether, because as we got into streets that grew steadily grimmer, I was dropping further and further behind. It wasn't a slummy area; just Victorian terraces behind the gasworks. But grim.

Then suddenly, he waved and left the gang, and cut up a side street, already getting his key out of his pocket, on the end of a long leather thong attached to a loop of his trousers. I had to run; or I would have been facing a closed front door.

He heard me coming, and swung to meet me. He was big for a fifth-year, taller than me, but lanky, with a chin like the bow of an old-time battleship. You could see the policeman in him, already.

'It wasn't me that was messing about, Atkinson!'

'I haven't come to see you about that.'

'What, then?'

'Have you ever thought of playing rugger?'

'Stop taking the mickey.' He dismissed me, and reached the key up to the front door.

'Look, I'm *serious*!'

'You're not *serious*, you're *fatal*.' It was an old joke, a very old joke. But I laughed. And a wrinkle of curiosity crossed his brow. As if I might just be human after all.

'Look,' I said, 'what you going to be doing once the rugger posts go up at school?'

'Not a lot.'

'Well, why not play rugger, it'll keep you in training.'

''Sa toff's game.'

'Look, you're good at catching the ball, diving at people's feet . . . it's just the same. Only the shape of the ball's different.'

There was a slight flicker of interest in his stolid blue eyes. 'Never kicked a rugger ball.' Then the flicker died. 'Everyone would take the piss.'

'Not on a Sunday morning they wouldn't. There'd be nobody there but you and me. We could have a kick around. See if you like it.'

'Go church Sunday.' It came out as a guilty mutter, eyes on the ground.

'*All* Sunday?'

'I could come Sunday afternoon. If me mam'll let me. She says Sunday's the sabbath — the day of rest. Even God rested on the sabbath.'

I was starting to lose him. So I said quickly, 'Well, I'll be there, two o'clock. With a ball. I'll wait till four.'

And then I was away, before he could say anything else. He did yell, 'Atkinson,' after me. But I pretended I didn't hear.

So I was there at two o'clock, sports coat over my strip, rugger ball tucked under my arm, lingering by the padlocked school gates.

He came promptly. But no kit, no boots, nothing. And wearing what appeared to be his Sunday best. Face very woebegone.

'Me mam says it's wrong to play games on Sundays. But I have to come and tell you sorry.'

I was that mad at his being so gormless; at letting his parents rule his life like that, and ruin mine. I began to play with the ball, to let off steam, spinning it between my hands.

Then I looked up, and his eyes were following the spin of the ball hungrily.

I threw it at him. He caught it beautifully. He had big bony hands, with long square-tipped fingers, and very marked joints. Pale, his hands were, with strong brown hairs on the back of them; and freckles.

'Here,' he said guiltily, and threw the ball back to me, in a lifeless way. 'Tara. Sorry!' He turned away.

I let him get ten yards away, then yelled, 'Bowes,' and threw the ball at him hard. It wasn't an accurate pass; it was too high and two yards to his left.

He picked it out of the air like an angel. What a pair of hands! What an eye!

He made as if to throw it back to me again.

'Not like that!' I shouted. 'It's a *rugby* ball. Like this!'

And I mimicked the motion in the empty air.

He copied me perfectly. The ball came whizzing back straight to my hands. I flung it straight back at him. The next second, we were bombarding each other with it, there on the pavement. I could tell he knew he ought to stop, but he just couldn't. He was hooked on that ball, like on a drug. Once the ball was moving, he just couldn't resist it. And all the time I was moving back and throwing longer and longer passes.

Then I changed tactics; a punt of the ball up in the air with my foot. But a bad one; it was spinning out over the road. He leapt into the road to catch it, at the same time as a car was whizzing straight at him.

The car did not miss him.

He missed the car. He saw the car in time, took the ball, swerved on one foot, leaned in to the kerb, all in one tiger-like movement. The car, with an angry screech of brakes, missed him by an inch, then drove on.

He walked across and put the ball into my hands.

'That was a *warning*,' he said solemnly. 'Not to play on Sundays.' And yet his eyes drifted longingly to the locked gate and the huge wide playing field beyond. All he wanted was to run and leap and kick and catch. What in God's name was wrong with that, even on a Sunday? I felt I could still tempt him over that gate . . .

And then I knew it wouldn't be smart. He'd arrive back home late, with grass on his best shoes and a guilty look on his face, and his stupid parents would *know*. And then they'd equate rugby with sin, and he'd never play again.

So I just laughed and said, 'OK, you win. No playing on Sundays. But,' I added, 'keep the ball for a bit. Get the feel of it. What about Monday after school?'

'Got me paper round. Got me homework.'

But all the time his eyes were on the ball in my hands. I felt like the serpent in the garden of Eden.

'Just take it,' I said, offering the apple a second time.

His hands came out of their own accord and took it. And I went off feeling peculiar. My ball, my best ball, almost my only ball. So what did I have to feel guilty about?

## 14: Big Practice

I didn't see hide nor hair of John Bowes for two weeks after that. I thought my plan had failed completely, and several times I almost went to ask for my ball. Only one thing held me back. Vague rumours that 'that Bowes type had been seen watching rugby. Not at school. At the big match when our county team got thoroughly thrashed by the Australian Touring XV at Gosforth.

'Standing there in his raincoat with the collar right up,' Jack reported. 'Nodding and shaking his head like an old gaffer. D'you think he's having a nervous breakdown, or just going for laughs?'

'Laughs,' I said lightly; because our gallant county side had lost 32–0 to the Aussies.

Then came the magic moment when the soccer posts were dismantled and the tall rugger posts went up, and we began to dubbin our boots and get serious.

That first big practice is always a shambles. Remnants of last year's first fifteen, last year's second fifteen, and a host of hopefuls who'd never been much good at soccer, and ten to one wouldn't be much good at rugger, either. I mean, some of them thought you kicked a goal under the crossbar rather than over it.

Bill Fosdyke waded through them, like a feeble shepherd among demented sheep, blowing his whistle for silence over and over and asking, 'What position do *you* play, where do *you* play?'

John Bowes stepped straight up and said, 'Fullback.' Bill Fosdyke didn't recognise him, because he likes to take part in the game, as well as being referee, and he wasn't wearing his spectacles. You can imagine what a good referee that makes him.

'Right,' said Fosdyke. 'Fullback for the Possibles, then.' He looked a bit pussy-struck. Nobody ever volunteered for the fullback position, because fullbacks pay the price of everyone else's sins. Either they're standing well back, miles out of the game, their muscles freezing up with cold, or else they're suddenly faced (at the point when their muscles have totally ceased to function) with a wildly bouncing ball, closely followed by six or seven large and angry enemy forwards. Being fullback for our Possibles is the nearest thing I can think of to Hell, a mere chopping block for the Probables who will make up next year's first fifteen.

We started; there was a scrum. Unbelievably, the Possibles pack heeled it, and I ran round and made a nasty face at their scrum half who dropped the ball in fright. I got a boot to it, and it shot thirty yards into their half, bouncing in all directions like a jumping jack on Guy Fawkes. I was going to score a try for certain . . .

And then a flying shape whipped the ball out of the air, sidestepped my attempt to clobber him, leaving me flat on my face, dodged round four more of our lot and put in a kick for touch that made the ball go so far and high it looked like a wartime barrage balloon.

The touch judge's flag went up, almost on *our* goal line, seventy yards behind our backs. The Possibles were in great danger of opening the scoring against *us*. And

John Bowes had arrived.

"'Sa fluke,' muttered Jack, after the Possibles had scored, and we watched John Bowes convert it for two more points from the touchline.

But, glory be, it wasn't. John Bowes caught and ran and kicked. We were penned in our own half the whole game. It was the only time in the history of the school when the Possibles beat the Probables — by twenty-five points to ten.

'He's like a flipping howitzer,' muttered Jack. '*Nobody* can kick that far.'

Just to prove him wrong, John Bowes kicked a drop goal from forty yards out, the last kick of the match.

Everybody gathered round him.

'What's your name?' asked Bill Fosdyke. A sure sign of someone being picked for the first team.

'John Bowes.'

'John Bowes? Are you any relation to the school goalkeeper?' (So Bill Fosdyke wasn't quite brain-dead, as people had suggested.)

'I *am* the school goalkeeper.'

It was a nasty moment. Soccer players, in Bill Fosdyke's book, were not as bad as murderers, but a lot worse than rapists. Now, he hesitated. But he who hesitates is lost.

'Didn't he play well, sir?' I bellowed. 'Just the fullback we need, now Smithy's gone! Lot better than Smithy ever was.'

Fosdyke went pale. Smithy had been one of his protégés.

'He's a *gift*, sir,' intoned Jack. 'A gift from heaven,' he added piously, which was a bit thick considering Jack was an atheist.

All the new first team growled in agreement. Fosdyke looked round the ring of hostile muddy faces . . .

'Won't the soccer team require his services?' he joked weakly.

'They don't play again till January,' we all assured him.

'Are you sure you know all the rules?' Fosdyke looked severely at poor John Bowes.

But John Bowes pulled a booklet out of his overcoat pocket. *The Rules of Rugby Football.* Something our lot, and probably old Fosdyke, had never seen in our lives.

'Know 'em off by heart, sir.'

We all cheered.

'But I've given the fullback position to Harper.'

'I'll play on the wing,' said Jess Harper. 'That Bramble's useless.'

Bramble was another of Fosdyke's protégés . . .

So we walked back round Fosdyke to the changing-room, rearranging the team between us. And Fosdyke was so flabbergasted, he hardly opened his mouth.

I walked home with John Bowes afterwards.

'How'd you do it?'

'Been practising wi' that ball o' yours non-stop. Down our allotments.'

'Who with?'

'By meself. Kick it up, catch it. You get weird bounces off the greenhouses and sheds and things. An' you've got to dodge the cabbages and stuff. Good practice. An' that Aussie fullback at Gosforth taught me a lot. Where to stand – he was never caught out of position. Wouldn't have learnt nowt, watching you lot. You do nowt but make mistakes. You want to go and watch the best. It's the only way to learn.'

I suffered a lecture on the finer points of rugger, all the way to his front door.

Next day at school, Bill Fosdyke caught me in the corridor.

'A minute, Atkinson!'

'Yessir?' I knew what was coming.

'I hear you encouraged Bowes to take up rugger?'

'Yessir!'

'Why?'

'Thought he'd be useful. We'll win a lot more games with him at fullback.'

'Has it ever occurred to you that there is more to rugby than *winning*?' He said it like he might have said 'masturbating' or 'picking your nose'.

'Like what, sir?'

'Sportsmanship. Giving the other chap a fair crack of the whip. Not taking advantage of his weaknesses. Playing for the sake of playing.'

'You mean, like against Newcastle Collegiate?'

He winced. Collegiate played beautiful rugger, the handling game. They always beat us about forty–nil, while Fosdyke smoked his pipe and fawned around their posh rugger masters, who were always discussing the All Blacks Tour of 1925 or something.

'I think we'll give Newcastle a fright, this year,' I said. 'Spring a few surprises on them.'

He gave me a look, with his nose up in the air, like I was a kipper that had been kept too long.

'I hope you won't have any *more* bright ideas, Atkinson, that's all.'

It was a warning. And it set me thinking who else we could usefully nick from the soccer team.

# 15: Music and Grief

'D'you *like* music?' she asked. And I could tell from the set of her mouth that she meant *real* music, not jazz.

'When I can get it. The "Warsaw Concerto", and the "Dream of Olwen". And that tune from *Gone with the Wind*. Stuff at the pictures . . .'

She sighed. 'What about in school?'

'Never get any. All he taught us about was crotchets and minims and quavers. He made us sing sometimes – "Cherry Ripe" but we sang "Cherry Tripe" and made up our own words. But it's not compulsory in the sixth, so we don't go any more.'

She sighed again. I said, placatingly, 'I heard "Fingal's Cave" once, I liked that. And that bit of *The Planets* – "Mars, the Bringer of War". That was terrific – made you want to go out and beat somebody up.'

'Atkinson, you're a savage.'

'Music soothes the savage breast.' I thought that was from Shakespeare or something. It made her laugh, anyway.

'Let's see what "Für Elise" will do for you.' She patted the couch next to her, invitingly, and went to dust the record and put it on.

I sat on the couch, all atremble suddenly. At the thought of sitting next to her.

But when I glanced at her, while the music was playing, I saw she wasn't being flirty at all. She had sat down in the furthest corner of the settee; she had picked up a big fat cushion and was cuddling that, as if her life depended on it. Her head was down, and her face oddly pinched. Almost as if she was punishing herself.

After 'Für Elise' we had some Chopin, and then she said, in a curious voice, 'Rachmaninov's Second.'

And all the time she got sadder. In the middle of the Rachmaninov, she reached out and held my hand and said, 'I'm glad you're here.' But it still wasn't at all sexy. Her fingers bit into mine, like hot bits of wire. She *hurt*.

And at the end, after a long silence, she said, 'I think it's time for you to go,' and then she couldn't get rid of me fast enough.

I was bewildered.

We had good nights and bad nights. Bad nights were when she played the music. I could have got mad at her wasting the time we had together, being miserable and silent. When we could have been putting the world right . . .

But I was fascinated by her unhappiness. It made her into a sort of tragic heroine. That bloke in the RAF who got killed, whose name I had forgotten. RAF blokes were still heroes in 1949. We had films . . . the tender last goodbyes on the runway. No point in being jealous; he was long dead. But, what had he been like? What had they *done* together? The darkness in her was an exciting darkness, that I longed to explore.

But she never let me in. Never said a thing. Just held my hand, so it really hurt. And soon we were having more bad nights than good nights, and I felt she was just but when . . .

One night, as she moved towards the big gramophone, I said, suddenly savage, 'Do we have to?'

She turned and looked at me; her big eyes were reproachful. 'I love music. But I can only play it when you're here.'

'How can you love it, when it makes you so flippin' miserable?'

'Do you want to be happy *all* the time? Like a pig in a sty?'

'Yeah.'

She gave me a long look I couldn't fathom. And then she came and sat back next to me. 'What shall we talk about then?'

So then we had a long painful silence. You always do, when somebody says something like that. Finally she said, 'I'm a selfish beast,' in a very small voice.

'No, go ahead. I like music, honest.'

'I've been using you.'

'I'm made to be used. Like boxes of matches.' Sounds stupid but I do really like being useful. Everybody else seemed to think I was a nuisance. To my mam I was a leaver of dirty socks under beds, to my dad a lunatic who was a Tory one day and a Communist the next. To my teachers a hander-in of late homework and an asker of awkward questions. I felt a Burden on Society. The idea that she might find me *useful* went to my head like strong drink.

In the ensuing silence, I gazed around to see if there was any way I could be even *more* useful. It was then that I noticed the upright piano for the first time. It had just been a piece of furniture, a thing to put flowers and photographs on until now.

'D'you play the piano?'

She gave a start, then said, 'Not for years. Not since . . .'

'Go on — you're always lecturing me about not burying my talents in the earth.'

Still she sat, hesitating. 'I must be *terribly* rusty. You don't want to listen to a lot of wrong notes.'

'You know me. I can't tell wrong notes from right ones!'

She seemed to come to some decision. Set her mouth grimly and got up. Moved the photographs from the piano lid, exclaimed about the amount of dust, and brushed it away with angry sweeps of her hands. Got a piece of music out of the music stool.

She played a short piece of something, full of stumbles. Then played it again, much better. I was so much on her side that I went to stand beside her. Like I sometimes stand beside Dad when he's doing a difficult repair, and might need some help. She gave me a swift, searching glance. The look on my face must have told her I'd come to support and not to criticise. Because she got out something else, almost gritting her teeth.

Beethoven's 'Moonlight'.

Her hands were surer now. The opening chords went right through me. I watched her face, set like iron, the little hooky lines round the corners of her mouth. But we were getting there. Together.

And then the strong climbing theme collapsed in a crash of discord. She slammed the piano lid shut . . .

'Go on,' I said. 'You were doing all right.'

Then I noticed the first drop of water fall among the disturbed dust of the piano lid. Then several more, like the start of a rainstorm. I looked up at the ceiling in alarm, but there was nothing visible, not even a crack in the plaster.

'Hey,' I said. And then I realised she was crying. Just sitting there silently with wet cheeks, and water dripping off the tip of her nose.

I wasn't used to crying. Nobody ever cried in our family, even when my grandfather died. Except my grandmother. And then my father had gone up to her and put his arms around her and sort of rubbed her back, and in quite a short while she stopped crying. I just thought that must be the thing to do . . .

For a moment, she sat on, rigid as wire with my hands on her shoulders. And then she got up and turned in one movement and sort of burrowed herself into me. I could tell how much pain she was in, from the way her fingers were almost clawing into my back. It hurt. But I just stood there, stroking her back and murmuring noises, because I hadn't a clue what to say. I mean, it just went on and on, getting worse and worse. She kept choking with it, snorting with it, her chest heaving against mine like a bloke who'd run a long long race. It was so ugly, I got a bit scared. Not knowing how it would end; half scared her mother would come and find us, and half hoping she would, so I could be out of it.

But the storm began to abate at last, as they say in the novels we have to read for A-level English. I just kept on murmuring and stroking her back. Finally, she gave a wriggle that said stop stroking, and I stopped and just stood there holding her.

She looked up at me and said, 'That was the last thing I played; before he left.'

And then she started crying all over again. But I wasn't scared any more; I knew it would end, without

114

my having to do anything worrying. And it wasn't half as bad as the first time. She was crying more comfortably, somehow. She wasn't tearing herself to bits any more.

When she stopped the second time, I began to loosen my grip on her. But she said, 'Don't go. Just hold me a bit longer.' And sort of rested, against my chest. It was very comfortable, companionable; even if my shirt was soaked down as far as my navel, where one little drop was hanging and tickling me.

Finally, she looked up at me and said, 'Thank you.' Her cheeks were flushed and wet still; her hair was all over the place; unshed tears made her eyes look enormous. And yet she didn't look a mess. She looked like a trusting little girl.

'He had eyes the same colour as yours,' she said. 'Tawny eyes, lion's eyes.'

I suppose I saw the gaping hole his death had left in her, that bomber-bloke whose name I had long since forgotten. All I can say is that it seemed such a terrible hole it had to be filled. Like you would want to close a big open wound. Such holes shouldn't be allowed to exist in the world.

That's why I kissed her, then.

It was as if a huge mass of feeling poured from me into her, and an equal mass poured from her into me. Something very warm and filling. It was like a bowl of good hot soup on a very cold day, when you're really famished, and you drink it so fast your mother tells you off. I was so greedy and she was so greedy, and our greeds fed each other, and a line of one of our Shakespeare plays came floating into my mind, something about an appetite doth grow on what it feeds upon. I had never known anything like it in my life before. And . . .

She pushed me away so hard I fell over the arm of the settee and just lay there staring up at her.

She was glaring down at me, as wild as a wild beast in its lair. Big though I was, it scared me. It crossed my mind that she was so desperate she might do anything.

But she just said, 'You'd better go home.'

Then she banged across to where her handbag lay on a chair, and began to open it, then dropped it and sat down, burying her face in her hands.

'What . . . ?' I bleated.

'Just *go*!' she said, very muffled, without looking up.

All shaky, I went and got my coat off another chair.

'I'm sorry . . .' I bleated again. 'I didn't mean . . .'

'Don't blame yourself. It's my fault.' But she still kept her face in her hands, so I could hardly hear what she was saying.

'Look, can't we talk about it?' I didn't know what was going to happen next, what had happened, how she felt . . .

'For God's sake, *go*. Haven't you done enough damage for one night?'

I was so scared I just ran away. Closing the door so quietly and tiptoeing downstairs in case her mother should come.

The letter came three days later; I didn't recognise the handwriting on the envelope. I'd never seen her writing before. It was on official school notepaper and it said:

Dear Atkinson,

I'm afraid I shan't be able to fit you in for any

further sessions of coaching in Latin. My marking commitments are growing, as the term progresses, and I have been invited to become an examiner with the Joint Four Board, which will require a lot of preparation and reading.

I feel I have seen you through the worst of your difficulties with Latin, and you should be able to progress satisfactorily from now on.

All the very best of luck with your applications for university. I feel sure you will be successful in gaining a place.

Yours sincerely,
Emma Harris

'What a charming letter,' said my mam, after she'd read it (we don't have private letters in our house). 'I hope you'll write back and thank her nicely. And I think you ought to buy her a big box of chocolates or something.' This last with a glance at my dad, who was pretending to read the paper and not be listening. He groaned and felt in his back pocket, and produced five shillings.

My heart leapt. I had an excuse to go round to her house again, see her again. I could explain. And she would give her old grin and raise one eyebrow, and call me 'Atkinson' sarcastically, and say I was like a wild beast, and it would be OK.

So I went to her door, with the great big box of chocolates beautifully wrapped up by Mam. And her mother opened the door, and I gabbled my piece, straining my ears for the least sound of her upstairs.

But her mother just took the box off me, and said I was very kind, and to give regards to my grandmother. And closed the door again, and that was that.

# 16: Out in the Cold

It was only after that that I learnt what she'd done to me. She's made me *grow* like that little bottle in *Alice in Wonderland*. She's made me grow so big that I didn't fit into anything any more. Every door into every other part of my life was now too small to go through.

The gang at school; they were just spiteful little pygmies, with their stupid bickering and stupider jokes. I couldn't be bothered with them any more.

And home. Home was like a tiny set of prison cells with carpets on the floor and wallpaper on the walls. The smell of my father's feet when he padded around in his socks; Mam's non-stop nagging, even the dog's occasional scratching drove me mad. The highly polished fender, those pictures on the walls — *The Boyhood of Raleigh* and the horse picture, *Mother and Son* — things that I'd loved since I could ever remember, became jailers. Even that radio serial *King Solomon's Mines* that I'd really looked forward to every Monday night, became no more than a bunch of men in lounge suits shouting into a microphone.

Only two things helped. Walking and cruelty.

I'd always been a walker. Especially on Sunday afternoons when my parents and Nana vanished under sheets of the *News of the World* and *Reynold's News* and snored their Sunday lunch off. I would watch their heads slowly drooping, and their mouths slowly falling open, and wonder if the end of the world would be like this.

Now I just walked all the time. Through the dark, the wind and rain. If I imagined that Emma was somewhere ahead, waiting for me, it made it all OK for a bit. I got an obsession that she would be in that pub at Old Hartley, on the coast, eight miles away. Just by chance . . . alone . . . lonely like me . . . a chance visit, impelled by fate.

Of course she never was. It was always full of strangers I didn't want to speak to. And I drank up my half-pint of shandy and shouldered my way out again, hating the drinkers for their cheerful carelessness. Didn't they know they were going to die soon, after a measured, counted, number of days? As I was. And the sand in the hour-glass of days was running out, never stopped running, like Nana's egg-timer that I'd played with for hours as a little lad.

I became obsessed that my body was only a machine, and like any machine it could stop at any time. The next heartbeat might not come, nor the next, nor the next, and then I would be dead. I started to worry about my breathing, about every breath I took possibly being my last. And when you start thinking about your breathing, you get the conviction that you can't *do* it. I stopped breathing for minutes at a time, until my heart began to thunder and my lungs felt like bursting, and then the animal inside me insisted on living, and took a great gulp, and then I was panting like I'd run a mile.

After the pub at Hartley, I'd weave my way down the coast, the sea-gale battering me in wild staggers inland.

119

And then it was Tynemouth pier, with the waves coming like pale ghosts out of the wild darkness and crashing over the wall, and half soaking me. That suited my mood to perfection; maybe one wave would overwhelm me, suck me back into the sea, and that would be an end of me.

And I would shout her name to the whole world, without any danger of anybody hearing me, the wind snatching my voice and tearing it to rags on its journey to the distant lights of Whitley Bay.

At times I would consider chucking myself over, but by that time my fury was spent, and I was suddenly quiet and peaceful with weariness, and would limp the last two miles home with a blister, feeling small, like a mouse going back to its hole.

My cruelty was vented on the Geography mistress, Winnie Antrobus. She was one of the younger ones, about forty, and had the misfortune to be a mate of Emma's. I knew Emma talked to her; they were always chattering and laughing when they met in the corridor. She was a tall, plump woman who might once have been a beauty, and she was a fool. Because when she made small mistakes in class, she would never admit it.

I mean, all teachers make mistakes sometimes. When we pointed them out to the men staff, they just said things like 'Thank you for your esteemed help, Atkinson, what would we do without you?' or 'I had a bit too much beer last night' and they'd get a laugh and we'd forget it.

But Winnie . . . one morning we were doing the fauna of North America and she announced that moose lived on 'herbage and small animals'. My hand went up like a shot, a most concerned and scholarly look on my face.

'Miss Antrobus, you did say small animals?' The class gave its hunting cry, very soft. She saw the trap; she turned pale, but set her lips and gave an emphatic nod.

'What small animals, Miss Antrobus?

'It doesn't matter. We must get on. Lots to do before the bell goes.' She glanced at her watch desperately. 'The next animal in size is the caribou . . .'

'Oh, but it does matter,' I said, all earnestness. 'It's *fascinating*. Are these *very* small animals, like mice? I mean, a moose catching a mouse? Does the moose pursue the mouse across the open prairie, or does it lie in wait for it concealed behind a bush? Like a cat? Does it pounce and rend the creature with its sharp claws?'

Even the prissy girls were starting to titter.

'And,' asked Jack, 'how many mice does it have to catch in a day? Several hundred for a good meal, I would imagine?'

'A herd of moose would need millions,' added Rita Davies, the boldest girl. 'This is so *exciting*. I hope we get an A-level question on it.'

'I meant *insects*,' said Ma Antrobus desperately. 'Insects are animals too. Insects crawling on the grass the moose eats.'

'Ah,' said Jack, 'but does the moose *know* it's eating the insects? Does it say to itself, "I'll just stroll down and chew a few insects this morning"? Because that would make it insectivorous. Wouldn't it, Miss Antrobus? But if it just eats them by accident, without knowing . . .'

'George the Fifth once ate a caterpillar by accident,' added Rita. 'It was on his salad . . .'

'Hang on, I must write this down. George-the-Fifth-was-insectivorous. Isn't geography fascinating?'

'Miss, if a moose ate King George the Fifth . . .'

But Miss Antrobus was no longer with us. Eyes brimming with tears as usual, she was swirling out of the door with her gown flying out behind her.

Jack spent the rest of the period drawing a diagram on the blackboard of a moose eating King George the Fifth. Still wearing his crown.

I sometimes passed Emma in the corridor. I'd look up, and see that beloved shape, and I'd suddenly stride towards her, smiling the smile we'd always smiled at each other in the corridor, small, discreet, but warm, eye to eye.

But now she swept past me in a swirl of academic gown, barricaded behind an armful of books, eyes snootily above the heads of the common herd. It was like being kicked where it hurts most.

I grew desperate. It could go on like this for ever, till the end of the summer term swept us apart for good. I had no *reason* to speak to her ever again. Sometimes I mourned her as if she was dead; sometimes I hated her in her snooty impregnability. But all my emotions got me nowhere; at the end of them I was still only a sixth-former, a scruffy working-class kid who'd somehow got above himself, who'd shit in his own nest, as my father always put it. That phrase of Winston Churchill's, about broad sunlit uplands, haunted me. I'd lost mine.

And yet, there were moments of wild hope. My grandmother told me that her mother said she'd not been well. How I clutched her illness to me; hoping against hope that I was the cause of it!

And then one day in the changing-room, after a particularly vicious private rugby practice, when I'd kicked a ball so hard it had landed through somebody's greenhouse, Jack said to me, 'I didn't know Ma Harris was keen on rugby!'

I just grunted.

'She was watching us today. She stopped and watched for five whole minutes.'

I was quite sure she'd been watching me.

It was then that I resolved to hunt her down, like a beast of prey. She was weak, behind her wall, and I would get her through her weakness. I would touch her if I wanted to, where I wanted to, when I wanted to. Be damned to what *she* wanted.

I grew cunning; I worked out the one place where she couldn't escape me, where she couldn't run away, or catch a bus, or go into some place I couldn't follow.

In fine weather, the whole school moved out on to the playing field. And the staff on duty had to move out with them. They did it in pairs, one man, one woman; once a fortnight. And she was on with Conk Shaw . . .

Most pairs of teachers just strolled together, talking and laughing in the sunshine, trusting in their very presence to maintain order. But Conk Shaw was a bossy-boots, all over the field, telling kids to pick up bits of litter, and even interfering with the little football games, when he thought they were getting too rough.

The day they were on duty, I followed them up the touchline of the first-team soccer practice, a big book in my hand, keeping a discreet distance. In no time at all, old Conk was away, striding across the field, clouting ears left and right.

I smiled, and pounced. Thrust the book into her hands.

'What's this for?' She did look very pale; her eyes went very wide, and dark suddenly. Her pupils very big.

That was the first time I'd ever seen that in a woman; but I seemed to know it was a good sign, by instinct.

'That's for us to pretend to talk about,' I said. 'You don't want them gossiping about us, do you?'

She set her lips in a tight line, but started walking on slowly, holding the book open, and I walked with her.

'What do you *want*?' she hissed.

'To see you. To talk to you. That's all.'

'That's quite impossible.'

'*Why* is it impossible? I was only trying to cheer you up.'

'Is *that* what you call it?'

'You asked me to hold you – to go on holding you.'

'Keep your voice down. D'you want the whole school to hear you?'

'Let me see you, then. I promise I'll behave. I promise never to touch you again.'

'It's quite impossible.'

'But *why*? We used to have such good times. All I want is to talk.'

'You'd better be off – here's Mr Shaw coming back.'

'Not him. He'll be clouting heads till the whistle goes. *Why* have you turned against me?'

'You know I haven't turned against you.' She said it in such a low wretched voice, I was certain I was going to win.

'What harm will talking do? If only you'd explain to me what I've done, I could say I'm sorry. Even if it was just the once, we could part friends. I don't *understand*.'

She turned and faced me. I realised she was making a big effort, for she closed her eyes . . . and I realised with horror that I had lost. By a whisker. The final 'no' was coming.

And then . . .

And then the first-team fullback, under pressure from enemy forwards, made a wild and desperate kick into touch. And the ball came flying straight for her head . . .

I caught it before I knew I'd caught it. I had never done anything so neat and amazing in my life. A few specks of mud and grass landed on her forehead.

I went wild. I went up to that fullback, and slammed the ball into his chest and shouted, 'Can't you bloody look where you're kicking? You nearly seriously injured a *lady*.' I kept on slamming the ball into his chest and yelling at him. Till the master who was refereeing came up and took the ball off me and calmed things down.

I turned away in despair, knowing that she'd have taken the chance to slope off, expecting to see her retreating back halfway into school.

She was standing there laughing.

'The white knight on his steed! Damsels in distress a speciality. Oh, you looked so *cross*! I thought you were going to murder that poor lad.'

'Mindless soccer-playing twit.'

'Oh,' she said, 'you're only a boy. I've been taking you much too seriously. And myself. I'd forgotten how *funny* you are. I could do with a good laugh.'

'I can come then?'

'Just this once. If you *solemnly* promise to behave yourself and make no attempts on my virtue.' She was suddenly terribly solemn.

'I promise,' I said. The awful frozen hell was over; all over the world the ice was melting. I'd have promised her anything.

'Tuesday, then. And take this silly great book away. You know I have no interest in William the Conqueror, you *silly* child.' She was as happy as I was, and I knew if I played my cards right that one more meeting could turn into any number.

The bell went, the whistle went, and, kicking their footballs ahead of them, across the stud-muddied yard, the school went back to work, and I, dazed, overjoyed, with them.

I was even good and kind to silly Ma Antrobus, when she feared more trouble. I might even have been kind to Tony Apple, or the devil himself.

I went back, and it was different. Why did she make it so hard for me? We sat in our same old places, her on the couch, me in her father's chair. But it was the *way* she sat; it wasn't tarty or provocative, but it was *fashionable*; the stylish way women sat in magazines. Legs crossed, arm along the back of the settee. And her clothes; she was either spending a lot more money on clothes, in spite of clothes rationing, or she was using all her wardrobe on me. In the old days, I hadn't watched her more than I might have watched my mam, or a mate. Now I watched her all the time; noticed things I hadn't noticed before. How small and neat her ears were; the small creases at her wrist and elbow; the way her little finger curved, and was more separate from the others, when she put her hand on a page; the beautiful almond shapes of her fingernails.

There was always a hint of perfume now; and she kept having her hair done different ways. There was a perm, that didn't suit her, and made her look middle-aged and frumpish, which put me in a bad temper. But it was quite gone by the following week . . .

Her manner had changed, too. She drove me much

harder with the Latin; I was getting really good. And she took to referring to me, when her mother came up, as 'young Atkinson here'. And the number of times she told me I was only a boy, or still wet behind the ears, or had a lot to learn. She was worse than my mam and dad. And it stung; what especially stung was her new habit of leaning over and brushing my hair lightly with her hand, when she was cross or especially pleased with me. The same gesture the games masters used on young kids when they'd been a bit hurt in a match, but decided to struggle on bravely. It made me *feel* a little kid; a nothing . . .

And then, when I had my coat on, and was leaving, she would say, 'You may kiss me goodnight,' and hold out her curved cheek, as if she was my mother or aunt.

I was different too. I hadn't forgotten the feel of her weeping in my arms; the more I thought about it, the more I liked the memory of it. But I kept my word, for I was in terror of being flung out of paradise again; the cold airlessness of being alone. I didn't put a foot wrong, though there were times saying goodnight in the narrowness of her hall, when she brushed against me by accident, and I would tremble from head to foot.

# Part Three

## 17: Joyce Adamson

Well, if I couldn't touch her, I would touch some other woman. Anything that was going. And I had a ready-made subject for experiment to hand. Joyce Adamson. Ever since Clatterburn, she'd been giving me yearning and reproachful glances across the classroom.

A few of the lads had taken Joyce out. Mainly because her father, who was reported to be stinking rich, owned an aeroplane which he flew with the Aero Club at Newcastle aerodrome. Only an old ex-service Tiger Moth he'd got cheap after the war, but an aeroplane was an aeroplane, and after you got asked home for tea, you just might get offered a flight . . .

But nobody got asked home for tea, even. And the reports of Joyce's conversation out of school were worse than those inside school. Bill Tewson said all she'd done was to ask the time three times, and on the last occasion, said it was time she went home. Even the possibility of a flight in an aeroplane couldn't make that kind of boredom supportable. I know they say men prefer dumb blondes, but that's a different sort of dumb.

Anyway, one Monday night, which was a night when nobody else had any money, and everyone was safely doing their homework, I took her to the Carlton. It was a movie called *Flying Tigers* starring John Wayne and

Anna May Wong, which I wanted to see anyway, so the most I would have wasted was one and ninepence. The film finished with everything getting blown to bits, which was rather enjoyable, like that stall at a fairground where you can break crockery with wooden balls.

Early on I'd put my arm around her, in those twin seats that the Carlton had in the back row of the stalls. And she'd put her head on my shoulder, and that was that. I emerged with a very stiff arm, and I wondered if she emerged with a very stiff neck. We walked back in silence along the seafront. Halfway to her house, I dragged her round the back of a seafront shelter and put both my arms round her. I mean, if it didn't work, I wasn't in the mood to waste any more one-and-ninepences . . .

She didn't give any indication that she objected, so I kissed her. Our noses banged together painfully, so I showed her how to turn her head so our noses didn't bang together the next time we did it. She kept her lips together, like they all did, but her breath was sweet. So I loosened the belt of her coat; they were useful, those coats; they were tie-belts with no buttons. Still she didn't complain, so I put my hands inside and stroked her back; it was a bit like stroking a big friendly dog, but her shape was more interesting. Then I dropped my hands till I had them on her hips, and again she just stood there. So, greatly emboldened, I put one hand half on her upper arm, and half, accidentally-on-purpose, on her left breast, rather expecting to have my face slapped. But no, she just let me kiss her again, so I put my hand right on her breast. It was only when I started to undo the top button of her blouse that she pushed my hand away. Not nastily; not indignantly. And she went on holding that hand in a very friendly way.

Fair enough. I gave her about six more friendly kisses and then, squinting at my watch over her shoulder, I saw what time it was, and we set off walking again. I didn't want to miss the last bus; it's a long walk home.

By and large, I was pleased with her. She was definitely worth one and ninepence; she had nice big breasts. I'd ask her out again. I was so pleased with her I prattled on all the way to her gate. About blokes in our rugby team, and our chances for the new season against Whitley Bay Grammar, and about various teachers.

She even volunteered one remark of her own; that she liked Mr Blake, she thought he was a good teacher.

We had another kissing session on her doorstep. I didn't undo her coat again, because her father might emerge. But I pressed both her breasts through her coat, just to remind her. Then I asked her out again, the following Monday, and she just nodded. Then her father put the front room light on, so I scarpered.

I caught the last bus, and rode home feeling like a man of the world. I hadn't thought of Ma Harris for at least an hour.

I took Joyce out twice more. We established frontiers. She didn't mind me stroking her neck and face. She didn't mind me laying hands on her bottom through her rather thick skirt. She didn't even mind me finding her navel, through her jumper. That made her giggle which was at least cheerful. Actually, I tickled her a lot, in non-sexy places, like armpits. She liked being tickled; she had rather a good giggle.

And she showed a quick grasp of the rules of rugger,

so she could understand how I'd scored my tries last season. She said the rules were quite different for hockey. She also told me her father went away on business a lot, all about her young brother's awful habits, and that she adored Humphrey Bogart. Which was more than anybody else had ever got out of her. We became quite good friends. I think she was truly grateful someone was taking an interest. Two of her mates had seen us out together, and that had sent up her status quite a bit. She always gave me a very nice grin when we met on the steps of the Carlton.

It was a pure fluke that I was tickling her under the armpit, as we walked back along the seafront with our arms around each other, that last night when we met Emma. I mean, I suppose it looked worse than it really was . . .

Emma was standing under a street lamp, ten yards ahead of us, when I saw her. She'd been taking her dog for a walk. It was a golden cocker spaniel, and it had wrapped its leash half-round her legs and was pulling like mad but not getting anywhere. Except I was scared it was going to pull Emma off her feet.

I stopped tickling Joyce instantly; and Joyce shoved my arm away from round her. My whole side felt cold for the lack of her. But then my whole *being* felt cold.

We all just stood there, about five yards apart, staring at each other. With the tall yellow street lamps like a dwindling chain along the edge of black sea and sky. And an occasional gust of wind shaking the street lamps and making them sway, and bringing the noise of waves breaking, out there in the dark. I could not read the expression on Emma's face. The swaying light of the street lamp cut her face cruelly into triangles of yellow and darkness.

Then, after what seemed for ever, I said nervously, 'Good evening, Miss Harris,' and Joyce echoed me, even more nervously.

There was another pause, then Emma said coldly, 'Good evening,' and let the dog tow her away.

We walked on, far apart. Joyce said, 'She won't report us. She's a good sort. Not like the old ones. Not like Katie Merry.'

It was the longest speech she'd made yet. I couldn't say anything. I just walked.

After another hundred yards, Joyce said, 'We weren't *doing* anything. Just having a laugh. It's not like she caught us in the *shelter* . . .'

I was still unable to say anything. Joyce said, 'After all, we weren't in school uniform. We could've been *anybody*.'

We reached the cover of the shelter, and Joyce ducked behind it, out of the wind. It was the first time I hadn't pulled her in. She went in of her own accord. That was the first time it occurred to me that Joyce might actually like the things I did to her; didn't just see them as a reluctant payment for trips to the cinema. It surprised me a bit; half the kick for me was that I'd thought her a reluctant, unwilling victim . . . the other half of the kick was just exploring, which you could do with any girl.

I followed her in, and just stood next to her. I didn't feel like doing *anything*. After a moment, she stood a bit closer; put a timid hand on my arm. It was a bit like our dog nudging your arm, when it wanted its ears played with.

'Not tonight,' I said gruffly, feeling a bit shifty. Joyce looked back along the empty seafront.

'It's all right, she's gone. There's nowhere to hide. Anyway, she wouldn't spy on us. She's not that sort.'

Still I stood.

'Give us a kiss,' she said. 'Please!' She sounded really worried now. So I gave her a reluctant peck.

'That's not much of a kiss!'

It drove me mad, her nagging at me when all my mind and body was on Emma. So I gave her a kiss just to shut her up. The kind of kiss I'd once given Emma. She sort of went rigid with shock, but I didn't stop. She began making incoherent protest noises, and then she put both hands against my chest and pushed me away really hard. We stood glaring at each other, under the windy sway of the street lights. Her eyes were accusing, as Emma's had been.

'You know I don't like that sort of thing!'

'What sort of thing?' I was spoiling for a quarrel now and she sensed it, and cooled down a bit. She knew how thin her hold on me was.

'It . . . upsets me. I'm not . . . ready for it.' There was a quaver in her voice that excited me. A crack in her shell, in the shell of silence she always kept up.

But I said bitterly, 'I kiss you gently and you don't like it. I kiss you rough and you don't like it. You don't know what you want.'

'I just want it to be like the other times.' It was a bit pitiful, really. But I wasn't in any mood to have pity. Because I was bloody sure Emma wasn't going to have any pity on me. So I looked at my watch and said, 'We'd better get cracking. It feels like rain. And I don't want to miss my bus.'

She guessed then I wouldn't be seeing her again. 'Oh, *Robbie*,' she said, and there was real sorrow and real affection in it.

'Let's go.' I turned on my heel and began to walk.

There was another seafront shelter, just before we reached her house. As we neared it she said, in a very low voice, 'You can kiss me roughly, if you like.'

We both stopped. We stared at each other. With her eyes full of distress, she was a handsome piece. And a surrender is a surrender, even if you don't really want it . . .

So I took her in and kissed her roughly many times. She even let me undo three buttons of her blouse before a desperate hand stopped me, and clutched my hand and wouldn't let go.

'Please, Robbie, be *patient*. I have . . . to get used to it.'

'Oh, all right.' I just stood there, feeling desperately weary. She was as scared of losing me as I was scared of losing Emma. We were both in the shit together, and I felt a sneaking sympathy for her I'd never felt before. And if Emma did give me the push, Joyce'd be better than nothing. A lot better than nothing.

From far away, as if to confirm my judgement, there was a low growl of thunder.

'We'd better run,' I said, quite gently. 'Or we'll get soaked.'

We ran, arm in arm. On her father's doorstep, I said, jokingly, 'Well, you've found your tongue at last!'

She just stared at me. The hall light was on, flooding through the oval window of the front door, and by its glow, I saw to my horror that tears were trickling down her face. Hell, if her father saw her like that, World War III would break out, and I'd never be allowed to see her again. Even my little female insurance policy would be gone. I grabbed my hanky out to mop her down, but she took it off me and dabbed very cautiously. God knew what she was doing to her make-up . . . just *everything* was going wrong tonight.

And then, blessedly, it started to rain. Whole stair-rods. My own face and hair were soaked in an instant. Saved. There was a sudden brilliant flash of lightning somewhere out over the blackness of the sea. Thunder rattled, deafeningly.

Footsteps thundered up the hall, too. Her father yanked the front door open.

'What are you standing there for, you ninnies? You're getting soaked.'

'We were watching the lightning,' I said. Just then there was another spectacular many-branched flash.

'Well, come in where it's dry,' he said, quite impressed by the lightning in spite of himself. We stood in the darkened front room for ten minutes, watching the display fade away out over the sea, as if it was a fireworks night. By the time it was over, we were both totally calmed down, and her mother sent Joyce upstairs to change, before she caught her death of cold. And gave me a good hot cup of cocoa.

Joyce came down again, in blue pyjamas and a thick blue dressing gown. She looked OK in a cosy domestic sort of way. I had a brief vision of spending my life with Joyce in a dressing gown every night. Not exciting but . . . cosy. Could do worse.

I felt so relieved, rescued, that I chattered away with them, ten to the dozen. We got on like a house on fire. I even heard her mother mutter to her father in the kitchen that I seemed quite a nice boy. Her father replied I seemed a bright spark, anyway. They seemed relieved that Joyce hadn't done worse for herself. Her father even got out his car to drive me home.

He wasn't all that impressed with where I lived. But he could see it wasn't a slum; all our door knockers are polished every day, and the privet hedges are cut regularly.

And you can't have everything.

# 18: Hothouse

It was Emma who opened the door to me, not her mother as usual.

'Good evening,' she said, distantly.

'Is you~ mother all right?' I asked nervously. I couldn't think of anything else to say.

'She's gone with my aunt to the Essoldo at Newcastle. They're showing *Gone with the Wind*.'

'Oh.' I was even more disconcerted, because I'd just noticed she was wearing a brand-new polo-neck sweater. Dark pink; knitted from a soft, clinging wool, angora I think my mother calls it. Polo-neck sweaters were the latest craze. Some American film stars wore them, like Lana Turner who was called the sweater girl. We had a joke going the rounds. Why do sweater girls wear sweaters? Three reasons. One is to keep them warm. The other two reasons are perfectly obvious . . .

Emma settled at our work-table. Her other two reasons were more than obvious; they were delectable. And the dark pink of the sweater seemed to reflect up into her face.

'Right,' she said, even more brisk and schoolmarmish than usual. 'Virgil, Book Six for you tonight, m'lad. C'mon, Atkinson, gather your wits. I'm not doing this for the sake of my health, you know. Start at the beginning. *Sic fatur lacrimans . . .*'

' "Thus weeping," ' I stumbled, ' "he gave free rein to the fleet, and came at last to the Euboic shores of Cumae." '

She leaned forward, pointing with a finger. 'I would rather say, "the Cumaic shores of Euboa". Don't you agree?'

Was she trying to drive me *mad*? Her left breast hung less than three inches above my hand where it rested on the tatty-paged book. If I lifted my hand as if by accident . . . but I knew that that would settle my fate once and for all. She would quite rightly sling me out on my neck.

'C'mon,' she snapped. 'We can't spend all night drifting round the Cumaic shores of Euboa.'

I made a very poor show that evening. I couldn't think about anything but that sweater. And she'd rolled up its sleeves, so that the creamy skin of her arm showed, where the near-invisible down glinted in the light of the desk lamp . . . what would it be like to touch?

And yet she was as correct in her speech, as sharp-tongued, as Katie Merry. And then the little jokes about Joyce started.

'The Delphic Sybil, wrapping up the truth in obscurity. Sounds a bit like your little friend, doesn't it? Only she wraps up the truth in total silence.'

I just sat there and *writhed*. Then there was that bit about the death of Icarus.

'Icarus . . . poor young man,' she said, looking at me with those great dark eyes at a distance of less than a foot. 'He had those wonderful wings, but he was too *arrogant*. Flew too near the sun, and the wax that held them on his back melted, and he fell headlong to his death in the sea. Beware of arrogance, Atkinson . . . take it from *Daedalus, ut fama est, fugens Minoa Regna.*'

' "Daedalus, as the story goes, fleeing the Minoan Kingdom . . ." '

' "The Kingdom of Minos", if you don't mind. Even your wonderful Joyce wouldn't have got that wrong.'

It was the last straw. I don't know what it was, the sweater or the taunting, or even the knowledge that the rest of the house was empty . . . but I just blew. Jumped to my feet. Roared at her.

'For pete's sake, leave Joyce alone. Stop picking on her. What's she to you?'

She bristled at my rudeness; but it wasn't quite a schoolteacher's bristle.

'She's nothing to me, and less than nothing. A mere pupil. As you are yourself.'

I expected her face to go pale at my shouting, like my mother's does. But it stayed quite a bright pink. And her eyes were very bright too. Somehow I knew she *wanted* a fight.

'Joyce is a mate of mine.'

'I hope you'll be very happy together. I'm sure you have the most *fascinating* conversations.'

'There you go again! There's more to life than conversations.'

'Obviously. There couldn't be less in her case. I have never known her make an intelligent remark.'

'She's nice to *cuddle*,' I shouted, fit to bring the house down. 'At least she's not scared to let me touch her!'

'*Fascinating*!' Did she flinch? 'You *are* making good progress. You must have winning ways. Are you *quite* sure she doesn't mind you *touching* her? Or is she just putting up with you?'

'She doesn't move away, so she doesn't mind.'

'How *romantic*! It wouldn't have done for me, as a girl. I saw off a wretched Frenchman once, who thought like you. I was walking along the Champs-Elysées in a sleeveless dress, and he began walking beside me and stroking my bare arm. Thinking he was irresistible, just like you. I never even looked at him, just went on talking to my friend. In the end he screamed some silly remark about *les Anglaises* and whirled away into the road, right in front of some passing taxi. I was kind to him, after that. Visited him in hospital; took him some flowers. He was in plaster from head to foot, so he'd forgotten all about being *sexy*.'

'Big deal!' I shouted. '*La Belle Dame Sans Merci*.' (We had been doing the poem for A-level.)

She knew the poem too. That one went right home. She stood up. I thought she was going to slap my face. I knew I had given her the excuse to throw me out for good. She'd got what she wanted. I despaired. I half raised my arm to ward off the blow.

But she was trembling from head to foot. Inches away from my upraised hand, her left breast hung like a ripe lovely apple.

I knew it was my last chance to do the thing I'd been wanting to do for all those years, since I was a little kid.

I put my hand on it. It gave slightly; a softer elasticity inside the elastic of her bra.

She glared at me, and I glared back. It was the biggest battle of wills I was ever in. But I knew a trick; you don't look the person in the eyes, you look at the bridge of their nose, and then it's easy. I could still see the cruel red mark on the bridge of her nose, where she'd just whipped her spectacles off. And one little curved dark hair, at the end of her eyebrow, that stood alone from the rest.

I knew I'd won, when she gave a shudder. It was a terrible shudder, as if something had collapsed inside a building, and the whole building was going to fall.

And then she slapped me. God, it hurt so *much*. I put my hands to my face.

The next second she'd pulled my hands away from my face, and was kissing them, and tears were streaming down her own face.

'I'm sorry, I'm sorry, I'm SORRY. I'm a *bitch*. Here, sit down. I'll get something to ease the pain . . . I'll make you a cup of tea . . .' But she didn't move from the couch.

Now she was like a mother, pulling down my head between her breasts, stroking my hair, murmuring soothing things as to a little child. I stayed where she wanted me. It seemed the safest thing to do. I was totally bewildered.

I just lay there, smelling the smell of her body, feeling her tears falling on the back of my neck and trickling through my hair. They tickled. And listening to her voice going on and on, as much to comfort herself as to comfort me.

'Oh, this is ridiculous. I'm old enough to be your mother. I'm a *teacher*. We're supposed to stand *in loco parentis*. What's got into me . . .'

She went on like this for a long time. But her hands went on stroking my hair, as if they had a life of their own. I began to get pretty excited, smelling her, moving my head a little, so that her breasts moved too. They were startlingly warm, through the wool of her jumper.

And then her voice suddenly changed, became

brisker, as if she'd made up her mind about something. And her body stiffened, and she pushed me upright, holding both my upper arms.

'Robbie – look at me!'

Her eyes, full of tears, looked enormous, wonderful. They seemed to fill the world. Their pupils were enormous. And she didn't look at all miserable and pinched, but softly flushed. I had never seen her look so beautiful, even if her hair was all over the place.

'I know what's the matter with us. We've spent too long cooped up together in this room. We need to get out . . . do things together. Fresh air and exercise. Being cooped up's unhealthy. Like living in a hothouse. Feelings . . . get out of control. We're being silly, so very, very silly. We're ruining a lovely friendship. Being in the fresh air will make us good-tempered with each other again.'

A pain was gnawing at my stomach that I'd never felt before, except when I'd got kicked in the wrong place playing rugger. But it wasn't as excruciating as that. More warm and draggy. I was so full of feelings I couldn't say anything. I just let her go on talking.

Finally she said, 'We are going to be sensible. We are going to behave properly, like sensible people. Agreed?'

From the cosy place, I nodded my head. I'd have agreed to anything, while she went on holding me.

'And we shall have our day out. Where would you like to go?'

'The Wall,' I mumbled. 'Somewhere on the Wall. That hill above Vindobala. Where we made you into a human sacrifice.'

She laughed, a little shakily. 'Yes, we had a good time there, didn't we? Well, we shall have good times again.

142

And be sensible about it, too. I hope you'll go on seeing Joyce. I'm sorry I was so rude about her. She's a nice girl. Promise me you'll go on seeing her.'

'Don't you mind?'

'No – I was just being silly. I *insist* you go on seeing her. She's good for you. Not a tear-stained old hag like me. God, I bet I look a mess. Here, sit up, will you! I can't *move* for you, you great lump! How much do you weigh?'

I told her I weighed twelve and a half stone, while she peered in the mirror, and groped for her make-up and comb in her handbag, and tutted and made other exasperated noises. And yet, I thought vaguely, she sounds so *satisfied*. She sounds so . . . comfortable with herself.

'I'll go and make us some tea.'

I went on lying on the couch, waiting for the pain in my stomach to go away.


So, if we had agreed to be sensible people, and all above board, with nothing to feel guilty about, why did we then start to plot like burglars?

'Do you ever go off for whole days on your own?' she asked, as she sipped her tea. 'Walking? Or cycling?'

'I'm famous for it,' I said. 'I once walked thirty-three miles. Last August Bank Holiday. I had blisters for a week after.'

'Why did you walk so far?'

'To find out if I could.'

'Do you always go on your own?'

'Nobody's daft enough to come with me.'

'D'you enjoy it?'

'Not much. The start's nice, being in the country, if

the sun's shining. After that, it's just a bit of a slog. The last bit's OK, when I'm looking forward to flopping out on the bus home, knowing I've done it.'

'Well, you'll travel in luxury with me. By car. I'm not a masochist. Will next Sunday do you?'

'Yeah.'

'Fine. Where shall we meet?'

'Well, we don't want nosy eyes . . . I'll set off north, through the pit villages. Nobody from our school lives up there, and nobody *goes* up there, either. I'll go through New York and Shire Moor. And you can overtake me and offer me a lift. What could be more innocent?'

# 19: The Kingdom

'Where you off to today, then?' asked my father at breakfast.

'Roman Wall,' I said, through a mouthful of bread and bacon.

'Make sure you don't fall off the top, then.'

'It's only about five feet high.'

'That was a joke.'

My mother wasn't in such a joking mood. 'It's not natural, the way you go off on your own all the time. When I was your age, we went round in a gang, all the lads and lasses together.'

'You mean in a gang, like robbing banks?'

'Don't be cheeky,' said my father.

'And take your raincoat. It looks like rain. Don't come back here soaked to the skin an' gettin' a cold and expecting me to nurse you.'

'Which part you going to?' asked my father. 'In case you fall off an' break your neck, and we have to send out a search-party.'

'Getting the bus to Hayden Bridge. Doing the bit round Housesteads Fort.'

My lies seemed to boom in the air like a great gong. But neither of them heard it.

'I'll go and water me chrysants, then,' said my father.

'Don't do anything I wouldn't do.'

'We used to have so much fun going round in a gang,' said my mother. 'Those were happy days, happy days.'

I picked up my old Boy Scout rucksack. It was just big enough to carry a sandwich tin, a Thermos flask and a great big old trenchcoat my uncle had given me. This, together with a pair of ex-army boots, an ex-army balaclava rolled up on my head, and a Bartholomew's map of Tyneside, was my complete hiking gear.

'Tara, well.'

I went off at a great pace, feeling like a spy. Every lace curtain seemed to twitch at me. Every old granny was on red alert as if it was some national emergency. I went through New York, which was named after the American New York, but had no other claim to fame. American soldiers, in the war, were always turning up there for a look-see. They didn't stay long; it was only a single street of collier's cottages, and a pub that sold very warm beer.

In Shiremoor, a black car passed me and then pulled up with a toot-toot. Through the small yellow back window the dim blur of a woman's head turned round to look at me. I had the door open and was shouting, 'You made it, well-timed, what did you tell your mother?' before I realised with a terrible shock that the woman inside was a complete stranger, offering me only a smile and a ride.

There seemed no possible explanation I could make, so I just shouted, 'No thanks,' and slammed the door on her and walked on stiff-legged, staring sweating at the sky. She gave me a very funny look as she passed again; probably thought I was an escaped inmate of Morpeth Asylum, and she'd had a lucky escape.

Beyond Shiremoor it began to rain, and I began to despair of her. Her car wouldn't start. Her dog was ill. Dead. Her mother was ill. Dead. She'd had a crash and was lying bloodstained amidst wreckage and broken glass. Or I'd explained the route wrong or the time wrong, and we were doomed (by some Omniscient Being whose eyes were as evil and carping as the rest) to spend the whole day seeking each other, unavailing. And I'd return footsore and weary from a day of colliery villages, to hear bad news of her.

Her brisk toot-toot as she passed me sounded like an angel's trumpet. But I still opened her passenger door with the smile of a polite stranger; you don't catch me that way twice.

She was wearing dark glasses, as we'd agreed. I just hoped the sun would come out soon. But her lips were unmistakable. It's funny, I hate men who wear sunglasses, they look so sinister. But with women, it just makes their lips look more beautiful.

'Sorry I'm late,' she said. 'I couldn't stop my mother fussing. You'd think I'd never left home for the day, before; have I got this, have I got that? I just drove off and left her talking, in the end.' She gave a slightly uneasy laugh, and I got in. The car sagged beneath my weight. It seemed very small and narrow and dark, even if it did have four doors. The smell of leather and petrol made me feel a bit sick.

She zoomed off; it would have seemed a real gangster getaway, except she missed a double-declutching, so we nearly stalled. And me staring out of the back windows, making sure we hadn't been noticed and weren't being followed . . .

It was a pretty tight fit. Our shoulders touched; her

hand bumped into my knee every time she changed gear. Her skirt kept on riding up a bit, showing her own shapely knees, and she kept taking one hand off the steering wheel to pull it down again. I could smell her hair, through the leather and petrol smells. But sadly I put such thoughts out of my mind; we had agreed we were innocent.

'I'm sorry you're so cramped,' she said apologetically. 'This was Daddy's last car, an Austin Ten. 1935.' She said it very wistfully, like a little girl. It suddenly brought the ghost of her daddy into that brown-windowed space. Made her seem vulnerable, young. But I just thought, your daddy's dead, but *I'm* here.

She gave me a map to hold on my knee. Bending my head to it made me feel even more sick in that petrolly interior, as we worked our way through that unlovely network of slagheaps and electricity pylons, that had given us such good cover, but had suddenly become intolerable for me. If we broke down here (and the old car made constant and frightful noises) our precious day would shatter into a thousand fragments. And the car, under her white-knuckled hands, rattled and jerked and ground on, in a way that was far from reassuring.

Slowly, by many crossroads, we worked out of the cinder tracks, rows of outside privies, bright-striped pigeon crees and rusty roadside signs for Bovril and Numol. At Heddon, the rain stopped, and the sun came out, and the road stretched before us, straight as a ruler.

'This is Wade's Road,' she said. 'Built by General Wade after Bonnie Prince Charlie's rebellion.'

I said, 'Please, miss. Yes, miss,' in my best primary school impersonation. She giggled explosively, and reached for my hand and gave it a squeeze. It was only the solidarity of successful spies, who have completed their mission, but we were suddenly light-hearted now. The dross of pit heaps was left behind; we were new-born, clean out of our everyday lives. Eagerly watching through the brown-edged windscreen for the new gifts that our new-found land presented to us. I wanted nothing from the past, not even the things I normally clung to, like my brilliant O-levels, or my rugby triumphs, let alone parents of soul-destroying aged dullness. I wanted only what this land was giving us. This shepherd, with his greasy grey cap and paw-poised dog was *our* shepherd; with all his twelve newly clipped sheep thrown in for good measure. This farmer's wife, hanging out her clothes in her front garden with her mouth full of wooden pegs, was *our* farmer's wife. The golden misty morning sunlight was *our* sunlight; and the dark hedges, their swathes of cobwebs glinting with new-minted raindrops. This was our land, and we would rule it wisely as king and queen.

'Happy?' she asked, with a bright sideways glance, squeezing my hand again.

'What have I been doing with my life until now?'

She coloured slightly, and turned her eyes to the road again. But there was no harm in it; we had agreed innocence. My body was quite calm; my fumblings with Joyce now seemed beneath contempt; with all the rest of Tyneside's squalor.

A pub appeared, standing on the crest of a rise, solitary as a sentry. Old grey walls, long rows of windows, a sign so weathered it told us nothing. A pub without cars or dogs tied up outside. A pub existing only for us. With a weathered grey bench in the garden.

'Drink?' I asked, being greatly daring, grown-up.

'Why not?' she said. 'Only a half of cider.' And pulled in. I desperately hoped my four and elevenpence would be enough.

'Two halves of cider.'

He made a fuss about finding bottles; cider was a rarity in pubs then.

'Does your girlfriend want ice in hers?' He was staring through the window at her. She was sitting on the old bench, flirting a bit nervously with three hens. In her ankle socks and stout walking shoes, and sweater, she did look like a sixth-former. There was no mockery in the landlord's voice. The dark glasses hid the lines under her eyes. On that golden morning, she could so easily have been seventeen . . .

'Yes,' I said. 'Ice.' Though I did not know if she liked ice or not.

'That'll be two shillings, sir.' Uttered in slow Northumbrian, it was a kind of blessing on us.

I carried the drinks out. She brought her eyes back from the low striding moors.

'It's so lovely,' she said. 'I wouldn't mind if you left me here. I'd happily die now.'

We pulled up below our hill. Far above, the sunlit clouds blew past the dark needle of stone where we'd made her into a human sacrifice.

'D'you think I should take my raincoat?' She squinted at the sky.

'I'll carry it for you. Better safe than sorry.' It was one of those white rubberised riding macs, with a red lining. I rolled it into a neat cylinder, and hung it in my rucksack straps.

'It fascinates me,' she said. 'You're so careless about

150

some things, and so meticulous about others.'

'Things that matter. Let's go.'

Halfway up, we came upon a long wide stretch of burnt heather. The farmers burn it, to give the juicy new shoots a better chance in the spring. Sheep like the new shoots, they won't eat the old. The old burnt heather was no more than tall black curved sticks, in a bed of black charcoal that crushed under our shoes with a squeaking noise. But those old burnt shoots were tough and springy still. They didn't snap off; they whipped us, as we passed.

'Oh look,' she said. 'The burnt heather is drawing in charcoal all over me. How am I going to explain *that* to my mother?'

I looked. She had pulled up her skirt. Her calves and knees were cross-hatched with black lines. But above, the inside of her thigh was a breathtaking soft white.

But there was no harm in it, just a lost sadness. For we had vowed to be innocent.

'Look at my trousers,' I said. '*My* mam will have a fit. C'mon, I'll give you a tow.' And slowly I began to tow her up the hill, by one hand. But she, perhaps to show independence walked out far to one side, so we were almost level.

Thus we climbed up into the silence, only broken by the lonely sound of the wind, and distant peewits.

Silence outdoors is a funny thing. If you don't want to be alone, it drains you of all life. If you do want to be alone, you drink it up like spring water. But if you're with somebody you like, it sort of presses you closer and closer together. In spirit, I mean. As if it too was blessing us and and what we were doing . . . I was very aware of her quickened breathing, as the hill got steeper.

151

And then, suddenly, shallower, and we were going faster and faster, and almost running as we flung ourselves down beneath the stone needle, where the heather had stopped and there was a ring of short soft grass.

She looked at the stone needle, and giggled, remembering.

'Let's have lunch. I'm starving.'

'Which way d'you want to face?' I asked, getting out my trenchcoat.

Southwards, far below, the excavated walls of Vindobala lay, like an intricate honeycomb, crawling with black swarms of schoolchildren.

'Not today,' she said with a mock shudder. 'Today I am *not* a teacher.'

'We'll face north. So we can spot the Picts and Scots coming to make you into a human sacrifice.'

'Not much future in being a human sacrifice. Less even than being a teacher.'

We opened our sandwiches. She'd made a lot, very dainty triangles with the crusts cut off. Mine were the usual self-cut slabs. I was suddenly ashamed, because she laughed at them.

'Better have some of mine,' she said. 'We'll save yours for emergency.'

'Mine *are* an emergency.'

Hers were nice. Ham. A subtle blend of cheese and chutney. Something she called 'Gentleman's Relish'.

'I know what gentlemen relish,' I said.

'Down, Atkinson, down! Remember your monkish vows.' She kept holding her sandwiches out to me, and I kept eating them. In between admiring the landscape. Afterwards, she said, 'Peaceful,' and stretched out her

152

legs and leant back against the stone pinnacle, offering her throat to the sun.

'Puts things in perspective,' I said. 'The rat race an' all that. What does time matter, up here? This view can't have changed much, since the Romans. I expect they came up here, for a bit of peace.'

She began to recite a poem. About some old centurion saying goodbye to the Wall. Housman or Kipling, I can't remember which. She recited it very well. After that, we just sat in silence, watching the huge cloud-shadows skimming north towards the Wall, passing through farmhouses and barns and coppices as if they were huge unstoppable ghosts. The wind, growing a bit stronger, did rude things to her skirt. She tucked it in beneath her legs severely, as if it was a naughty child.

She said, 'This is perfect. You can leave me here. I wouldn't mind being *buried* here.'

I knew what she meant. The sun and the wind for ever; away from all the filth and dross of school, the sneers and the jeers and the backbiting. And yet she had a sadness that worried me.

'Is teaching so bad; so awful?'

'Not you,' she said, 'never you.' She reached out and held my hand and gave it a reassuring squeeze. 'But being a teacher is such an *act*, from start to finish. You're on stage all the time, like a bad comedian. Only you don't get many laughs and they never clap at the end. You can never be your real self. I have to play the part of Ma Harris. I can never be just *Emma*.'

I said, timidly, 'Can I call you Emma?'

She looked at me, startled, halfway back to schoolteacher.

'Well . . . yes . . . when we're alone. But you'll never tell any . . .'

'My lips are sealed.'

'We guard our Christian names like gold. If the kids find out, they shout it after you in the street, and your discipline's gone.'

I said, in an attempt to pay her back for the great privilege, 'My parents call me Bob, my nana calls me Robbie and the common herd round school call me Akker. Take your pick.'

She pursed her lips, head on one side, considering me. Teasing, for she drew it out to a great length. Then she said, 'I'm not one of the common herd. And Bob's too short for you. It's a funny little name for a funny little boy. I shall call you Robbie.'

'You don't find me a funny little boy, then?'

'I find you large, and at times, alarming. I suppose that's half your charm.'

'Big and ugly; it helps at rugby. There, I've made a little poem for you.'

'Don't look so horribly smug.' She smacked my hand, in mock-punishment. 'Be nice.'

'I'm always nice to you. You're not a scrum half.'

'You're not always nice. You can be horrid.'

'How, horrid?'

'You were horrid to Winifred Antrobus. You had her in *tears* in the staff room the other morning. I couldn't do anything with her. You *can* be so sweet . . . *why* do you do things like that?'

I was tempted to take the 'bit of fun' line. To tell her Ma Antrobus made her own misery by not admitting ever being wrong. But that hilltop was a place where lies didn't work.

'I did it because I was mad at you, and she was your friend.'

A stillness and a sadness crossed her face. I suddenly felt cold. The very light seemed to have dimmed. And then I felt a dampness on my cheek. And realised that our latest cloud-shadow was lasting far longer than any other. I looked southwards.

Beyond Vindobala, the brown autumn hills were paler than the sky. The sky was filled with bulging slaty clouds, from which dense scarves of rain were already falling. On Vindobala itself, the swarming crocodiles of schoolchildren were already breaking up and running for the shelter of the hut. Faint screams came up to us, and the twinkle of white ankle socks on the feet of scampering schoolgirls.

'Blast!' I said.

'C'mon,' she said, gathering up the picnic things. 'Run for the car.'

'We'll never make it.' The car was a tiny black-beetle, far below. 'We'll be soaked before we get halfway.' I had a hiker's hatred of getting wet. 'Look, I can keep us dry. I've done it before. We'll make a tent. Sit down against the base of the pillar. Quick!'

She did so. The base of the pillar was about five feet across and four feet high. It would keep our backs dry, against the worst of the driving rain. I sat down next to her, and arranged my uncle's huge trenchcoat across our legs. Then I undid her riding mac from its straps, and hung it over our heads, with the open side to the front; and grabbed in the rucksack. The sandwich tins wouldn't come to any harm.

And then the squall hit us. There was a thunderous patter of raindrops on the riding mac overhead.

'How ingenious,' she said. 'You are a clever young thing. But the rain's still coming in the front.'

'We'll have to sit closer.' I put an arm around her, to pull her in tight, and rearranged the mac, leaving only a tiny slit, out of which we both peered, as the view to the north disappeared under the driving rain.

'Snug,' she said. 'I love rain when I'm not getting wet in it. How long will it keep us dry?'

'Forever,' I said. 'I once spent three hours under my uncle's coat like this. It's harder if there's just one of you.'

'Ow! Ow!' she said, turning to me. 'A drop of rain just hit me.'

I turned to look. I meant to say, 'It's coming through the pocket of your mac,' but I never got further than 'It's'.

Because my mouth was against hers.

And the bomb we'd been tinkering with all those weeks finally exploded.

It was nothing like the torrid love scenes in the books I'd read. Nothing like the sloppy corniness of my mother's books, and nothing like the more gymnastic scenes in the dirty books my father occasionally kept hidden under the family biscuit tin in the sideboard in our lounge, which I'd discovered at the age of twelve and had been keeping an eye on ever since.

There was only one story I'd read that was anything like it. That was 'The Door in the Wall' by H.G. Wells, which is about a man, who, as a kid, comes upon a white wall with a green door in it, and goes through, and finds a magic enchanted garden, which he eventually loses and can never find again, until he dies in

156

the attempt.

I could tell you of the little things that surprised me; that a woman's skin is so much hotter than a man's, and so much smoother. I could tell you that the sounds a woman makes, her very breathing, is more like a symphony than anything else; but a symphony that you can understand far more easily than you can understand Beethoven. Listen and you always know where you are with her. It tells you when you are winning, and when you are losing; like hunt the thimble, you are always getting warmer or colder. But those are just details.

The real thing is that you are journeying, exploring, into a country that you don't know, but a country that is entirely on your side. Where you are absolutely safe. You pause, and wonder whether you dare go on. You creep on in fear and trembling, but there is no flare of sudden resistance, no sudden sniper's bullet of protest out of ambush. Instead, a little arching of the back that leads you to the bra hook, and a long silent patience while you fumble with it, and curse yourself for a blundering idiot who deserves a clout. There is a knee digging hard into your thigh, so it hurts and you reach down to move it gently, and then you realise that is a *knee* you've got your hand on and, above, the skin is even smoother.

And in that land you can raise storms, tempests, at your will, and you feel sick with power because you are a great magician.

And afterwards, a great peace and you could lie there for ever, because there are no longer two people, but only one, breathing quietly. And there is nothing else in the world; there is no world but this safe darkness. And all loneliness, and being sick to death of being fastened

157

up inside your body with all the nasty things that are you, are done away with for ever.

And then things start to come in from the world outside again. You realise with a start that that world still exists. The last few raindrops pattering down on the mac; a streak of sunlight through a crack in the coats.

'My arm's got pins and needles,' she said, sleepily, and moved. The mac fell open about a foot, and we peered out together at the world we had thought so lovely only an hour ago, so perfect; but which, by comparison with where we'd been, seemed cold and thin and a little scary.

'You all right?' she asked.

And I was all right. Safe and dry, and still inside my buttoned-up trousers. For there was a simple rule in those days; if you got a girl pregnant, you married her. Full stop. The only alternative was to leave home, family, friends and district, and that made you a pariah; who nobody would ever want to know again. The penalty was as inexorable as the death penalty for murder.

It had happened to a mate of mine, poor Benny Jobling. We'd planned to go to university together. But poor Benny was always talking about sex (we thought it rather ill-bred of him). And then, he got involved with Thelma Hargreaves, who we'd always known as the sort of girl who let boys do things to her. She wasn't even pretty; just willing. And poor Benny got caught.

No university for Benny. No more school, even. Down the shipyards at sixteen, apprentice riveter, having what was left of his brains hammered out by the noise inside a ship's hull when fifty riveters are going full out. And when he came home, it was to one room in his mother-in-law's house, and a kid that never stopped bawling, and a wife who had gone to bits with having the baby, and went about in curlers, nearly as fat and slovenly at seventeen as her mam was at fifty. He didn't even give his pay packet to his wife; he had to give it to her mother. And she gave him back five shillings a week; not enough to keep him in Woodbines. And that was for the rest of his life; two women nagging at him non-stop and he couldn't even get a chair near the fire in winter. I crossed the road when I saw him coming; we all did. The misery on his face made any attempt at cheerfulness seem a deadly sin. It would have been like slapping a leper on the back.

Maybe it was the fear of hell that kept Catholic lads on the straight and narrow. With me, it was Benny Jobling. I'd rather have been a monk for life; at least monks got some respect, and some peace and quiet.

Emma said, 'I bet I look a proper fright.'

I looked at her. Her hair was a bit tousled, and the bandeau was all crooked. But her face was softly pink, and all the lines on it seemed gone, as if smoothed away with an iron. And her eyes were huge and dark and dreamy. She found her strappy handbag in the wreckage of the coats, and took out a comb and began to comb her hair. On and on and on, slowly, as if it gave her enormous pleasure; with her eyes on the horizon, so when she spoke, it was as if she was talking to somebody else.

'I wanted you to respect me,' she said. Then, 'I've ruined everything.'

'It wasn't you,' I said, trying to cheer her up. 'It was me. It was *my* fault.'

'Don't be such a ninny. Don't you know how women can make themselves *available*? It is all *my* fault. I used you. I'm a bitch. Like a bitch on heat. I shouldn't be allowed loose round young boys.'

How could words of such bitterness come out of her mouth, when she looked so well? So utterly content?

'I didn't plan this, you know!' She looked at me accusingly.

'I know. It was the rain. We should have let ourselves get soaked instead.'

'What must you think of me?'

'I think you're the most wonderful person I ever met.'

Was that a half-smile, or was she just biting her lip?

'You know we must never do this again?'

'Why ever not?'

'Because it's *wrong*.'

'Didn't feel wrong to me. Felt wonderful. We're not harming anybody.'

'Only ourselves. But if people *knew*? If they ever found out . . . You know I'd be sacked on the spot? Without a reference? I'd never get another job in teaching, not even in some crummy little private school. I'd have to leave the town . . . my mother . . . I think the disgrace would *kill* my mother . . .' Her face grew dark; she was going way from me; I was losing her.

I grabbed her arm. 'Nobody knows. Except us. It's our secret. We've been careful. We can go on being careful.'

'*God* knows!' She gave a little shudder; even looked up at the now harmless clouds that were drifting overhead.

'God says a lot of things. But folk don't take much notice.'

'Like what?'

'"Thou shalt not steal." My dad goes to church, but

160

he still buys things cheap at work, and he knows they've been stolen. God says, "Do not bear false witness," but people lie every day of their lives, when it suits them. The world runs on lies. If everyone told the truth all the time, World War III would break out in a week. God says, "Sell all you have and give to the poor." That'll be the day.'

She gave a short harsh little laugh. I took the chance to press the point home.

'What's so special about God and sex?'

'I'm old enough to be your mother!'

'You must have had me very young!'

She did laugh, now. 'Oh, Robert, what am I going to do with you?'

'Be kind to me. In secret.'

'Oh, the headmaster warned me about you!' But she was smiling ruefully now, and I knew the worst was over. At least for the moment. And just as well. Because life had not only returned to Vindobala, but a snake of children, under two teachers, was slowly wending its way up the heather of the hillside.

'Oh, how can I face them?' she asked. 'Let's get back to the car.'

'If we run away now, it will look suspicious.'

'But if it's somebody we know . . .'

'You wear your dark glasses, and I will give them a lecture on human sacrifice on this very spot.'

'Oh, you're *awful*!'

Luckily, it was no one we knew. And anyway, they were far too wrapped up in squabbling and keeping control to give us more than a cursory glance. I actually sat and finished the rest of her sandwiches, and waved to them idly.

We drove back into Tyneside in the dusk. The air smelt of tar and smoke, salt and rust. It was like driving into a hostile country.

'I'll probably burn in hell for what I've done today,' she said.

But she said it quite cheerfully, now.

# 20: Gaining and Losing

Peacefully, we lay in the long grass and stared at each other, sideways to the world.

'Why do you keep closing your eyes alternately?' she asked.

'Each eye sees you a different colour. My left eye makes you look pinker; my right eye makes you look yellower. D'you think I ought to go and see a doctor?'

'No,' she said, very solemnly. 'Sometimes I *am* yellower. My great-grandfather was a Chinaman!'

'Be serious!'

'If I was serious, I would say I was worried about you. These times are great for me, but what do *you* get out of it? It can't be much fun for you. I get everything, you get nothing. It's not *fair*.'

Her hand went out primly to pull down her skirt. But I caught her hand in time.

'Don't. I like looking at you.' She grimaced, but went on holding my hand, and I went on looking at her thigh.

'I like looking at you,' I said again. 'I like touching you and smelling you and listening to you. All your sexy moans. You're like a symphony by Beethoven.'

'Which one?'

'The "Pastoral". This is the shepherds' rejoicing after the storm.'

'Am I *so* noisy?'

'The last time, they could have heard you in Haydon Bridge. I like the way you call my name over and over; like you were falling over a cliff and didn't care . . .'

'It's not like falling, it's like *flying*.'

She looked at me like I was a beloved clever child who'd passed the eleven-plus, O-level and A-level all in one afternoon. Then she said, 'Don't you ever want . . . more? Don't you ever feel . . . bad-tempered . . . afterwards?'

'Only when . . . it doesn't work for you. Then I feel *useless*. If you're happy, I'm happy. I love the way you comb your hair, afterwards. I *like* making people feel happy.'

'Now I feel part of a great crowd. Who else have you made happy?' There was a little sharp edge in her voice. Though she was usually happy, afterwards, she was touchy, too. As if her skin had grown very thin. I groped in my lazy mind for a safe answer.

'Me mam and dad are happy, when I get a good report. Our dog, when he knows I'm going to take him for a walk.'

She let me off the hook with a gurgling laugh. Then said, a bit petulantly, 'You see plenty of *me*. I never see anything of *you*. Look at your shirt still all buttoned up. I'm surprised you're not wearing a *tie*!' Her hand came up and undid my top button. 'I don't even know if you've got a hairy chest!'

It made me . . . uneasy. What was mine was mine. My own private person. I felt suddenly a bit . . . invaded. But I just imprisoned her hand firmly, and turned it into another joke.

'I've got seven hairs on my chest. I've counted them.

I'm lucky – me dad's only got three. If we are the average of our parents, that means me mam's got eleven *somewhere*.'

She giggled. 'You are a fool!' But then her hand wriggled out of my grasp, and slid down inside my shirt, and tweaked with her fingers. 'I think I've found one of the seven. Shall I pull it out?'

'Don't you dare!' I grabbed her hand again, and transferred it to the raincoat by main force. It wasn't that I hadn't liked her touch; but I felt I was starting to lose control of the situation. Buttoned-up was safe.

But the edge had come back into her voice. 'Sauce for the goose is sauce for the gander. I was only undoing your shirt, for heaven's sake! I just wanted to see your chest, that was all.'

'I don't know why. It's ugly. I'm ugly.'

'Don't I get a chance to form my own opinion?'

Oh hell, this was real trouble brewing. Please don't spoil our lovely happy time. We've only got another hour . . .

I rolled over on my back and stared at the sky. 'OK, you can undo my shirt if you want.'

She giggled again, a lovely noise. I'd know that giggle in a thousand. 'You know what you look like? A Victorian bride on her wedding night. Lying back and thinking about England.'

'Get on with it.' I shut my eyes, and gritted my teeth. I felt her undo four more buttons; so deftly. Then she pulled back the halves of my shirt, heaving them out of my belt and trousers. The sun was warm on my chest; the breeze blew cool on it. I felt her eyes run up and down me, like tickling flies.

'Your chest isn't ugly, just big. You remind me of one

165

of those classical fountains; Neptune sounding his conch.'

'Yeah, Neptune.' That would do me. Not Apollo, not Adonis. Old Neptune. Why not? 'Have I got any moss or lichen on me? Could I do with a good scrub down?'

'I'll see.' She ran one finger daintily, tracing my muscles. My hands, by my sides, were clenched tight. I was losing my grip on everything. I'd gained a whole lovely new world, discovering her. But now I was losing the world I'd had before I met her; the only world I'd had since I was a little kid.

'What're you all tensed up for?' she asked, half laughing at me.

'It *tickles*. I can't *stand* being tickled.' I was on the verge of exploding into rage. She heard it in time.

She said, plaintively, 'Can't I just put my head on your shoulder? You smell so nice.'

'Oh, all right then.'

I felt the cool tickling shadow of her hair descend, and her arm go across my chest. Then we were quite still, listening to some curlews calling, across the hill, and the breezes sighing in the long grass.

'There,' she said coaxingly, like she was my mother taking a splinter out of my finger when I was a kid. 'That's not so bad, is it?'

''Sall right. But keep *still*.'

'You play on me as if I was a violin,' she said resentfully. 'But you just lie there like a block of wood.' Then she said, 'I can hear your heart beating. It's thudding like mad. Maybe you aren't a block of wood after all.'

God, women! Little busy fingers, trying to pry you open all the time. Trying to explore parts of you you've never even explored yourself.

'Maybe this block of wood is starting to feel like touching *you* again!'

She laughed, triumphant. '*I* don't mind. I don't mind at *all*!'

It had been a crazy half-term week. October week, the teachers called it; potato-picking week, we called it. A week of sunlight. We'd come up to the Wall three times, and it was still only Thursday. We'd have come on the Tuesday, too, only it rained stair-rods all day, and even I couldn't get away with going for a walk, crazy though my parents usually thought me. I had hated Tuesday; mooning around, feeling so helpless, staring out of the window praying for the rain to stop.

'You're like a caged tiger,' my mother had said, and even I had the sense to calm down and despair properly, and settle into a book about American bombers in the war, that I'd read a hundred times and knew by heart.

Things had changed with us. We no longer came to our hill. It was too popular, too public. We looked for places where nobody would come. Fields with sagging gates, wired up. Fields with long grass in their gateways, and no marks of tractor tyres. Fields with high dense hedges, full of winter cabbages the farmer wouldn't come near for months yet. Oh, we had grown very cunning, and we hadn't been caught.

'What about tomorrow?' I asked, as we packed up our things ready to go.

'No can do,' she said. 'Dentist's at twelve o'clock.'

I was outraged that she should let a mere dentist stop us.

'Can't we come here after?'

'I'm having a tooth out – a nasty one at the back. D'you want to kill me or something?'

'Saturday, then?'

'I have to go shopping with my mother, Saturday morning. *Every* Saturday morning. And my aunt and uncle are coming for afternoon tea.'

'*Sunday?*' It was a scream of rage and pain. It was as if I was a dying man, watching my life dribble away. Ahead, there was only winter; rain, frost, snow . . .

'I've still got marking to do. I've done nothing this week, thanks to you. And lessons to prepare. Life's got to go on, you know. It can't *all* be holiday. Even you must see that. Haven't you got any things that need doing? Homework?'

'Bugger homework. What's homework?'

'Look, you must have known we couldn't go on like this for ever. It's been a kind of lovely madness . . . a dream. But we've got to wake up now.'

'So you'd rather do marking than be with me?'

'That's not fair. The weather forecast for the weekend is more rain, anyway.'

'You've got it all planned very neat and tidy, haven't you? When can you next fit me in?'

'You're coming on Tuesday evening.'

'To do *Latin*?' I made it sound like breaking stones on Dartmoor.'

'We're happy, and then we have to go back into your little box. That's the price you pay. It *hurts*. Didn't you *know*? Oh, I'd forgotten how young you were.'

'*Thanks*. I'll just crawl away under a suitable slimy stone.'

'I'm sorry. It's my fault. I shouldn't have let it happen.'

168

'Not happen? But it's been the most wonderful . . .'

She clasped my wrist tightly. 'Life is wonderful; then it's terrible. You *must* accept that. Look, I'll tell you a story. That last night Reggie was on leave from the RAF – the last night before he was killed – my mother had gone out on purpose, and left us alone together. We were just going to make love, when there was a ring on the doorbell. Reggie didn't want me to answer it, but I did. It was my aunt and uncle. I couldn't just turn them away – they'd come to see me, to congratulate me on my engagement. They'd brought us an engagement present. They stayed the whole evening, till my mother came home. And Reggie was nice to them, and made them laugh. Even though he *knew* he was going to buy it, somehow. All I could do was play him that last piano piece, to say how sorry I was. That's how hard life can be. What would you have done?'

It silenced me. I killed my lovely mad dream of being always happy, of the world being made for us. Like killing a rabbit with one blow to the neck. Maybe that's what growing up is.

She said, fearfully, 'You could look in on Sunday afternoon, if you like. You haven't been for a lesson this week. You could have a problem with your Latin. I'll give you a cup of tea. I don't know what my mother will say. But it'll be all right, she likes you.'

'OK,' I said wearily. 'Sunday afternoon tea it is.'

The little box isn't so bad, once you've squeezed yourself back inside it. Old patterns take over, and you forget pretty quickly how it's been. Some things in that little box you even enjoy. Like our opening match of the rugby season.

It was straight after school on the Wednesday night. Against Garmouth School. We were Tynemouth High School. Garmouth School was fee-paying, and all boys, but only about three hundred of them, including kids of eight. They only played rugger, never soccer, which wasn't posh enough for them. They played very pukka rugger, and tackled bravely, and fell on the loose ball suicidally, and ran for the line, passing the ball with great precision, when they got it. Bill Fosdyke thought very highly of them.

We usually managed to beat them in the end (though they held up well till half-time). Because they didn't have any big nasty rough bastards like me.

It was a glorious evening, as we ran on to their pitch at Prior's Park, overlooking the Priory ruins, and the river and the sea. With the tall Georgian houses where they all lived, all around us, winking their big many-paned windows in the distance. There was a seagull perched on the top of every goalpost, come to see the fun. And more than a smattering of our own kids, since for once they didn't have far to walk, and they liked to see us win, on the few occasions when we did. And there were about six of our staff there, calling in on the way home, and I was surprised to see Emma among them, talking to Fred Wrigley, which made me a bit narked to start with. I vowed to play in such a manner as to take her eyes off him as quickly as possible.

It wasn't long before one of our backs dropped the ball, in our own half, as is their regular habit. I'd taken up the custom of running across behind them, to tidy up just such blunders. Now I grabbed the ball, expecting death and hell to fall on me at any moment, when I heard a clear small authoritative call of 'Akker'.

There, ten yards behind me, beautifully turned out in his spotless white soccer shorts, was John Bowes.

I gave him a lovely pass, straight into his big hands. The next second, there was a great thump, and the ball dwindled away heavenwards. I thought it might land on the top of Garmouth Priory, or even in the sea; but it plopped down nicely into touch, a mere yard from their goal line.

In the line-out that followed, one of their lot, a big beanpole called Wardle, caught the ball. But I pinioned his arms before he could think what to do with it, and he dropped it, and I fell on it.

A clear try. Everybody flung their arms in the air, and the kids on the touchline began shouting, 'Well played, Akker!'

That was until Bill Fosdyke, who for some reason known best to the gods was refereeing, ran up.

'No try. Knock-on,' he shouts.

'Who's supposed to have knocked on?' I asked. 'I never touched the ball till I fell on it.'

'Scrum,' he said. 'And don't argue, or I'll send you off.'

So the two packs scrummed down, and we pushed them clean over their own line. And scored. We had to do it three times, before old Bill Fosdyke would admit we'd actually scored. It was so boring . . . but good old John Bowes converted it with a big kick, for two more points.

And that was how it went on. John Bowes's big kicking, against Bill Fosdyke's bent refereeing. He let their side get away with murder, but he kept on whistling us up, and disallowing tries we'd clearly scored. It made our lot so mad, we began to play really well. I mean, the backs became so careful not to drop the ball. We really worked like a Swiss watch; we really looked like a rugger team for once. Of course, it was all John Bowes – he kept us in their half nearly all the time. Jack scored two lovely tries jinking and weaving, and even Tony Apple got one.

At half-time the score was 27–0.

Bill Fosdyke came across to us, while we were sucking our quarter-oranges.

'Just ease up now,' he said. 'Take it easy. You've won already. Just leave it at that.'

'It's not *gentlemanly* to score more than thirty,' mimicked Jack, behind his retreating back. 'Stuff him!'

The second half was a slaughter. I got two myself, and then, when they were disallowed, John Bowes began kicking tremendous drop goals instead. Forty yards, fifty yards . . . Even Bill Fosdyke couldn't find fault with those.

We ran off at 63–0. Bill Fosdyke turned away from apologising to the Garmouth School masters and said, 'Atkinson, I want a word with you.'

I just stood. It was hard luck on Bill Fosdyke that the rest of the team decided to wait with me. So all he could do was rail on in general about lack of sportsmanship.

I glanced across to where Emma had been, hoping for a smile or a wink. But she was walking off the pitch with Fred Wrigley. And he was holding her by the arm.

There was a sudden wriggle of unease in my gut.

# 21: Two Women

The next Saturday evening, I called on Nana with a bag of Brussels sprouts. Her face lit up.

'Bye, you've just missed your Miss Harris. She called here with her mother, for a cup of tea. She *was* looking bonnie, better than I've seen her in years. Ten years younger. Pretty as a picture.'

I tried not to smirk. But I was also relieved to have missed her. My nana has very sharp eyes and ears. What would we have dared say to each other? Still, it was nice to have been so close . . . I sniffed guardedly and thought I could still smell her perfume in the air.

'What did *she* want?' I asked, letting a bit of ungraciousness creep in. 'I didn't know she came to see you?'

'She doesn't, as a rule. But they'd been out shopping. Her mother said she'd been getting out a lot, over the half-term. It's done her good. She looked quite tanned.'

Inwardly, I gloated. If only they knew . . .

'Her mother says that Fred Wrigley is showing an interest again. He's taking her to the pictures tonight. I suppose she *could* do worse, at her age.'

I sat there, suddenly frozen. I couldn't move hand or foot. It was like a direct hit from a six-inch shell. And Nana didn't miss it.

'You all right, pet?'

'I got kicked in the match on Wednesday. In the back. It catches me, when I sit.' Somehow I blundered it out, screwing up my face and feeling my spine gingerly.

'You want to get to the doctor's. It's a nasty rough game, that rugby. Like some cocoa?'

She went off and rattled her kettle, while I fought with a black fiend inside me, the like of which I'd never known before.

How *could* she? After all we'd done and all we'd been? I'd made her happy, I'd put that look on her face, and bloody Fred Wrigley had come flapping back after her, like a vulture. I remembered his hand on her arm, at the end of the match.

I don't know how I struggled through Nana's usual chat. I kept on having fantasies of beating Fred Wrigley's head against the stones, outside the Rock of Gibraltar . . . oh, I'd have it out with her, I'd have it out with her.

As I got up to go, Nana said, 'Tek care, now. You do look a bit not yourself. Get down to the doctor's on Monday, if that pain's not better. You'll have your mam worried sick.'

How did I live, until that Tuesday night? Largely inside my head, playing out the same scenes over and over again. So I was word-perfect, when I got to Emma's.

Still, I remembered to be nice to her mother. Scraped a big smile on to my face, like a mingy ice-cream vendor giving you short-change with an ice-cream sandwich.

'Go up. She's expecting you.'

So she was expecting me, was she? Well, she'd get more than she expected . . .

She looked up from her desk. She looked fresh and young and glad to see me. But her smile was just a little bit apprehensive. She knew what she'd done. I threw my Latin books across into the chair. So hard one of them bounced out again, nearly into the fire.

'Robert! What's the matter?'

'You know bloody well what's the matter. Fred Wrigley's the matter. Back row in the Carlton's the matter.'

'We didn't go in the back row. Don't be so *silly*.'

'Did he put his arm around you? Did you hold hands? Or did he put his hand on your knee?'

'With half the sixth form watching? Don't be so ridiculous. And keep your voice down. D'you want my mother to hear you?'

'How could you? How *could* you?' I discovered how to have a row, in vicious hisses.

'Why shouldn't I? I've often gone to the pictures with Fred. He's a friend.'

'Well, that's one name for it. And he was *pawing* you in public at Prior's Park.'

'Pawing me? He had a hand on my arm, you silly boy.'

'Silly boy is it, now? I wasn't a silly boy on the Roman Wall . . . at Vindobala. Or was I? You were just *using* me. I was *convenient*. Does Fred touch you . . . ?' I couldn't finish the sentence. The vision I had conjured up choked me.

'Oh, Robert.' She came across and took both my hands in hers. 'You're torturing yourself. We just sat and watched the picture and he drove me home, and came in to have a cup of coffee with my mother.'

That made me feel better. But I wasn't ready to show

175

her that. 'My nana says you could do worse at your age than *marry* him.' I had a sudden vision of them getting into bed together. Of her having a baby. That vision was so awful, I was nearly sick on the spot.

'Robert, Robert!' She had clutched me by the upper arms, and was shaking me gently. 'You're beside yourself.'

'Well, it *could* happen.'

'Ninny. I only went with him because I wanted to see the picture. It's not much fun going on your own.'

I knew it was true. It was very comforting. And yet I would not let myself be comforted. Fred had a car; Fred had a good job, a university degree. All I had was an old bike and a tennis racket. I had the whole long journey to make. It could be twenty years before I stood where Fred Wrigley stood now.

'Come and sit on the couch. You've worked yourself up into a terrible state.' She sat beside me and put both arms round me. I suddenly felt very comfortable and terribly weary. But there were still questions . . .

'Has he *kissed* you?'

'Yes, many times. Usually on the cheek.'

The black fiends of hell had me by the throat again.

'But not like *you* kiss me. That's not his style. *Please*, Robert.' Her arms were tight round me. She was trembling. I suddenly grabbed her and gave her a tremendous furious kiss, a kiss like a punishment. And another, and another. And the more I kissed her, the more she trembled. Suddenly, she took both my hands very firmly in hers, imprisoning them. 'Not *now* Robert, not *here*.'

'Why not?'

'This was Daddy's room. And my mother is

**176**

downstairs.'

Somehow, they were reasons that sobered me.

'Promise not to see him again!'

'I most certainly shall *not* promise that. If he asks me, I shall go, like I always have. It's my life. You don't own me.'

Her face was pale, her lips were set, and I knew she meant it. I knew she wasn't in the least afraid of me; yet still she trembled.

Then she said, a little bitterly, 'If you knew how I *really* feel about you, you would stop worrying about Fred. It isn't Fred *I'm* worried about. Can't you *tell* the state you get me into? And what future is there in it, for me? A good chance of losing my job, if we get caught.'

I was answered; it was a gift fit for a king. Half-drunk with it, I said, 'I could marry . . .'

'Don't be silly. By the time you're ready to marry, I shall be an old woman.'

'Not so old. What does that matter?'

'It will matter. You'd be the laughing stock of the whole town. I know a man like that. People mistake his wife for his mother, all the time. You'd end up hating me. And I couldn't bear that.'

I thought of her, old and grey, like her mother. I couldn't bear that, either.

'What can we *do*?'

'Try to be happy, while we can. And when you're tired of me, just tell me. I hope we'll always be *friends*.' She suddenly looked defeated.

'I'll never get tired of you. How could I get tired of you? You're on my side, all the time.'

'I hope so,' she said, very doubtfully. 'And I hope

177

you'll be on my side. Please, no more rows, Robert. No more blow-ups like this. I can't bear them. I feel so guilty.'

'But I . . . feel so much.'

'I know you do. That's why I should go on going out with Fred, and you should go on going out with Joyce. We're like a pressure cooker. We have to let off steam sometimes.'

'Do I *have* to take Joyce out? She's such a bore.'

'If you just drop her, it'll hurt her so much. And she'll want to know *why*. And girls have very sharp eyes and very sharp noses. We don't want her as an *enemy*, do we? Whereas while everybody knows you're going around with Joyce, why should they ever get suspicious about *us*? *Give* them something to gossip about – you and Joyce. Then they'll stop looking any further.'

'That's damned *clever* . . .'

'I hope you'll be nice to Joyce. Girls have very thin skins at that age.'

'Oh, I know how to keep old Joyce happy.'

'Steady. Girls my age have thin skins too.' It was said with a thin smile. But it wasn't really funny.

Oddly, all the time I was at school now, I felt I was acting a part. Taking pleasure in acting it rather well. Doing an impersonation of myself, while my real life only started when I was with her. Still, acting doesn't take it out of you like real life does. Not even in a rugger match; not even against Whitley Bay. They were just a state school, like us, but in a posher area. Lots of tall long-legged girls lining the touchline, shouting for their lads in their red-striped blue blazers and red and blue scarves.

Their team was tall and long-legged and well fed too. There was a glossiness about them that we lacked. Their team strips were brand-new; their school had got past the clothing-coupon crisis somehow. Five of our lot had new strips, lovely green and gold. The rest of us had to make do with strips from before the war, their gold faded to cream, and their green to pale grey, and all of them carefully darned.

Whitley Bay always beat us; in a bad year 30–0, in a good year, just.

This year, we beat them. Partly it was John Bowes; they had nothing to answer John Bowes. And partly because I really hit their stand-off early on. After that, he was watching for me more than he was watching what he was doing. Mind you, I didn't mean to flatten him so much he had to go off for treatment. And mind you, Whitley Bay took their revenge on me. The elbow in the ribs in the line-out, the elbow in the eye . . . I ran off at the end, well, limped off actually, a mass of bruises from head to foot. But we ran off winning 22–19.

I was still aching from head to foot when I took Joyce to the pictures on the Monday night. And I took care to limp when I saw her waiting for me on the steps; taking a leaf out of Jack Dowson's book. I was desperate to convince her I was in no fit state for anything physical. The film was a rerun of the Marx Brothers' *A Night in Casablanca* and I followed every laugh with a pitiful groan. In the seafront shelter afterwards, she put a gentle hand on my arm and I said, 'Ow.'

'Oh, for heaven's sake, what's the matter with you, Robbie?'

'I'm paying the price of victory over Whitley Bay,' I

said feebly. Though I felt it had rather a Churchillian ring to it.

'I think rugby's a *stupid* game. Why do you play it, if it makes the rest of your life such a misery?'

You will note that her gift of muteness had somewhat departed.

'For the honour of the school,' I said stoutly. 'We've won two matches in a row. It's going to be the best season ever.'

'Well, I think it's a pain in the neck,' she said with heat.

'Perhaps you think I'm a pain in the neck?' I said, hoping to escalate it into a quarrel, which would get me off the hook altogether.

But girls are too cunning and patient for that. She went all gentle and lovey-dovey, and stroked the back of my neck as softly as a breeze.

'Well, you might *kiss* me. Your mouth isn't bruised.' She kissed me with slightly parted lips, and her tongue flicked out, timidly, momentarily.

'Who taught you that trick?' I demanded, with not-quite-feigned jealousy.

'Rita Tuxfield. She read about it in a book of her mother's. Don't you like it?'

''Sall right, if you like that sort of thing.'

She did it again, very gently. It was *very* provoking. This evening, in spite of all my good intentions, was not going the way it was meant to go, at all.

'There, that's not so awful, is it?'

'Damn you!' I tightened my hands round her waist. Her body felt younger than Emma's; leaner, more elastic. The comparison was very pleasant. Like an essay in English. Compare and contrast Emma Harris and

Joyce Adamson. I felt a totally disloyal rat, and I was thoroughly enjoying it. Well, Emma had said be nice to her . . . but I knew damned well she hadn't meant this sort of thing. Then I made a bad mistake. Quite out of habit, I did something to her that Emma liked.

'Ooooooh,' she said appreciatively. Then, sharply, 'Who taught you that?'

'Jack Dowson told me about it. He read it in one of his mother's magazines.'

'I don't *believe* you. They don't write about that kind of thing in women's magazines.'

'That was a joke, idiot!'

'*Don't* call me an idiot!' She sighed. 'But do it again.'

God, it was a minefield. What kind of things had I done to her, before I touched Emma? I couldn't concentrate. My hands seemed to have a life of their own . . .

I was rescued by a patrolling policeman, who stood about twenty yards away, staring, till we broke it up.

On her doorstep, Joyce said, 'You're a deep one,' very suspiciously. But it didn't seem to put her off me. Then she said, a bit querulous, 'Why didn't you give me a ring, last Thursday?'

'You said you were going on holiday with your dad.'

'Only a long weekend. I *told* you that.'

'Sorry. I got in a muddle.'

'And what were you doing in Shiremoor? Daddy saw you, when he was driving to work. He said a woman gave you a lift.'

I finally realised what that sheer cold sweat was, that novelists write about. Still, I have this quick tongue.

'I was walking to my cousin's at Ponteland. It was just some woman who gave me a lift.'

'You haven't told me about any cousin.'

'He's a bore, really, he keeps pigeons.'

'You prefer pigeons to me?'

I gave a sigh, without enjoyment, at how complicated life was getting.

'Reckon we'll manage against Hexham Grammar,' said Jack the following morning. 'If everybody's fit. Whitley beat Hexham easily. But Dame Julian's are going to *massacre* us, in a fortnight's time.'

Dame Julian's were the second-best team in the county; always had been. In spite of the fact that on the touchline, all their masters wore long black skirts under their overcoats. The lads were all Catholics and wore strips of a deep and marvellous blue with narrow gold bands which had some link with the Virgin Mary. So you felt a little uneasy about tackling them, in case some unwanted holiness rubbed off on you. Their school smelt funny, in a clean and holy sort of way, and people reckoned they had an unfair advantage as all their masters prayed for victory the night before. But that was just flannel, because the best team in the county, Newcastle Collegiate, nearly always beat them, and they were a totally godless Protestant lot who hardly prayed at all.

No, Dame Julian's were just *good*, and rugby-crazy little sods, a lot of them Irish. We knew Bill Fosdyke had to go cap in hand to them, to get us a fixture. Some years they couldn't fit us in. They thought we were a drag, because they had always beaten us at least 30–0, as far as memory stretched back, at least ten years.

'We need more life in the forwards,' said Tony Apple, nastily. I bristled, because the forwards were my responsibility. 'Can't you field Joyce Adamson? You seem pretty thick with her, and she's a good size.'

'Now *look*,' I roared, leaping to my feet and reaching for his dangling tie across the library table.

'Will you sit down and be quiet,' called Ma White, the librarian. 'You should be setting an example, Atkinson. *If* you're still a prefect.'

Tony Apple gurgled with delight. You see how unfair life is?

'Look,' said Jack, placatingly. 'Why don't you try the soccer team again? John Bowes was a good idea . . .'

So I strolled down to watch them practise, that lunchtime. They were not like us. We practised twice a week, at most. They played every second God gave them, breaks, lunchtimes, after school. They played with scruffy old tennis balls, and even tin cans on the way home. They'd sooner have given up breathing than soccer, even in the cricket season.

But at lunchtime they played on the Diggings, a half-pitch carved out with great labour many years ago, from the shallow lower slopes of our local pit heap. It was either huge tufts of wicken grass, or pools of mud, which was why their school uniforms were well mud-spattered in winter.

I lingered behind the goal, which was marked out with piled blazers, which got trampled on and spread during the course of the game, and led to many quarrels about whether it was a goal or not. They even keep tally of the goals they've scored when they're kicking a tin can down the street. John Bowes and I exchanged distant nods. Playing for us had not helped his popularity with them, and he dreaded being accused of being 'one of those rugger snobs'.

They played in a very flashy show-off way; they seemed to be even keener at beating each other with the ball, than in scoring goals. There was one kid in particular who seemed to have to beat all the opposing team twice before putting in a shot. John Bowes, who was no fool, saw me watching that particular kid. Who had quite amazing ball-control . . .

'You're welcome to him,' said John Bowes. 'He's nowt but trouble. Selfish little sod. Rather lose the ball than give a team-mate a pass. We've tried him on the team three times, but he's just too selfish. Thinks he's a second Stanley Matthews.'

But I was weighing this kid up. You could tell he was not from a cultured background. His hair was cut so short it stuck up like a dirty brown greasy lavatory brush. He was pale and had nicotine stains on his fingers. His eyes were reduced to calculating slits, and he seemed to have scars on his face. He was middle size, and not very well muscled, but you could tell he was a hard kid, by the way he blew his nose without a hanky, closing one nostril with a finger and shooting the contents of the other straight on to the ground.

'What's his name?'

'Jeff Cullom. They reckon he nicks things out of cloakrooms. But they've not caught him at it yet.'

But the boy was quick, so quick. Quick with his feet and quick with his elbows, if anyone came near him. And the ball seemed to stick to his toes. If anyone could master a wildly bouncing rugby ball, it was this one. And the way we played, there was plenty of wildly bouncing ball.

'Don't *touch* him,' said John Bowes. 'He's pure

poison, I tell you.' He picked a savage shot out of the air, and punted the ball to the far end of the field. He must feel so cramped, on this half-pitch . . .

# 22: Cullom

I went back the next day, casually carrying a rugger ball under my arm. It got quite a lot of rude remarks.

'Just laid an egg, Atkinson?'

'Your balls are the wrong shape, Akker!'

But I could tell they were watching me like hawks. They knew what I was after. They were wondering who . . .

Just then, Jeff Cullom scored another goal, and came back to the touchline for the restart.

'Not a bad goal, that, Cullom!' I said cheerily.

'How would you know?' He spat on the ground.

'Course, anyone can judge a *round* ball,' I said. 'Bounces true every time.'

'On *this* pitch? You're potty. You should be shut away in Morpeth.'.

One or two of his mates had gathered round, grinning, to enjoy the fun. Which was exactly what I wanted.

'Bet you couldn't control *this* ball!'

'Wouldn't want to, mate. I'm not a rugger ponce.' But his eyes lingered on the ball under my arm, speculatively. Just like John Bowes; any ball fascinated him.

I tossed it to him. 'Go on then. *Show* me how well you can control it.'

'Go on, Cullom! Show the silly bastard!' Now his pride was involved. He spun the ball in his hands, tentatively, weighing it up. Then he put it down and tapped it with his foot. I noticed he hit it on one side, putting a sort of spin on it, that seemed to bring it back to his feet. He took it ten yards down the touchline, while we all watched.

''Seasy!'

Then the ball hit a tussock, and remembered it was a rugger ball, and leapt over his foot at a weird angle. He pushed up his foot to claw it back, so high that he fell over, getting the back of his grey shirt all muddy. Now his little mates, with all that typical schoolboy loyalty, were laughing at *him*.

He got up, mustering what dignity he could. 'Just a matter of practice. Give me a week . . .'

'I'll lend you that ball for a week. Bet you still won't be able to run the length of a pitch without losing it.'

'What you bettin' then?' His eyes were tiny slits of calculation.

'Ten bob,' I said. That was two weeks' pocket money.

'Ten *bob*?' he ridiculed. 'I can make that in Woolworth's any lunch-hour.'

'What, then?'

'Your prefect's badge!'

That was a punch in the gut; and he knew it. My name and the year were engraved on the back of it, but I wasn't at all sure it was mine, till I left school at the end of that year. The head had taken Teddy's and Tony Apple's away from them already. And the amount of trouble Cullom would be able to cause, swanking with it on his lapel round the school . . .

Now they were all starting to laugh at me. The

moment was slipping away. All I could do was to put my faith in the cantankerous nature of rugger balls.

'Done,' I said. 'And if you *lose*, you play for my rugger team. *If* they'll have you! *If* you're good enough!'

He went even paler than he normally was. Whoever lost this bet would be left with no pride at all; would be a pariah. He hesitated. Then one of his friends said, 'No guts, Cullom?'

That did it.

'Yer on,' he said, and picked up his blazer and slouched off with the ball under his arm.

His mates watched me, and murmured. The bet would be the talk of the school, in half an hour. I only hoped nobody on the staff heard about it.

My only consolation that week was the fact that we played well against Hexham at home, and ran out victors at 27–15. They were not at their best, that year, and really had no answer to John Bowes's kicking. Fifteen of our points came from him. We'd probably have lost if we hadn't had him.

And the Tuesday evening with Emma. Latin was quite impossible; impossible to be near her, and not to reach out and take hold of her hand, or squeeze her knee with all the joy of a landed proprietor. And that set her mind in a whirl as well.

But neither could we misbehave much, in that august room, with her father's books lining the shelves, and her father's photograph staring down at us from the mantelpiece. We were simply cosy. She let me lie with my head in her lap, and stroked my hair. I'd used Brylcreem on it, up till then. But now I just washed it every Sunday night, when I had my bath, so it was still soft and dry and shiny on the Tuesday. And we could listen to some records now, without sadness creeping in. Modern stuff, Rimsky-Korsakov's *Scheherezade* and *The Firebird* and Holst's *Planets*, that her airman had never liked or never heard.

There's one movement of *The Planets* that was used for the hymn 'I Vow to Thee My Country' that I knew by heart. And I was so happy, I just sang it, lying there. And she listened.

When I got to the verse, 'And there's another country, I heard of long ago,' she said suddenly, but gently, 'Robbie, you're *crying*!'

I shot bolt upright. 'No I'm not. My eyes are watering, that's all.'

'You *were* crying. Why are you ashamed of it?'

'Lads don't cry. I haven't cried since I was *seven*.'

'*Why* were you crying?'

'It's that line about "another country". I've always wanted another country. Where people are really decent to each other, and aren't always cutting each other to pieces. There's *got* to be something better. Then I found it. With you.'

'Oh, my *love*! I'm not perfect. I . . .'

'You're a lot better than Tony Apple and that lot.'

'It's only because they're boys . . . and young. They'll grow out of it.'

'They'll not. They're getting worse. Anything for a laugh. *Nothing's* sacred. Except you.'

'Oh, my dear.' Were her eyes wet now? 'What about your parents? They love you.'

'Then why does my mother nag all the time? And the old man make sarky remarks, then?'

She held both my hands, tight. 'I expect they're a little

189

scared of you. Have you ever thought of that?'

'There's nowt in me to be scared at. Our dog knows that. *He* trusts me.'

'Your dog hasn't got to listen to you, talking about things he doesn't understand. Supporting the Communist Party and wondering if God really exists. You are quite a handful, you know. Even for me, and I'm used to it.'

'Yeah, I suppose so.'

'And what about all those poor little scrum halves you terrify? Or poor Wilson? And poor Winnie Antrobus?'

'Yeah. All right. You made your point. I can't help being what I am.'

'I expect Hitler told himself that, too.'

'Damn you. You tie me up in knots.'

'Somebody has to, or we'd get no peace.' But her smile was very warm and loving. I caught myself wishing my mam and dad had looked at me like that. Just once or twice . . .

Quite a little crowd gathered, to watch Jeff Cullom make his famous dribble down the touchline. The only people who didn't turn up were the staff. My so-called friends of the rugger team hovered in the distance, equally ready to rush up and get into the action, if I won; or slope off out of the way if I lost.

I could tell Cullom was taking it seriously. He had taken the trouble to change into shorts and soccer boots. He looked pretty pale and he was spitting on the turf a lot. I had a feeling that ball had given him a rough time, and he was none too sure of himself.

Anyway, he lined up with the ball, and looked at me, and I said, a little shakily, 'OK, off you go then,' and one of his silly little friends blew a referee's whistle.

He started off. He took it slow; little delicate taps with the outside of his boot, putting spin on the ball, so it went away out, then curved back in to him. He speeded up a bit, as he reached the halfway line, and I fingered my prefect's badge nervously, in spite of swearing not to.

Just over the halfway line, the ball hit a tussock and reared up into his face, but he used his chest cleverly, arms outstretched, to bring it back under control.

Then it reared up again, suddenly to his right. It was past his shoulder . . . then his right leg whipped up, almost level with his ear, and came back with the ball, as if it was glued to his boot. Oh, he was a lovely ball player; a maker of miracles. How I longed to have him . . .

But he was three-quarters of the way there now; all his mates, every kid in the school going wild, because the fifth-year trogs were going to win, and it was revenge for every little kid who'd ever had his ear twisted by a prefect or been given five hundred lines to be handed in by the morning.

Whether it was the cheering that turned his head, or whether he just wanted to get it over with, I shall never know. But he suddenly speeded up for a flying finish, and the ball began to bounce high again. It was the point, in a rugger match, when you grab the ball with both hands, and run for the line. But he couldn't. He only had his feet. Twice his foot reached it, almost recovering control, and then the ball hit another tussock and went seven feet in the air, right over his head, and in trying the impossible, he fell over the goal line and went full-length in the mud.

A groan arose from the workers' proletariat that might have accompanied the fall of Moscow. They immediately began to shout insults at their late hero, as he lay there, winded.

'Crap!'

'He could never hold his place in the soccer team anyway!'

But I remembered a phrase of Winston's. 'In victory, magnanimity.' And I rushed down to him and helped him up and said, 'Welcome aboard!'

He gave me a very suspicious look, from under lowered brows, with his pale, pale eyes. I think he thought I was taking the piss as well. In his world, everybody took the piss at every opportunity.

But I smiled at him, as genuinely as I could under his withering hate, and said, 'Keep the ball. You'll be needing it. First practice is Thursday. Twelve o'clock, sharp. You'll be playing alongside me.'

'Right,' he said, and walked straight through the rugger team, who were now rushing up to inspect their new acquisition, without raising his head.

As we walked out to the practice, I tried to explain the rules to him.

'Don't bother,' he said. 'I borrowed Bowesy's book.'

'Are you sure?'

'We can bloody read, even in the D stream.'

'Well, when I tackle somebody, and knock the ball loose . . .'

'I know, I've watched you play, you dirty bugger.'

What more could I add, after that?

He was wearing an old grey washed-out rugger strip he'd scrounged from somewhere. He was smaller than our average player, so Bill Fosdyke, without specs as usual, didn't notice him. Cullom had done his homework well; I suspected he'd had a chat with John Bowes; certainly he fitted in from the start. I suppose, when you play one ball game really well, you can soon pick up another. And he was quick, and he had that wonderful eye for a ball.

He scored with a magnificent forty-yard dribble, in the first ten minutes. He caught the ball as it began to bounce high, and made for the line like a terrier.

After that, he was everywhere, except offside. He even got flattened a couple of times, by bigger lads; but just picked himself up without a murmur, and spat on the grass philosophically. A hard kid. He scored twice more, good tries. And Tony Apple had to fall on the ball so much he was caked with mud by the end. Altogether, very satisfying.

Until Bill Fosdyke asked his name.

'*Cullom?*' he said in tones of doom. Even Bill Fosdyke had heard the name Cullom.

'He's been dropped by the soccer team, sir,' said Jack helpfully. 'He's looking for a new way to bring glory to the school.'

'We could bring him in as wing-forward, sir,' said Wilf. 'Bob Cutter's not got over that clogging that Hexham gave him.'

'Cutter may still be pronounced fit,' opined Bill Fosdyke desperately.

'Well, we can take Cullom along as reserve,' said Jack. 'Just in case.'

# 23: Dame Julian's

Jack Dowson sat with his strip off, so we could all see the three creases in his flat belly. He had one muddy boot off and one still on.

'Hell,' he said. 'I still don't believe it. Twenty points to fourteen. We *done* it!'

'I'll bet *they* can't believe it either,' sniggered Tony Apple. 'He dribbled seventy yards for that last one. *Seventy* yards!'

'They never knew what hit them,' said Teddy. 'And he flattened a couple of them. He's a nasty tackler. Worse than you, Akker. That fullback could hardly walk.' He did his usual war dance, stark naked apart from his socks and boots.

'Did you hear Fosdyke apologising afterwards?' asked Wilf. He did a fair impersonation. 'He's really a *soccah playah*, you know. But we thought we'd give him a *chahnce*.'

'I'll bet the Pope won't be pleased,' said Jack. 'Perhaps they won't tell him till he's finished saying Mass in the Vatican.'

'We shall all be excommunicated for not playing a straight bat.'

'No, it's not cricket, old boy, it's not *cricket*!' Jack really was on top form. We all fell about.

Then a frozen hush fell, as Bill Fosdyke darkened the doorway. His face was flushed and sweaty. He looked slightly insane, with his spectacles awry.

'I have never been so ashamed in my *life*!' he said. 'That display was disgusting. Rugby football is a *handling* game. You play against one of the best sides in the county, and you turn it into a *farce*. We shan't be invited here again, I can tell you that.'

'Why?' asked Jack. 'Are they scared of being beaten, sir?'

I thought Bill Fosdyke was going to have a fit.

'It's not a matter of *winning*, Dowson! There's more to life than *winning*. Especially the way you did it.'

'We didn't break any rules, sir,' said John Bowes stubbornly. His big jaw was stuck out; he was really roused, and no wonder. Because he'd played a beautiful game; never put a foot wrong. We reckoned now he might make the county all-age side.

'There's the letter of the law; and the spirit!' shouted Fosdyke. 'I have run this side for ten years . . .'

'And hardly won ten matches,' muttered Jack.

I don't know how it would have ended. Because at that point, two of the Dame Julian's masters appeared, black skirts down to their cracked shiny black shoes, and expressions as dire as if someone had laughed in church on Sunday. They drew Bill Fosdyke outside. From the low apologetic muttering, we could tell this was worse than any mere 20–14 defeat.

Fosdyke came back. He was as pale as death now, and trembling. He licked his lips.

'One of the Dame Julian boys has reported a very expensive watch missing from his blazer in the changing-room.'

Why did we all look at Jeff Cullom? He had just emerged from the shower, looking as scraggy and ribby as ten-penn'orth of cat's-meat, with a very thin worn towel wrapped round his skinny middle.

'Oh hell,' I heard John Bowes whisper. 'I meant to watch him. But you wouldn't stop talking tactics, Akker.'

'Stand aside, Cullom,' said Bob Fosdyke. He stepped forward like an officious copper, and began to finger through Cullom's clothes hanging on the peg, his bag, his filthy rugger kit still lying on the floor under where he'd sat.

It was a bit pathetic. We stood expecting the worst at any moment. But what Fosdyke piled on the bench, for everyone to see . . . A packet of Woodbines, and a box of matches. A crumpled paper bag with two squashed jam sandwiches inside. A page torn out of a magazine, with a well-crumpled busty nude blonde smiling invitingly from a pink couch. And in a used envelope, a French letter . . . All under the eyes of those two priests, who none of us dared look at.

'Nothing,' said Bill Fosdyke, in disgust. He flapped around the whole area where Cullom had sat; as far as the next lads' heaps of clothes. But there was just a bare wet concrete floor, a slatted bench, a blank white-tiled wall. 'Nothing.'

Then he turned to Cullom again and said, 'Let's see inside that towel of yours.'

'No,' said Cullom. He was as pale as death.

'I insist,' shouted Fosdyke. And reached over and began to pull the towel off him. We just watched, as Cullom resisted and twisted his body, and Bill Fosdyke's big meaty hands tugged and tugged. Finally, the towel tore, leaving just a tiny piece in Cullom's hand.

No watch fell out from the folds. Instead, we all looked on Cullom's nakedness. It was big; and very curiously twisted. Really *deformed*. We all knew why he'd been hiding it. He must have spent agonising years in changing-rooms, desperately trying to keep his secret from prying eyes. And now it was out, and he knew it. Somebody among the seventeen of us would blab. It would be all round the school, the source of endless jokes. Maybe the source of a new and hideous nickname . . .

Bill Fosdyke just stood. He didn't know what to do next.

John Bowes did. He stepped up to Fosdyke, whipped away his own towel and gave it to him, disclosing that he was as normal in that department as he was in everything else.

'Search me next, sir!'

The rest of us couldn't disrobe fast enough. Then we turned our pockets inside out, our socks, our shorts, our bags. I have never seen a display of hate like it. And the great fool just stood there with his head down, alternately going white and red.

And then one of the Dame Julian's lads came and tugged at his master's coat.

And there was a watch in his hand.

'It was down a crack in the back of the bench, sir. Under where my clothes were. I don't know how it got down there. I *swear* I put it in my blazer pocket.'

'You are a *fool*, McHugh,' said their master viciously. 'You will see me in my study, *first* thing on Monday morning.' He turned back to us.

'How can I ever apologise enough, Mr Fosdyke? That *stupid* boy!'

But it was lost in the sound of our cheering. We turned to Cullom and slapped him on the back, and wildly threw our muddy kit in the air.

Fosdyke turned to Cullom. Even then, he had a chance. If he'd said sorry . . .

But all he said was, 'I'm confiscating these, Cullom,' and picked up the Woodbines and matches, the dirty picture and the envelope with the French letter. Even those priests were shocked.

Then one of them said, and it was a sort of apology, 'I hope you'll still join us for a cup of tea, boys? We've got a nice display of cakes – the mothers do us pretty well.'

He wasn't a bad bloke. So we went. And got in a huddle with the Dame Julian's lot, and told them what a sod Fosdyke was. Loudly. They totally agreed.

You could have cut the silence in the coach going home with a knife. I was sitting next to John Bowes; I suppose I was getting pretty fond of him. He was a bit of a prude, a bit of a stuffed shirt. But a nice guy, all the same.

He muttered to me, *sotto voce*, 'I'll keep an eye on Cullom in future.'

'But he was innocent . . .'

'Was he hell! I reckon he took that watch, and hid it where they found it. Afterwards he'd pretend he'd forgotten something, and nip back to the changing-rooms, and lift it, if nobody had found it. He's very cunning, is Cullom. I told you he was poison.'

The head had Jack and me into his study, on the Monday morning. Captain and vice-captain of rugger.

He didn't keep us standing there on his hearthrug, like naughty boys. He invited us to sit in the chairs that parents sat in. Cunning old sod.

'Now, gentlemen.' What followed was a whole lot of hot air, wrapped round the idea that we mustn't choose Cullom to play rugger again. For the honour of the school.

We heard him out in silence, to the point where he just had to ask us what we thought. He didn't *want* to ask us, but he did.

'We've played four matches and had four wins,' said Jack.

'And got yourself a thoroughly bad name. These schools don't *have* to play us, you know. Very soon now, Mr Fosdyke is going to have to start sending out postcards requesting next year's fixtures. It won't be your concern. I expect you two will have gone on to university by then. If I can write you a good enough reference. Which I am busy compiling at the moment . . .' He let the implication of that sink in. Then he added, 'We only have two matches left this term. One against Gateshead Grammar, which Mr Fosdyke assures me will be a walkover; and the one against the Old Boys, which we have never won, and will never have a chance of winning.' He gave us his most charming smile, palms uplifted. Implying we were all men of the world, who knew the score. It was true enough. The Old Boys were *almost* the first fifteen of the local rugger club. It was more of an exhibition match . . . with us as the chopping block.

'And it's soccer, the first half of next term,' said the head. 'By the time you come to play again, I'm sure things will have . . . blown over.'

What Jack said then, I admired him for. I thought it very cunning.

'Cullom's got a swollen knee,' he said. 'I don't think he'll be fit anyway. But when he is fit . . . I reserve the right . . .'

'Yes, yes,' said the head. 'I'm sure that's the right decision. I'm sure the whole thing will blow over, given time. Meanwhile, give some other deserving chap a game.'

Heads take short-term views. They have to, poor sods.

'You crafty bastard,' I said to Jack, as we crossed the hall. 'What a brilliant idea.'

'What?'

'What you said about Cullom.'

He turned and looked at me, a frown between his eyes. 'That wasn't crafty. It was *true*. I met Cullom on the way in, this morning. He could hardly walk. Got it in a back-lane clog-in on Sunday afternoon.'

'Oh.'

'Sometimes, Akker, I think you try to fiddle everything in this world. It'll get you into trouble, sooner or later.'

He walked away without another word. As if I'd said something indecent to him.

There's nothing more to add. Except we duly beat Gateshead Grammar 32–8, and the Old Boys wiped the floor with us, as usual.

## 24: Christmas and After

'I've brought you a present,' I said to Emma, the last Tuesday of term. 'A Christmas present.' I'd been meaning to keep it till Christmas, but it was finished, and I couldn't bear to wait to see her reaction any longer. I'd slaved over it. It was a picture I'd painted myself. I'd done O-level art, but given it up in the sixth form, when I put away childish things. And it wasn't really *my* picture exactly. It was a copy of one my dad had. By a famous local artist. *Old Shields, the Fish Quay and Trawlers*. But I'd copied all the artist's tricks very carefully, and my mam and dad thought it was nearly as good as the original, and my dad had framed it for me.

I now produced it from behind my back and handed it to her, carefully wrapped in Christmas wrapping paper by my mam.

'What *is* it?' she asked, a bit nervously.

'Open it and see.'

She surveyed it. I'd been quite honest. One corner had my name, and the other 'After Victor Noble Rainbird'.

'It's very nice,' she said doubtfully. 'I didn't know you could paint.'

'I can't. I'm just good at copying. That's why I gave up art. I hope your mother likes it.'

'Do you mind very much if I don't show it to her?'

'Why ever not?' I was *outraged*. 'Isn't it good enough?'

'She'll just tell everybody. It will set people *talking*. And we don't want that, do we? It's too . . . personal, Robbie. I'm sorry. I know how much work you must have put into it. When I'm on my own, I'll get it out and enjoy it.' She gave me a big kiss, as an afterthought. 'Thank you ever so much. It must have taken you *ages* to do.'

'I nearly kept it till next week, real Christmas, but I couldn't wait.'

'Then it's just as well. I can't see you next Tuesday. Or the Tuesday after. We've got family parties.'

'Can't I come some other time?'

'Well . . . not really. Christmas is a busy time. We've got all sorts of friends and relations coming. Haven't you?'

'I suppose so,' I said sullenly.

'We *never* coach pupils in the holidays. It stops with term time.'

'Oh, so I'm just a *pupil* now, am I?'

'You know you're not. Don't be unreasonable.'

'Three weeks without seeing you!'

She was silent. Then she said, 'It'll be more than that. When we get back, it'll be mock A-levels. I'll be up to my eyes in marking, I'm afraid. And you'll be swotting.'

'You're getting tired of me.'

'Don't be so *silly*. You get on with your revision. You are going to revise thoroughly, aren't you? It's *terribly* important for you. The time will just streak past.'

'Thanks!'

'I'm afraid I haven't got you a present, to repay your lovely one. It wouldn't be proper. We don't give *pupils*

202

presents, no matter how fond we are of them. It would cause talk. Sorry.'

'Are you going to be seeing Fred Wrigley over Christmas?'

'Oh ... I expect he'll call round for a drink sometime.' She said it with a certain false lightness.

'And you're going to the pictures with him ...'

'He hasn't asked me yet. But I'll probably go if he asks me. Now *please* don't start that again.'

I looked at her, hard. There was a hint of smugness in her, a hint of let's-be-sensible. I just knew she was looking for a chance to ... stuff me into a handy little box ... get me into perspective ... somehow *reduce* me.

'Why don't you take Joyce out — have a bit of fun? Relax.'

'I'll take Joyce out when *I* want to. Not on your say-so.'

'Robbie — don't be like that! I'm only trying to help.'

I couldn't have stayed in that room. The air would have choked me. I stood up, put on my coat. At least that got through her smugness.

'Oh, don't go. I thought I would give you a glass of port; for Christmas. We could drink a toast together. My mother's baked some mince pies specially for you.'

'I don't come here for mince pies,' I said. 'In fact, you can stuff your mince pies where they hurt most.'

'*Robbie* ... !'

But I was already halfway down the stairs, going full out.

As I reached the bottom, her mother opened her sitting-room door, a question on her face.

'Sorry,' I said. 'I can't stop tonight. I've got to help my

mother with *Christmas*. Merry-Christmas-and-a-happy-new-year-all-the-best.'

And with that I let the front door slam behind me. They could sort that one out between themselves.

It was very different with Joyce. In the shelter, as we were buttoning up our coats again, she said anxiously, 'I am going to see you in the holidays?'

'Thought you'd be too busy,' I said bitterly. 'Family parties and all that.'

'Good heavens, not *all* the time. I'm going to spend most of my time swotting.'

'Sounds thrilling.' My heart was in my boots.

'Oh, it's fun the way we do it.'

'*Fun*? Sitting in your cold bedroom copying things out, over and over? I can't do it. I spend most of my time hitting a tennis ball against the wall. Drives my dad mad – makes dirty marks on the wallpaper.'

'Margery and I have invented a new way. We turn it into a competition. We both put up five shillings, and Daddy gets us a big box of chocolates, and we ask each other questions, and whoever gets the most right, at the end, gets the chocolates.'

'Lucky sods.' It sounded pretty weird, but a lot better than endlessly copying notes out and hitting a ball against the wall and having rows with my dad about it.

'You can come, if you like. D'you know Margery?'

'Seen her around.' Margery was a large plump girl with curly black hair and a jolly laugh. I liked her because she was the first to laugh at my jokes, in class. I could put up with Margery.

I went down first on the Monday before Christmas. We thought we'd make a start. It was Mrs Adamson who opened the door, and you could have knocked me down with a feather. The last, and only, time I'd met her, she'd been wearing baggy slacks and slippers, a pinafore and a loose woolly cardigan. And spectacles.

Today . . . well . . . I hardly recognised her. No spectacles. A very smart dark-grey business suit. Nylons. High-heeled black patent-leather shoes.

I realised, with a start, that she wasn't much older than Emma. And her figure, well, it made both Joyce and Emma look lumpish. Slim as a pencil where she should be slim. And wearing that kind of blouse that secretaries wear (not school secretaries) that's a bit too tight and creases when they breathe, in all the right places. Her hair was up in a chignon, without a strand out of place. Blue-black and shining. Her ears were so delicate – ears always get me – with little pearl earrings. And her skin was like creamy velvet. And the perfume . . .

'You must excuse me,' she said, with a bright smile. 'I'm just going down to the shop.' Joyce had told me she ran De Reske Fashions, which was the priciest dress shop in town. My mother always looked in their windows, but never went in, and my father whistled over the price-tags.

I just stood there, thinking women were magicians. How could they look so frumpish and then suddenly look so beautiful?

'Aren't you coming in then?' she asked. 'Joyce has just nipped down to the shops for me. She's calling for Margery on the way home. They won't be long.'

I followed her into their immaculate lounge, wondering what the hell I could find to say to her. My eyes, roving desperately, alighted on a picture on the wall. A sailing ship in full sail, beautifully painted, and it wasn't a print, either.

'I like your picture.'

'Oh, that!' she said. 'We picked that up in Scarborough, on holiday last year. He's caught the sea rather well, don't you think?' We wandered on, looking at other pictures, and I managed to say something intelligent about each. In spite of the fact that I was struggling to keep my eyes off her, and not succeeding very well. Mums oughtn't to be allowed to look like that. There should be a law. Mums should look like mums.

We reached the last picture, and I began to wonder what I would be able to find to say to her after that. And she kept standing too close to me, and the scent of her perfume . . .

'Oh, that *was* a perceptive remark,' she said. 'I never thought of that. But you do art at school, don't you? Joyce told me.'

'Used to,' I said. 'Gave it up. I was only any good at copying. Never had any ideas of my own.'

'You're too hard on yourself,' she said. 'You're full of ideas.'

And she put a slim white hand on my arm . . .

I just stood there, unable to move.

'We had Joyce painted in oils, last autumn. By a man from London. Would you like to see that?'

'Oh, yes please.' I managed to choke it out.

'It's upstairs. I'll show you.'

I followed her upstairs. Under her dark nylons, the slim muscles moved softly, like cream. I thought wildly, I spend my life following women upstairs. Where have they *got* this picture? In the bathroom . . . in the toilet?

Some rich people thought it amusing to put precious things in their toilets.

She pushed open a door. Beyond, wall-to-wall blue carpeting. And a double bed with matching blue silk coverlet. God, you *never* got asked into people's bedrooms . . .

'This is our room. You'll have to excuse the mess.'

I couldn't see any mess; unless you counted a pair of white furry slippers under the edge of the bed as mess.

'There's Joyce. He's caught her well, hasn't he? That way she has of biting her lip.'

And there was Joyce to the life; looking a little bit younger and pretty bored and fed-up. But she was no help at this moment. She was just paint on canvas. And she was hung over the top of the bed. We had to stand next to the bed to see it properly.

And she was standing even closer. Inches away. Hand on my arm again. Raising her lovely face trustingly, questioningly to mine. And that perfume . . .

Then I thought of Joyce. And suddenly I got mad. It was all so bloody unfair, having a mum like that, more glamorous than you. A mum who appeared to be . . . trying to *steal* your boyfriend?

So I said, very stiffly, 'Very nice. Do you mind if I use your toilet?'

She smiled at me; a very . . . knowing . . . grin. 'Second on the left, as you go towards the stairs.' Then she started for the door, saying, 'I must be getting on.'

I heard Joyce and Margery arrive, while I was still lurking, wondering how long I could be in there, before I had to pull the handle and wash my hands and emerge. What was her mother thinking about me? Would she think I had constipation or something?

I came downstairs, searching desperately for the reassurance of Joyce's face.

'Oh, here he is,' said her mother, pulling on her gloves. 'I was wondering where he'd got to. I thought he'd pulled the chain too soon, and got swept down to the sewage farm.' She seemed to think the whole thing very funny. Then she added, 'I think I've shocked your young man, Joyce. I don't think he *approves* of me taking him into the bedroom, even to see your picture. Very stiff he was with me. You've got a real old Northern puritan there. See you later; have fun.' And then with a last swirl of her dark-grey skirt, and a last view of one beautiful leg, stocking seam as straight as a die, she was gone.

I descended the last few stairs, blushing furiously.

'Don't mind Mummy,' said Joyce. 'She will have her little jokes.' From the look on her face, she seemed very aware of what form the jokes took.

But Mrs Adamson never tried anything like that on me again. She was always just very friendly and ordinary after that. After a lot of thought, I came to the conclusion that she was trying me out, testing me. To see if I was safe, to leave alone in the house with Joyce. I mean, if I'd been a knowing little twerp like Tony Apple, I might have tried to kiss her or something, and got a hand-off for my pains, and told never to darken their doors again.

As it was, I darkened their doors quite a lot. I had tea there about four times, and even lunch twice. I never saw much of her father, and he never had much to say to me. He used to ask how my schoolwork was going, and how the rugger team was doing, but I never bothered to tell him much, after the first time, because he wasn't really listening, just making the right noises.

Both her parents were out quite a lot, which left us alone. With Margery, of course. I got to like Margery, though she was too plump for me ever to have taken her out. A bloke has to have some pride . . . but I was sorry for her being like that. If she could have lost a couple of stone, I think she would have been pretty popular. But then maybe she wouldn't have been Joyce's friend. Girls don't like their girl friends to be too attractive, I've heard.

Anyway, I got a lot more swotting done than I would have, hitting a ball against a wall. And we remembered the things we asked each other questions about. I'll never forget the industrial products of Czechoslovakia, as long as I live, because I lost three points over it, when I was already twenty points behind the pair of them. And I'll never forget which scene and act the ghost first comes in in *Hamlet*, because I nailed Margery for two points with that one.

In the end, after a lot of laughs, Margery won the chocolates on the last day. She had 419 points, to Joyce's 400, and my 399. Still, she shared the chocolates around pretty liberally, and we nearly finished them off.

And I got asked to the Adamson's New Year party, as Joyce's young man.

'You don't have to come,' said Joyce starkly. 'Everybody gets awfully drunk. It gets pretty embarrassing towards the end. I always go to bed, once we've seen the New Year in.'

She looked so desperate, I said I'd come, to keep her company.

## 25: Celebrations

It was pretty ghastly, all those middle-aged businessmen in lounge suits and their plump wives dolled up to the nines. I don't know which was the worst. The start, when they were sober, and could only talk about deals they'd done, and the new car they'd wangled, or, in the women's case, the difficulties of keeping a good charwoman. (And every single one asking you how you were getting on at school and not listening to the answer.) Or when they got really drunk, and began taking off their jackets and loosening their ties and kissing each other's wives. I mean, when adults begin behaving like stupid kids, it's a bit like the end of the world. And then, towards midnight, they gathered in a sentimental heap round the piano, and began singing 'There's an old mill by the stream, Nellie Dean' and 'I saw the old homestead and faces I loved'. I was just glad to be there, to see Joyce through her suffering. I took all the drinks they insisted on me having, and left the full glasses standing on windowsills behind the curtains for the charlady to find in the morning. I hate drink; I like having my mind clear.

There was only one bloke who interested me. A bloke who was as wide as a barn door, and played for the local rugger club. He was an old boy of our school. We had a nice long chat, because we were both forwards and knew the heat of the day, and what idle idiots the backs were.

After midnight had struck and been duly welcomed, he came and embraced me and said, 'In eleven hours, we shall be taking the field against Highcliffe.'

I gave him an odd look; by that time, he was so drunk he could hardly stand.

'We'll loosh,' he said, staring at me owlishly. 'We always loosh on New Year's Day, an' you know why? Because they'll all be *pished*. Two or three of the buggers will be so pished they won't even turn *up*!' He looked into his beer mug, as if seeking consolation there. He swilled the contents round and round and then said '*You'd* do all right. You're shtone-cold shober.' He then went in for another thought, mumbling to himself softly. It took a long time working its way into the light. But in the end he tapped me three times on the chest with his enormous index finger, and announced, 'Why don't you turn up tomorrow morning? Leven o'clock. You'll get a game for shertain. Always short, always short, on New Year's Day. And have you got a *friend*? Nice little wing-threequarter? Bring him, too. Losh of tries for him. Losh of tries.'

I felt a little prick of excitement. I could do with a game, to keep me in training. It must be their third or second fifteen or something. And old Jack might be interested.

'I'll try,' I said. I still didn't really believe it.

'Bring your kit,' he belched. 'And say I sent you. Tony . . . Tony . . . Bereshford's the name.'

Then he fell flat on his face.

\* \* \*

211

I was home by one, and up by eight, on the phone to Jack from the call box at the end of our road.

'I don't believe it,' he said, suspiciously. 'Pull the other leg, it's got bells on it.'

'You didn't *see* him,' I said. 'If they're all like him . . .'

'All right, I'll come. We can always *watch*.'

We turned up, wearing our overcoats, with our bags of kit swung ostentatiously from our backs. At first we thought there mustn't be a game on. There were very few cars about. The admission gate was swinging open. The stand was empty of spectators.

But the door into the changing-rooms was also open; and a low sound emerged. Not the usual yells and thumps of boots being thrown, and obscene songs about the foe.

More a low moaning.

Then an old bloke in a trilby hat emerged, looking very worried. He stared at the gate, fiddled indecisively, and went in again.

Three more times he came out and went back in.

'That's the *first* team coach,' said Jack, in an awed voice.

The next time he came out, he surveyed us in a very snooty way. Came across and said, 'Are you the Highcliffe reserves?'

'No,' I said. 'We're at the grammar. First team. Mr Bereshford . . . Berisford said that if we turned up, we might get a game.'

'Don't be so ridiculous.' He was deeply offended, and he showed it.

'This lad played for you once before,' I said, pointing at Jack. 'When your winger got hurt.'

'That was an *away* match,' he said. 'An emergency.'

'He scored a *try*.'

'Mug's luck.' I have never seen a man so contemptuous; or so disgusted. He went inside again.

'Let's go and sit in the stand,' said Jack wearily. 'At least we haven't had to pay.'

But at that point, a massive figure in a hooped strip appeared in the doorway. Held himself up by gripping the door.

'Bloody hellfire,' said Berisford. 'Why do we do it? Why do we *do* it? You haven't got an Alka-Seltzer on you, have you? I had three, but I've taken them already.' He was a delicate pale green in colour.

Then a dim light seemed to dawn in his brain.

'You're . . . the lad . . . from last night. You left *early*.' He stared at me accusingly. 'I didn't get home till half-past shix. Had a hair of the dog. Had no breakfasht . . . very unwise . . . to have breakfasht.'

'Why?' asked Jack.

'You'll shee. You'll shee!' He nodded very slowly; like a clockwork model of Wise Old Owl that is running down. 'You know what our bloody fullback did last night? Climbed into the Municipal Baths and dived in. Didn't get wet though. Know why not? No water in it – closed for the winter. Silly sod didn't even notice – broke his wrist. And the shtand-off wrapped his car round a lamp-post. He'll be playing a long way back today. In Preshton Hoshpital.' He gave a noise, like a hen laying an egg with great difficulty. After a while I realised he was laughing. 'Why don't you and your friend go in and get changed? Your country needs you!' He shook Jack's hand many times, as if it was a pump handle. 'You're a great little winger – a great little

213

winger. Friend told me. Besht winger in the town today.'

We went in. Immediately the worried elderly man accosted us. 'What are you lads doing in here?'

Berisford butted in. 'They're friends of mine, Maurice, and they're playing. I'm the captain, and if I bloody say they're playing, they're bloody playing.'

The players slumped around on their benches raised their heads. I noticed one was trying to put his right boot on his left foot.

'Let the kids have a game,' shouted one.

'What have we got to lose?' shouted another.

Maurice muttered, but finally gave in. Jack was to play at stand-off. They tried to give me fullback, but I nervously insisted on wing-forward, my usual position. Their wing-forward said he didn't care where he played, except he'd rather be in bed.

'Right, lads,' shouted Berisford. 'Let's get it over with.'

They got to their feet, levering themselves up with hands on their knees, like old grannies. Such a chorus of coughing, groaning, belching. We stood back, watching our heroes, the giants of many a game, stagger forth. Jenkins, the old Welsh international centre, his bald head in a pale sweat. The six-foot-three forward, McGregor, limping along using a mate's shoulder as a crutch. Only Wilford, our scrum half, looked merry and rosy-cheeked, boasting he'd been for a training run to see the New Year in; and the bookish solemn fullback Stephenson, saying he'd been in bed by half-past nine with the latest Agatha Christie.

I must say, as we lined up, Highcliffe didn't look a lot better. But they had a kid on the wing who'd obviously got his beauty sleep, as he was vigorously running on the spot.

'Better nail him early on,' muttered Jack.

It was a game played in a dream; a game played in slow motion, except by us few. Only a few incidents remained in my mind.

Jenkins, suddenly alive, twisting and jinking through the Highcliffe defence, with me trailing behind. Then suddenly stopping dead and handing me the ball, saying, 'Carry on, kid, I'm buggered.'

I ran on, through lumbering, chest-heaving Highcliffe giants who flung out feeble imploring arms to try and stop me, as they stood rooted to the ground.

Their goal area was as empty as a haunted house. I had difficulty deciding where to put the ball down for a try.

'Kick the conversion yourself, kid,' said Berisford. 'I'll start walking back to the halfway line. Don't be too quick with your kick. Give us a breather.'

And Jack, picking up the ball nearly on our goal line and running the whole length of the field, his famous lock of hair flogging on his brow, while the rest of our team just stood and watched, shouting him home like he was the winner at Newmarket.

On the other hand, that young winger of Highcliffe's ran through us four times and scored tries.

I don't know where the hip-flasks appeared from at half-time.

'Enjoying yourselves?' enquired Berisford grimly, from where he was lying on his back in the mud. 'I'm glad some bugger is.'

The second half was worse. When the two packs scrummed down they weren't pushing against each

215

other, they were propping each other up. Several times the whole lot just fell down. Wilford scored a couple of nice tries, and the studious Stephenson dropped two goals.

Jack scored again when their fullback, nicely placed to tackle him, suddenly bent double and began to throw up instead.

'I'm just knackered with running,' said Jack. 'It's like playing five-a-side.'

After another ten minutes, people began shouting at the ref, 'How long to go, Herbert?' and 'Have a heart, man!'

'What's the score?' shouted the ref. He looked like he had no puff left to blow his whistle.

'Call it twenty-nine all,' shouted Wilford.

'Done,' shouted the opposing captain.

The ref blew a long blast. Everybody cheered up no end.

'Hope they've got the bar open.'

'I could do with a jar after that.'

Jack and I looked with great eagerness for the account of the match in the local paper, the following week.

None appeared. Apparently the chief sports reporter had been locked up for cuddling a policeman, early on in the night's festivities.

The last day of the holidays, Margery didn't turn up. Joyce said she was staying home to revise French, which we didn't do. We had a feeble go at Latin, but neither of our hearts was in it.

'Let's go in the lounge,' suggested Joyce. 'There's a nice fire. We can lie on the sofa.' I gave her a look. That was a very pushy remark for her to make. But she just

216

looked weary, pale, with little blue shadows under her eyes.

We got ourselves arranged comfortably, and I started to play with the buttons of her blouse. But she just pushed me away, saying, 'Be nice.' And then snuggled in closer.

I was totally baffled. She didn't sound at all mad at me. She wanted to be close, more than I'd ever known her, but . . . I just lay there, with my hands flopping in the air, like bunches of withered bananas.

'What's up?' I asked, trying to be patient. 'Worrying about the mocks?'

'No,' she said, and gave a deep sigh. Sort of contented and doomed at the same time. 'Put your arms around me, tight.'

We lay there for about ten minutes. She said, 'You can stroke my back. Gently. *That's* nice.'

'Are you going down with flu?'

'No-oh.'

'What, then?'

'It's something only girls know about.'

'Hell, you're not preggers? You *can't* be preggers! We've not . . .'

She smiled up at me; a smile infinitely superior, knowing, a bit like the Mona Lisa. 'If you promise to lie still and be nice, I'll tell you.'

'Oh, all right then.' I wriggled a bit; my right hip was killing me. 'What?'

'It's . . . the wrong time of the month for me. Usually it hurts a lot. But because you're here, and being nice, it hardly hurts at all.' She smiled at me gratefully, and snuggled in a bit tighter. 'Go on stroking my back.'

How can I explain it? I felt so *privileged*. I felt so

217

*needed.* I felt I was making a difference to the universe. What did it matter, that my left arm was aching like hell and my right foot had pins and needles?

'We can have the radio on, if you like.' I crossed over the carpet and switched on, and tuned it till I got Mantovani, whom I normally regarded as gilt-edged slush.

'Clever boy,' she murmured as we got back together again. Then she simply fell asleep. I watched the bits of her I could see, without wrecking my neck. Her graceful calves and nyloned feet, as they draped up on the far end of the couch. Her slim smooth hand clutching mine. The rise and fall of her breasts, that made the little crucifix she wore move around the hollows of her neck. The faint blue of her eyelids, the way her lips trembled as she breathed. I felt like the captain of a ship, with a whole precious cargo. Utterly trusting me. All mine. It was so peaceful I wanted it to go on for ever.

I must have dozed off myself. Because the next thing I knew was her mother saying, 'Wake up, dream-boats!'

'Oh God!' I started awake in horror.

But her mother was smiling at me, with a very soft look on her face. 'You were *snoring*, Robbie.'

'Sorry . . . I . . .'

'Take your time. Swotting's a tiring game. I'm just going to make us a cup of tea.' She went, with another smile.

Joyce murmured my name, and grabbed my hand tighter.

'Wake *up*, your mother's home.'

So we sorted ourselves out, and grinned sheepishly when her mother came back.

'I'd better not tell your father I caught you sleeping together!'

But it was all just a joke, a soft female joke.

On the bus home, I fell to thinking about Joyce and Emma. I suppose I was pretty pleased with myself, having two women on the go, when most of our lot hadn't even got round to kissing one yet. And it was nice to compare them. Joyce was all gentle and peaceful and legal. Her mum probably knew how far we went – but she didn't mind. I wasn't minded to push Joyce along any faster. I supposed we might get there some day . . .

But Emma . . . I began to remember being with Emma and my eyes and ears just blanked out, so the bus conductor had to ask for my fare three times before I heard him; and the two shop-girls across the aisle began to giggle.

Emma thought she could push me into a little box when she didn't need me, like a favourite toy.

I'd make Emma pay for that, when I got my hands on her again. I'd show her who was boss . . . until she yelled for mercy.

No mercy for Emma.

But she'd like it . . .

I nearly went past my stop.

# Part Four

## 26: *The Pub at Old Hartley*

It was the end of January when it happened. I can't imagine now how I was happy till then. But there was Joyce and her family, and the mocks to get through. And all the money I had stored up in the bank, with Emma, waiting for me.

The mocks had gone so smoothly. Normally I did quite well in exams, in spite of not being able to swot. I had a glib way with words; I could start writing while the rest were still chewing the ends of their pens. I could dress up nothing to really look like something. But this time, thanks to Joyce, I had no need to. All the facts were there in my brain. When my results came out, I just couldn't believe them. Neither could the staff. They gave me some very funny looks, as they threw my papers back to me. Joyce did pretty well too.

I suppose I'd been getting a bit anxious about Emma, underneath. No word came from her. Her marking and the reports must be over by this time; I had my report in my pocket, ready to screw a quid's reward out of Dad, five bob out of Nana. I didn't seem to meet Emma so much round the corridors; and when I did, she never seemed to see me. Kept her head down. But I told myself she must be busy, tired.

And then that night after school, I saw her. Leaning

220

on a radiator; listening to Fred Wrigley. Never seen Wrigley so animated; he almost gave the impression of being actually alive. He was making jokes.

And she was laughing at them.

I stood and watched, from the shadows further up the corridor. It was well after four, and nearly everybody had gone home. I'd been having a clog-around in the yard, with Jack and Tony Apple and that lot, and had come back to our classroom for a book I'd forgotten. I stood and I thought, you *bitch*! So we have to be patient, do we, show self-control for both our sakes? Well, I've been patient, like you wanted, and I've shown self-control, and you just spend it laughing with Fred Wrigley . . . I stood there and shook with a black fury that scared even me.

Then Fred said, 'Till tonight, then,' and she turned towards me, all smiling and happy, and went into a classroom. And he wandered off down the corridor, whistling. It was lucky neither of them saw me, because I couldn't have moved an inch to save my life.

All I could think of was that she *belonged* to me. She was my property; and he'd stolen her. I felt I was nothing, and less than nothing. The world was a mountain built by grown-ups, from which they could sneer down on the young who were trying to climb it. Stamp on their hands as they struggled. Kick them in the teeth if they tried to get too high.

Hate is a sour taste in your mouth.

Two nights later, I was sitting in that same old pub at Old Hartley; with that same old half-pint of cider. There weren't many in the bar that night; it was an appalling night, throwing down rain in sheets. My trenchcoat (that same trenchcoat from Vindobala, I realised bitterly) was sodden, and dripping on the floor. Every time somebody came in, they brought the sound of the pounding waves and the howling wind with them. The rain drummed on the windows; the gale hooted in the chimney, making the fire spit and flutter.

My moods kept changing, like the scenes of a play. Hated Emma Bitch, dearest Emma, poor little Emma. At the moment I was having that disgusting childish fantasy that she would suddenly walk in the door of this pub.

How low can you *sink*?

What's the point of having money in the bank, if you can't spend it? Better to throw your bank-book away and forget it.

And then the mad thought came to me, sitting there dripping. I would spend all the money I had left in Emma's bank, in one great binge. If it was worthless, I would know it was worthless. And if it wasn't worthless, she'd be walking in that door in ten minutes, and the fantasy wouldn't be a fantasy any more; it would be *real*.

There was a red phone box outside the pub.

I would ring her up.

I had bought fags and matches tonight, with the cider.

I used up nearly all the matches, finding her number in the phone book in that gale-blasted kiosk.

It was she who answered the phone. I imagined her standing in their draughty hall.

'It's Robert . . .'

Long silence.

'Are you bloody there?'

'Yes, I'm here. What do you want?' Her voice

222

sounded a bit hostile. 'What's that noise?'

'The wind,' I said. 'And the waves.'

'Where are you?'

'Old Hartley.'

'Old Hartley? What're you doing *there*?'

'Walking.'

'On a night like this? You must be mad.'

'Maybe I am.'

'You must be soaked.'

'To the skin.'

'Are you going home?'

'Along the cliffs.'

'But it's dangerous. You might get blown over.'

'Yes.'

'Whatever's the matter with you?'

'*You!*'

'Oh, Robbie, don't be silly.'

'I have a right to be silly, if I want to. It's my life. I can do as I like with it.'

'Oh . . .' She was starting to sound really anxious, which was balm to my soul.

'Your time is up, caller,' said the operator, breaking in.

'Cheerio,' I said.

She gave a gasp. 'No, don't cut us off, operator, I'll pay for the call.'

The operator, satisfied, departed.

'Do you want to come here, Robbie? To my house.'

'Too late.' I only meant it would be too late by the time I got to her house; it was already gone eight. But, delightfully, she took it the wrong way.

'Robbie . . . you aren't going to do anything silly, are you?'

223

'I might. I feel like it. What do you care? Go off and marry Fred.'

'I have no intention of marrying Fred.'

'You could have fooled me. I'm going now.'

'No . . . wait. It's an awful night. I'll come and get you. Drive you home.' She was really frantic.

'OK.' I said. 'I'll wait fifteen minutes. Then I'm off.'

'I can't do it in fifteen minutes.'

Full of black glee now, I hung up.

She made it in sixteen, by my watch.

She came in looking angry and wary, in her white riding mac. She stared furtively round the bar, in case there was anyone there she knew. Did she think I was a fool? There were only three old geezers, and a couple of young fishermen, playing darts. Nobody we might know; I'd checked.

She came and stood over me, looking magnificent in her anger. I just enjoyed looking at her; I'd almost forgotten what she looked like. She hadn't even waited to powder her nose or put on lipstick. The wind had blown her hair about; I wanted to touch it, run my hands through it.

'C'mon,' she said grimly. 'Let's get you home.' Putting on some kind of social-worker act.

'Let me get you a drink,' I said, indicating the distant bar with a grand gesture.

'No time for that. I've got things to do, before I go to bed.'

'Have a drink, or I'm staying put.' And I meant it.

We glared at each other, then she sat down wearily.

It was the first surrender.

She sat and tried to drink it quickly. But I could see

her remembering. The pub on the way to the Wall. From happier days. There was a traitor inside her; all I had to do was encourage the traitor.

I drank up eventually; there was nothing more I could do here. We walked out to the car park, and the wind came round the corner and blew us together, so we had to cling for a moment, till it passed. My heart leapt. Even the gale was on my side tonight.

In the car, as she reached for the self-starter, our shoulders touched. That asthmatic old sewing machine coughed into life; she reached for the gear stick and touched my knee, as she'd always done. A tension grew between us; nobody saying anything. We set off for home, the wind catching the car and making it sway, and the dim headlights flicking about all over the road.

'I must be mad,' she said, 'coming out on a night like this.'

'It's just nice to see you.'

'Look! The less you say, the more you'll shine. I'm *very* angry with you. I always knew you were a fool but . . .'

'How else was I to get to see you?'

'You could have come to our house.'

'You could have asked me. I waited and waited. I was *patient*, like you said.'

'I haven't had any nights free.'

'You had for Fred Wrigley.'

'Oh, so *that's* it. You've been snooping. Well, we're going to settle this once and for all.' She braked and pulled in to the side of the road, and applied the handbrake with great force, as if she wished she could wring my neck. Oh, fool, Emma, fool! If you were going to finish with me, you should have done it at our front door. Not here on the lonely deserted road between Old Hartley and Whitley Bay.

We sat silent, like two armies waiting to attack. The wind came off the sea, and rocked the car on its springs. It was my ally; it was as wild outside as I was wild inside.

'Listen.' She took my hand, as she might have taken a naughty child's. But hands are hands, Emma. Hands remember . . . 'Listen. If you think you're ever going to get me again, into the state you had me before Christmas . . . I must have been *crazy*. Out of my senses.'

'I love you, Emma.'

'If you really love me, then leave me *alone*. You've got your whole life ahead of you. Your exam results were *brilliant*!'

'Oh, so you *noticed*, then?'

'Of course I noticed. I do care about you, you know.'

Her hand, as if it had a life of its own, gave mine a little desperate squeeze. 'And you've got Joyce, now.'

'What's Joyce to me?' Oh, I felt a rat at that point. But a hungry rat. A rat that wanted to conquer the universe. Not a rat to be trifled with. 'It's you that I love, Emma.'

'I wish you *didn't*.' It was a squeal of pain. 'But I'll have to live with what I've done. And so will you. People survive. Nobody ever died of a broken heart. Now I'm taking you home.'

Oh, Queen Emma, so safe in your kingdom, with everybody in authority on your side. The head, the Church, the flipping King himself would applaud what you're doing. You are being sensible. But there's more than good Queen Emma in your kingdom. There's the girl who lay with me on the hill above Vindobala, and

226

the woman who went mad when she saw me tickling Joyce on a night not unlike this. Deep down, they're stirring, remembering. There's going to be a revolution in your kingdom, and you don't even know it yet . . .

'OK,' I said. 'If that's all you've got to say to me, I'll walk home. Along the *cliffs*. Good*night*!' I reached to open the car door. Slowly. Giving her plenty of time. If my hand reached the door and I opened it and got out and walked away, that would be it. We'd never speak again. The gap would be as wide as the sea.

My hand moved down on the door handle, before she grabbed it.

'For God's sake be reasonable,' she yelled. But she was no longer reasonable herself. I felt the tremble in her hand, in her whole body accidentally pressed against mine.

I gripped her hand tight, and kissed her. Don't think I have any truck with force. Force, to me, is a waste of time. If you batter a woman's defences down by force, you'll find nothing left inside worth having. If she'd frozen up then, if she'd pulled away with that slight shudder of distaste women are so good at, I'd have sat quiet and beaten, and let her drive me home.

But through her lips, I felt the walls crumbling, the proud queen falling, the dark savage little women casting her down from her throne.

'Oh *hell*,' she said. As if she'd dropped a newly made trifle in a glass dish on a stone floor. 'Oh hell, why did you have to do that?'

I let her pull away, now it was too late. She sat huddled, staring at me, her eyes just dark patches in the white of her face. The wind came again, rocking the little car on its springs. A strange car swept past us, its headlights splintered to fragments by the rain on the windscreen. Her face, in the glare, was white and detailed; her mouth a little open, her pupils huge.

'It would have been the best way,' she said. 'We could have parted good friends. There would have been no *mess*.' But she was already talking in the past tense.

'I love you,' I said again, taking one of her hands very gently.

'I wish to hell you didn't. I wish to hell *I* didn't.' There was the beginning of tears in her voice. She was asking for comfort, and I had so much, of the wrong sort, to give.

A long time later, another car came past; and she cocked her head and wrist-watch to the light that came through the steamed-up windscreen.

'God, it's gone *eleven*. What will your parents say?'

'They'll probably have called out the police, the fire brigade and the coastguard.' I was exultant. I had her now; she could never escape me. Wrigley was destroyed for ever. The things she'd said about him; when we'd talked, in between! I almost felt sorry for him; but not quite. The misery he'd caused me still lingered as a shadow.

'I must be *insane*,' she said, rearranging her dress and coat, touching her hair, coming back to this cold world. 'My mother . . .'

'What did you tell her?' Suddenly I was anxious for our defences.

'She was out at my aunt's. I left her a note saying I was going to see Winnie Antrobus. But she'll be worrying by now. I can't find my other shoe. Is it your side?'

228

'They'll get over it. Here's your shoe.'

'Don't sound so damned smug. You don't know what you've done tonight.'

'What have I done?'

'You've made me feel . . . *different*.'

'A change is as good as a rest.' I was still smug; but the note in her voice *was* different. Warm, deep . . . almost broody. A tone I'd never heard before. Well, women, you could understand them so far, but no further. And this was my night to howl. Wrigley was no more. I'd fought Wrigley for her, on the battlefield of her body. And won.

'We'll have to talk, I think. But not tonight.' She started up the car, after several unavailing pulls on the self-starter, that had my heart in my mouth, at the sudden imminence of disaster. 'No, not tonight.'

That deep broody note in her voice was there again.

We were silent, all the way home; though from time to time, she reached out and grabbed my hand and squeezed it tight. She dropped me at the end of our street, and I ran all the way home, looking at my watch as I went in.

Twenty-five to twelve. The parents were sitting each side of a nearly dead fire, but that wasn't the cause of the sudden coldness in the room. But I was full of myself, and took the offensive.

'I've walked twenty miles tonight!' On to old ground.

'Your coat's *soaked*,' said my mother. '*Sodden*. Get it off this minute.'

'I knew you didn't have much sense,' said my father, 'but this takes the biscuit. Your mother thought you'd gone off the end of the pier. I was just going up to ring the police.'

I didn't bother to point out that if I had been swept off the pier, there wouldn't have been much the police could do about it. I just sat and let them beat me up in the good old way and thought about Emma.

Again, when I went down on the next Tuesday night, it was different. Nothing to grumble about. We made no further attempts at Latin. Just had coffee and talked and listened to music. But she was ... slower, somehow more certain of herself. She lingered over kisses, long after I needed to breathe; she held on to my hand when I was ready to let go. And whenever I looked up at her, she'd be watching me, with a look on her face I couldn't read. That Mona Lisa sort of look, that reminded me a bit of the look on Joyce's face, that afternoon she felt rotten and we fell asleep on the couch. I caught her watching my hands, the back of my neck with its folds of flesh, which was the ugliest part of me.

What had I to grumble about? And yet it felt ... oh, come into my parlour, said the spider to the fly ... that old rhyme from childhood kept echoing in my head. I felt the need to be flippant, to chatter a lot about people at school, or the world situation. Even about the forthcoming match against Newcastle Collegiate, though I knew it bored her stiff. To talk about anything but *us*.

But I still ended up sharing the couch with her, with my head in her lap, as we listened once again to Gustav Holst's *Planets*.

My favourite movement clicked to an end on the record-player. Click, click, click. I lifted my head so she could get up and change the record. But she said, 'Don't move.' And then, casually, 'Do you ever go hiking for a whole weekend?'

'Yeah,' I said, a bit baffled. 'Sometimes. I'm in the Youth Hostels Association. Why?'

'I'd like us to have a whole weekend together.'

I had a lovely vision of sunlight on mountains, and us climbing in the Lakes together, sitting on top of Helvellyn.

I sat up. 'Great. Are you in the YHA too? I could teach you how to rock climb.'

She shook her head. 'I didn't mean that kind of weekend. But my mother has to go to London in two weeks' time, to stay with my grandmother. And I'm staying behind to look after the dog.'

'You can't take dogs to Youth Hostels.'

'I don't want to. I mean, you could come *here*. Stay. For a whole weekend.'

I looked at her, wrinkling my brow. 'Wouldn't people notice if we kept going out and coming back?'

'I wouldn't want to go out.' It was her smile that told me what she meant. A huge soft warm hand seemed to be squeezing the life out of my guts.

'I want to spend a night with you,' she said. 'A whole night. Wake up and see you in the morning.'

If there's one thing I've always hated, since I was a little kid, it's sharing a bed with anybody. Sometimes my cousin Ronnie used to come to stay, and share my double bed, and I hardly got a wink of sleep. We each occupied the outer edges, so we were in great danger of falling on the floor. And still it was all sudden bony elbows and knees, or suddenly waking up to find you were glaring at each other, about two inches apart. And he snored like a pig. And I always hated being looked at, first thing in the morning; I look like death warmed up, my mother says.

'Don't you want to sleep with me?' She'd read the look of panic on my face, and her face was suddenly so sad, I couldn't *bear* it.

'I'm an awful person to sleep with,' I said. 'I toss and turn and I snore. Horribly. You wouldn't sleep a wink.'

'All right. I could make up our spare bed for you. For . . . afterwards.'

Still I pretended to be so naïve. 'After . . . what?' I mean, I knew. Her face grew sadder still.

'Don't you want to make love to me . . . properly?'

'It's not *safe*.' Suddenly all the memories of my poor old friend who got caught came flooding back. I even leapt to my feet. God; get me out of here!

She grabbed my hand. 'Hey, steady down. Can't we just *talk* about it?'

'Look,' I said, 'I can't get anything. The only people who sell them are the barbers, and there's always loads of old gaffers sitting around waiting to have their hair cut and listening to every word you say. And nasty old newsvendors who work the queues after the United match, at the station. One of them offered some to Tony Apple. He nearly *died*. Anyway, I don't think he really had any – he was just doing it for a laugh, to embarrass Tony.'

'Steady. Don't shout. You'll have my mother up, thinking you're murdering me.' She seemed to be finding me amusing.

'*What* then?' I glared at her.

'There are certain times of the month, when it's safe for a woman. Didn't you know?'

'How can you *know*? How can you be *certain*?' Oh

God, university . . . teaching . . . all my chances to get out of this crummy town. It wasn't worth it, it just wasn't worth it. Suddenly I wanted to be free, having a laugh with Jack and Apple, playing rugger, getting into the ordinary kinds of trouble I'd always got into. It suddenly seemed to be the most blessed thing in the world. Paradise.

'You don't really want to, do you?' Her voice was still low.

'I'm not ready for that kind of thing.' Suddenly I remembered Joyce's similar bleat, that night on the seafront.

'Then why on earth did you *start* it?' She was angry now. 'You wanted me enough in the car, the other night. Or that's how it seemed from where I was sitting.'

'Oh, I *do* want you. But not . . . in that way. Yet. I just want to talk to you and have you here and the music and . . .'

'And?' she said dangerously.

'Why can't you leave things as they are? Why do you have to *spoil* everything? For God's sake, I'm *seventeen*. I haven't been to college, I haven't done my National Service, I shan't be working for another six or seven years.'

'It's a pity you didn't think of that the other night. What on earth did you think you were *doing*?'

'I was angry with you. About Fred Wrigley.'

'You mean you were a little boy and Fred Wrigley had stolen your toy?'

I took a great breath and said, 'Yes.'

'Oh well.' Her voice was even lower. 'That's it then. That's the end of it.'

I thought for a silly moment I had won; but even I

couldn't ignore the tone in her voice.

'The end of *what*?'

'Us.'

'You mean . . .'

'End. Finish. I can't go on like this. You getting me worked up and then not doing anything about it.'

'You seemed to like it. You didn't complain.'

'You didn't see me afterwards. I didn't sleep a wink. I could have screamed my head off. You're never doing that to me again.'

'But,' I said, horrified, 'we can go on being *friends*?'

'It's much too late for that.'

'You mean – never seeing you again?'

'Yes. That's the only way I could stay sane.'

'But I never meant . . .'

'It serves me right,' she said drearily. 'Mucking about with little boys.'

'I'm sorry. I didn't understand. Please forgive me.' I grabbed her hands.

'Oh, I *forgive* you. But that doesn't make any difference.' Then she said to herself, 'I've been such a fool,' and stood up and began gathering up the coffee things. 'You can see yourself out. I'd probably fall downstairs.'

I said, suddenly desperate, 'There must be something we can do.'

'But you have just told me quite clearly that you don't want to do it.' She looked pale and pinched, weary and somehow old. 'Of course it's for the best. I just wish you'd realised that before that night in the car.'

I felt . . . so sorry for her. So sorry for me. So sorry for the whole bloody world.

So I said, 'If you're sure it's safe, I'll . . . do it.' I felt it was being dragged out of me with pincers.

She looked at me, one eyebrow cocked. 'Some people have been known to find it quite . . . pleasant. Do you have to make it sound like the end of the world? It's not very flattering.'

But life was coming back into her face, and she rushed tightly into my arms, and that was all that mattered then.

# 27: The Dog and After

'It's a funny time of year to go youth hostelling,' said my mother.

'It's *not*,' I said. 'The hostels are open. Some of them. It's a lovely spring day. I can't wait.'

'The weather forecast says rain.'

'Oh, I feel all cooped up. I could do with a change.'

'You can say that again,' said my father, rustling his paper. 'You've been prowling around like a caged tiger all week. It's time you got it out of your system.'

If he only dreamed what I was going to get out of my system. If he only knew how I'd been praying for rain, snow, blizzards, floods all week. But, no such luck. It was fine. I would have to go through with it. I'd given my word now.

'I've put you a little tin of Spam in,' said my mother, looking at my packed rucksack. 'You didn't have enough to feed a fly.'

'Thanks. I'll be off then.' Picked up my fake rucksack, stamped my fake boots, which would go no further than Emma's hearthrug, kissed my mother, and went.

'Don't break your neck,' shouted my father after me.

If only it was that simple.

I felt that every curtain in Tennyson Terrace concealed a

236

watching eye. Emma opened the door almost before I'd rung the bell.

We embraced lightly. Then she said, 'Take your boots off and leave them with your rucksack in the hall. Those hobnails will ruin the carpets.'

Feeling half-naked already, I followed her into the kitchen. From his bed in the corner, the dog gave a low growl, not at all welcoming.

'He's a bit insecure with my mother away,' Emma said. 'And he's a bit jealous of me. Better not touch me while he's around. Would you like a cup of coffee?' She sounded so matter-of-fact, as if she was getting ready for a morning of dusting or something.

I sat at the table, and drank my coffee. We weren't in a talking mood. She bustled around, doing the washing-up, going out to hang up a few bits of washing in the back garden. I tried to read her *Manchester Guardian* but kept wildly skipping from one article to another. Anyone looking in would have thought we were totally bored with each other. She was dressed for housework, wearing an apron. I even began a fantasy that nothing was going to happen after all.

Then she said from the sink, without looking at me, 'You don't have to go through with it, you know. Not if you don't want to.'

I thought about that. Thought about the idea of actually going hostelling, which is what I would have to do, if I said no now. It didn't appeal. I felt so lazy, even weary. If I walked a mile it would kill me.

'No. It's OK.' In spite of the coffee I'd just drunk, my mouth was bone-dry.

'You might as well go up and get into bed, then. You know where my bedroom is.' She still didn't look at me.

'Right.' I reached the hall, with an effort, and picked up my rucksack.

'What do you want that thing for?'

'Pyjamas,' I said defensively.

'Dear God,' she said, and leaned against the doorpost with her head turned away from me. I thought, in the gloom of the hall, that her back was shaking. I became terrified that I had upset her, that she was crying. But when she turned her head, she was laughing.

'What's so funny?'

'I'll ask you just one thing. Can you imagine your hero Heathcliff wearing *pyjamas*?'

I dropped the rucksack and stamped upstairs. She was so confident now, so brusque and businesslike, it was pressing on me, so I felt as flat as a pancake.

I got undressed, piling my clothes on a pretty little chair that vanished under the bulk of them. But I was reluctant to get into bed. Once in bed . . . I drifted towards the window. The curtains were half-drawn, making the room darkish, so the bedside light had been left on. I peeped round the corner of the curtain. There was an old lady coming up the road with one of those shopping baskets on wheels. She stopped to talk to a black cat, that rubbed against the basketwork enthusiastically.

The outside world never looks so dear as when you are going to jump over a cliff. I might come back to that dear world, but I would never be the same . . .

I did not hear her come upstairs; not till her voice said, outside the door, bossy and yet conspiratorial, 'Are you in bed yet?'

I scampered into bed like a naughty child. It was freezing. My teeth began to chatter.

She came in. She was wearing a blue dressing gown now, that almost came down to the floor. Her hair was combed out and back and lay on her shoulders, and she didn't look like a housewife any more. She looked like a cross between a triumphant queen and a mischievous little girl. She came to the bed and stood looking down at me. Then she thoughtfully undid the tie of her dressing gown.

I thought, when I saw her in the glow of the bedside lamp that every day we saw *bits* of women. Faces, hands, legs. And the bits never join up together, and it's as well for us blokes that they don't. I mean, even bathing costumes *chop them up*. And photographs of nudes are like dried flowers and worse than dried flowers, dead flowers that have never been alive, grey ghosts. And even the flashes we had of girls playing netball in the yard were like . . . picking little bits off the Sunday joint and never being asked to sit down and eat.

'Do you mind moving and letting me into my own bed,' she said at last. 'I'm freezing. Are you going to lie there and stare for ever? I feel like a peep-show.'

And with a sudden break in her grandeur, a sudden flurry of embarrassment, she bundled into bed and we lay there touching hands and shivering and laughing. I think she must have been pleased with the look on my face, though, because she was in a very good mood.

And then, downstairs, the damned dog began to bark.

She just lay there, listening to it.

'He'll quieten down in a minute,' she said.

But he didn't. He went on and on and on.

'Doesn't he ever shut up?' I asked. I put one hand around her ribs, and tried to draw her timidly to me. She didn't respond. She was giving the dog all her attention.

'He doesn't like being left alone,' she said. 'He gets lonely. Normally, he never leaves my mother's side, he goes everywhere with her.'

'Well, I wish she'd flippin' well taken him to London.' It was so provoking having her within a foot of me, so I could feel the heat radiating off her body, and not even be able to do anything.

Finally, she jumped up and put her dressing gown back on, and said, 'I'll give him his dinner, early. Perhaps that will quieten him down.'

I was left staring at the ceiling.

Finally, she came back and sat on the side of the bed, listening. I tried to reach inside her dressing gown, but she pushed my hand away. 'Be *patient*!'

After a brief bit of peace, the barking started again.

'Oh, *leave* him,' I said callously. 'He'll get tired of it before we do.'

'I can't. Miss Morrow next door can hear him. She's always complaining. And she knows my mother's away. She'll be round in a bit to find out what's the matter. I'd better go and get dressed so I can answer the door to her.'

And my vision departed abruptly. After about three minutes, I heard her go downstairs, and the barking stopped. I lay a bit, and then it all seemed pointless, and I got up and got dressed myself. I entered the kitchen to see that stupid spaniel actually trying to lie on her lap. It kept half falling off, the great stupid thing, and licking her face. But when it saw me, it gave me a treacherous sliding look and low growl.

'He's not very keen on me,' I said, for something to say.

'He's jealous of everybody, except my mother and me. He sleeps on her bed every night, and when she's away, he sleeps on mine. *Usually.*'

'What are we going to do then?' I mean, you screw yourself up to jump off a cliff and then . . . and that ache in my guts was starting.

'If I let him up on to the landing . . . where he could hear and smell me through the door . . . he might settle. He mightn't bark, anyway. Shall we try it?'

We tried it. I lay there and heard her cooing soothing words to him, then she came in with a rush, and slammed the door.

My second view of her getting into bed did not have the same impact, but it was still very nice.

'Let's snuggle up and get warm,' she said.

It seemed a good idea. Until the dog began scratching on the bedroom door. I felt her interest drain away again.

'He'll mark the door. My mother will notice.' Even her retreating bottom was so nice. Apple-shaped.

'Why don't you get a bit of old clothesline and tie the sod up?'

'Don't you talk about my dog like that. There, there, precious. Is the nasty man being rude about you?'

I *hoped* she was being funny.

The clothesline idea didn't work either. He began to *howl*.

'Perhaps if we took him for a walk on the beach? Up on the links towards Blyth. It might tire him out.'

'It might tire me out, too. I wish we could give him some kind of sleeping tablet. Hey, you haven't got any, have you?'

She frowned. 'I have, actually. Now. I never used

them before you turned up. I still don't take them every night.' Her face was suddenly bleak. Everything was going horribly wrong.

'If we shoved one inside a piece of meat . . .' I suggested, desperately.

'But he's just had his dinner.'

'Raw meat,' I said, suddenly the dog-expert. 'No dog can resist raw meat.'

She looked doubtful. 'I don't want to *poison* him.'

'Give him half a one. He's a big dog.'

'The only raw meat I've got is a bit of steak for your supper.'

'I'd rather have *you*!' Surprisingly, that seemed to cheer her. She went and fetched the bottle of sleeping tablets and the steak from the larder. I cut off a piece, and slit it open, and shoved the half-tablet well inside. Then I cut off two more small bits. 'Feed him these first. Then he won't worry about the bit with the tablet.'

It worked. All three vanished down his gullet. He didn't even bother to chew them. Like feeding Smarties to an elephant.

'Would you like another cup of coffee while we wait?'

We had to wait a long time. Old Bonzo had a lovely time; he loved having all her attention lavished on him. But he still found the odd moment to raise a wrinkled lip at me, exposing very nasty yellow fangs. The one thing he did not do was show any sign of wanting an afternoon nap. After an hour, he seemed as eager for her fondlings as ever.

'Let's try another half-tablet,' I suggested callously. By that time I was finding waiting to jump off my cliff pretty wearing. I was starting to have doubts that I could, even if Bonzo slept for a hundred years like Rip Van Winkle.

She eyed him with doubt and love. 'I don't think we ought to risk it.'

We risked it in the end. I wondered what we were going to have for supper now. But, no sooner had he swallowed the second half-pill, than he yawned three times, and got off her knee and staggered towards his basket.

'Night-night, Bonzo,' I said.

'Don't be so heartless,' she said. 'And don't call him Bonzo. His name is Benny.'

Still, she came upstairs willingly enough, holding my hand. Sharing that feeling of something attempted, something done.

We were just getting really cosy when she shot upright and said, 'I hope he's OK. He's very *quiet*.'

I just stopped myself pointing out that was what we'd hoped for.

'I'll just go and check.' I was getting quite a connoisseur of that retreating apple-shape.

The thud of her feet on the stairs sounded panicky.

'Robbie, I can't wake him up. I've shaken him and shaken him, but he just goes on snoring.'

'Well, that's what sleeping tablets are *for*!'

'Not like that. When I take one, I still wake up in the middle of the night to go to the loo.'

It was at that point that the last romantic feeling flew out of the window.

'He could be *dying*!'

I did not feel unduly stricken with grief.

'That's a horrible look on your face,' she said. 'You have such horrible ideas. You're *heartless*!'

'Why don't you ring the vet?' I suggested feebly.

'What could I *tell* him? He'll think I'm insane – not fit to keep an animal.'

'Tell him the tablet fell off the table into the dog's bowl while he was eating, and he ate it before you could stop him.'

She gave me a long hard look. 'You're a brilliant liar, aren't you? I sometimes wonder how many lies you've been telling *me*.'

'All right, think of something better.'

'I can't think of anything better. You're in a different league.'

But she rang the vet. And, amazingly, the vet was in and said bring the poor doggy down straightaway.

'Shall I come with you?'

'Certainly not. The vet knows my mother well. And God knows what fresh lies you'd tell *him*.'

'What shall I do, then?'

'Oh, go and read a book.'

So I helped carry the snoring Benny to the back of her car in the garage. Then I went and got a book off her shelves.

*Married Love* by Dr Marie Stopes. I love reading travel books; especially for countries I'm never likely to go to.

I must have fallen asleep. It was no criticism of the literary powers of Dr Marie Stopes. I was just worn out.

I was delightfully awakened by two loving arms coming down over the back of my chair and cradling my head.

'Mmmmmph?' I said.

'He's going to be all right. But the vet is keeping him overnight for observation. He told me I was a very silly

244

girl to leave sleeping tablets lying around where *children* could find them. I think he meant you!' She giggled delightfully. 'Come to bed. I'll make it up to you.'

And she did. I fell asleep reckoning that that poor dead RAF pilot deserved my gratitude for more than just dying for his country.

Birds sing in the middle of the night, while it's still dark. We lay coiled round each other. I pushed the bedclothes back a bit to get cool, and we listened.

'Is that the dawn chorus?'

'It's not dawn for hours yet.' She looked at the luminous hands of her watch, which she'd kept on. 'Four more hours yet.' The four hours lay snugly on us, like warm heavy blankets. Four hours more of the safe kingdom of the dark.

'I wish you hadn't put your hand over my mouth like that. You nearly choked me.'

'You were making such a racket. Miss Morrow came round from next door with the police, while you were asleep. I told them it was a purely private murder.'

She giggled. 'I'm sorry. I can't help it. And you're *such* a liar!'

Why did I have to make a joke of the way she called my name, over and over, as if she was dying of me? Feeling a bit guilty I said, 'Your watch hands look like little fireflies in the dark.'

'Have you ever seen a firefly?'

'No, but I'd like to. I'd like to go out into the country and make love all night under the trees. And foxes and rabbits would come and look at us – we'd see their red and green eyes.'

'According to you, I'd scare off everything for miles.'

'And I'd like to make love in a cave by the sea, with the sound of the waves. And on a mountain top, to watch the dawn. On a South Sea Island . . .'

'Dreamer!' There was a little tiny edge in her voice, as if she was frightened of being whirled away, to where she couldn't get back.

'Why shouldn't we, if we planned it?'

'This is enough for me, Robbie. I'm thirty-two years old, and it only happens to me now. When I'm middle-aged. Still,' she grabbed my hand warmly, 'it might never have happened to me at all. I suppose it never does happen, to some people.'

'Poor people. I heard my mum laugh once, like you laughed. In the middle of the night. I'd got up for a drink of water. I didn't know what it meant. Why did you laugh like that?'

'Just because you'd made me happy. And because I'd taken thirty-two years to find you.'

'Well, you have found me, now.'

'Yes.' Her voice went low, and a bit sad. 'But God knows when I'm going to find you again. This weekend was a pure fluke – everything coming right together. We can't expect that again. My mother hardly ever goes away.' It was as if she'd opened a little door, and let in cold and loneliness and a hint of fear into our cosy kingdom.

I reached for her. 'Don't fret. Don't waste this. We've got hours yet. We'll work something out.'

'Oh, the optimism of youth.' For a moment she sounded just like my mother. 'Oh, we'll have to pay for this, some day.'

Her body felt cold and stiff and reluctant, as if some frost had got at it. For a moment, I despaired, then she

246

said, 'Oh, you clever little devil,' and gave a great wriggle, and then it was all right again.

I awakened around dawn. At least grey light was just creeping round the curtains. Normally I dislike waking up. I feel a lot has been happening to me in my dreams that I can't remember, and wouldn't enjoy if I could. I usually wake up feeling like a drifting boat without oars that's about five hundred miles from land.

Not that morning. I stretched gently and yawned like a cat. I was full of memories of a small very warm body curled against me, first against my back, and then against my front. Delicious. We had even learnt to turn over together in our sleep, without waking up. And memories of the sounds she made in her sleep. Little 'Hmmmphs' and 'Ums' that seemed to contain the very essence of her mind, which was talking to itself.

I turned so I could look at her face on the pillow. Her closed eyelids were faintly blue; a stray strand of dark red hair fell across one eye, and moved gently in the breath from her nose. Her face looked as if all the wrinkles had been ironed away; she looked as innocent as a little kid. She had the faintest possible smile on her face.

I lay watching her, and idly tried to take stock of my life. With about a tenth of my mind, because the rest was still firmly and peacefully attached to her.

I tried to think about the match against Collegiate, but it just seemed piffling, something kids did. I tried to think about my A-levels, but that seemed a thing kids did as well. I thought about my mam and dad, probably getting up together at this very moment, to get him off to work on the six till two shift. I wondered if they'd

247

ever felt like this.

I wondered what they'd think of me, if they knew where I was now . . . World War Three!

But that was an unthinkable thought. I had set my will, my cunning, against them, and my will and cunning were a great safe wall. So many things I'd done, smaller things, that they'd never found out about. It was a way of life, now, deceit. It was simply a matter of taking infinite care and not making any mistakes. I began to make up a story for them, about my trip to the hostel. Blokes I'd met, meals I'd disliked, seeing a sheep giving birth to a lamb. All drawn from other trips.

But this was only with a tenth of my mind. The rest was full of the way she pressed against me as she breathed.

Perhaps she sensed me looking at her. She murmured, 'Not time yet. Go back to sleep.'

But I reached for her, and she said, 'Oh, Robbie, not *again*,' with a kind of hopeless delight.

We finally got up about five on the Sunday evening. She had to pick up her mother off the 6.30 from Newcastle, and fetch the dog from the vet's before that. She offered to drive me home, but it was raining and I thought I'd better walk. It would look better if I arrived home well soaked with a tale of woe.

We kissed a long last time on her doormat. She said, 'I don't know how I'm going to manage. My legs are so shaky I can hardly walk.' Then she gave that lovely laugh. I wondered sadly when I would hear that laugh again.

Then she opened the door and the rain and dark blew in.

248

'Take care,' she said, suddenly solemn and little and scared. 'Will your parents . . . ?'

'Leave them to me,' I said, and shouldered my rucksack and went. Didn't even stop to wave at the gate. Some old biddy might be snooping.

I was glad of the dark and the wind and the rain. The darkness a friend to cover my face, and the wind and rain enemies to fight against, grow angry with. It only came to me then how angry I was with life most of the time; now I wasn't angry at all. I suddenly felt in a hostile place, and lost without the weapon of my anger. I tried to work up some anger in myself, before I got home. Or they'd notice. But every time I tried, soft memories of Emma kept blossoming in my mind, making me soft and thin-skinned again.

The huge packet of chocolate digestives we'd lived on all day, because we couldn't bear the waste of time cooking and eating. The laughs about crumbs in the bed. Our delightful discovery that male nipples are just as sensitive as female . . .

God, I *couldn't* get my anger back, no matter how I tried.

I tried thinking about Katie Merry, only to slide into thinking she must have been young and lovely once. I even tried thinking about the Black Fan . . . but I knew he really loved his son, who'd left school last year.

Hell, here *was* our house, with the wide green in front, the panes of the bay window catching the lamplight. And I was still a great bulgy thin-skinned balloon of happiness. My lips kept smiling, of their own volition. I could feel the glow on my skin as well as the great soft ache in my whole body that was almost blissful. Even my blind parents couldn't miss that. How was I going to get through the four hours to bedtime, when I could be private to remember Emma again? Should I take another turn round the block, to get myself wetter? But if anyone saw me walking *away* from the house . . . questions, questions!

Feeling utterly naked, utterly doomed, I lifted the sneck of the back door.

But the door didn't open. And though the reading lamp was on in the sitting room, there was no sound of the radio.

Then the dog barked, and I knew from the sound he made, edgy, fierce, that the house was empty.

But they *never* went out on a Sunday evening! Mam would never miss her programme of Mantovani. Some dreadful disaster must have happened, some dreadful punishment for what I'd done . . . Mam . . Dad . . . Nana. I burst in frantically.

There was a note in Mam's handwriting under the table lamp.

Nana had bilious attack. Have gone down to see her. Your supper is in oven. See you later. About ten.

I was saved. By ten, I could, without causing comment, be in bed with a book.

I switched on the radio, hoping for some news that would help bring me back to earth.

'If we play John Bowes at centre against Wallsend . . .'
said Tony Apple. We were in the school library, at the
table furthest from Ma White. We were supposed to be
doing silent private study, but as usual, we were
tinkering with the first rugger fifteen, as if it was a
clapped-out old car going in for the big race at
Silverstone.

'But he's great where he is,' I said. 'Why change a
winning combination? We'd beat Wallsend; even if we
didn't have John Bowes at all.'

'All the more reason to experiment while we can,' said
Apple.

'Will you lot shut up,' said Big Bunty. 'Some of us
have work to do. *Serious* work.'

'This is serious.'

'Kids' stuff!'

'What is?'

'Rugby Union. You ought to try playing Rugby
League.'

We all stared at Big Bunty with much distaste. Rugby
League was not a gentleman's game. They only had
thirteen players a side, instead of fifteen. They had to
*pay* their players to play. They had stupid different
rules. They played in front of massive crowds of the

workers in cloth caps, in Lancashire and Yorkshire. They said things like 'eeh by gum'. They were beneath contempt. Trust *him* to bring the subject up.

'We're talking *serious* rugby,' said Jack, snootily.

'Rugby League's a lot more serious than Union,' said Bunty. 'Ask my Uncle Tommy. He played scrum half for Batley. Brok' his left leg twice, right leg once, collarbone three times. He hadn't a whole bone left in his body by t'end. You ask him.'

Jack shuddered gently. 'Did your *grannie* play Rugby League? The one that got married again?'

Big Bunty's face became as black as thunder. 'Don't you knock my grannie! Or Rugby League! It's a hard game. I've played it, so I know.'

'What – *professional*?' Jack was at his most mocking, now. Good sport was in prospect. 'Don't tell me, you played for Bradford Northern when you were still in nappies.'

'I played until we came up here last year. Every week. Down there, schools play Rugby League, an' all. Our Roy played as well.'

He glanced affectionately across the library, to where their Roy was frowning over a book on elementary atomic physics for kiddies or something. We never mentioned brother Roy; he was on the science side; in the lower sixth.

'Why don't you play at this school?' asked Jack suspiciously. 'If you were any good?' It was impossible to imagine Big Bunty playing. He was huge, a man-mountain. Not fat exactly but . . . he had big clumsy hands like hams.

'Not allowed to. Once you've played League, the Union won't let you play wi' them. Union thinks

League's the Black Death or somethin'. Besides, Union's a kid's game, a toff's game, a don't-get-your-shirt-torn game.'

'What a load of tripe,' said Jack. 'Bet you never played a game in your life. Those cigars of yours would break anybody's wind.'

'How much you betting?' asked Big Bunty.

'A quid,' said Tony Apple nastily. He always had too much money, burning a hole in his pocket.

'Done,' said Bunty. 'When's your next practice? Me and Roy'll show you.'

'Thursday,' said Jack, his eyes glinting, savouring the moment. He couldn't lose, whichever way it went. Either Big Bunty would make a fool of himself; or Tony Apple would lose a quid bet. That was really the kind of situation Jack loved.

I had a nasty feeling Apple was going to lose his money as soon as Bunty and Roy came out of the changing-room, and stamped their feet like carthorses, to knock the dried mud off their studs. They were wearing rather sinister short black shorts, and strips and stockings striped in yellow, green and black, as vicious as wasps. And they had numbers on their backs, eleven and twelve; which we never had. They *looked* professional somehow. And Bunty, all six foot-two of him, looked a lot more formidable stripped than in school uniform. He had legs like tree trunks; the size of his thighs, covered with black hair, made me blink in disbelief. And what had looked like his paunch, under his white school shirt, did not wobble now. It looked horribly like a barrel of muscle.

Roy, nearly as tall, was slimmer; and he would be

faster too. Six foot one to Bunty's six-two; fourteen stone to Bunty's fifteen.

Bill Fosdyke did not react to the viciously-striped strips. He just put them into the second row of the second-team pack. The second team were always short; glad to get anybody who turned up.

I'll never forget that first scrum-down. Bunty and Roy put down their heads like bulls about to charge, and drove our first-team pack back fifteen yards, till we broke up in confusion.

'That's a quid you owe them, Apple,' called Jack happily.

But it was the first time Bunty got the ball ... He wasn't expecting it to bounce into his hands; I saw his Brylcreemed cannonball head jerk back in surprise. But then he was off; with all the grace of a one-legged kangaroo, like Mount Everest going for a canter. It was hard just to believe it. But worse was to come. For Apple, probably in a desperate attempt to save his quid, flung himself forward into the tackle.

It wasn't that Bunty was exactly *fast* (though he certainly wasn't slow). But he ran pulling up his knees right to his chest almost, like a high-stepping horse. Which made him a very nasty prospect to tackle head-on. Also, he didn't slow up at the moment of the tackle, like all our players did, to avoid injury. (All Union players do that; you'll see even internationals do it, if you watch carefully.)

But not Rugby League. You could see why his Uncle Tommy had broken his right leg twice and his left leg once. But it was not a flying knee that got Apple; he never got that close. A massive arm shot out, at the last moment; a ham-like open hand slammed full into

Apple's chest, and Apple fell over backwards on to his bum.

Bunty crossed the goal line under the posts, bending down delicately to place the ball on the grass with one hand. Having left a welter of our recumbent first-team bodies in his wake. Then he went and helped Apple up, and said, 'You owe me a quid.'

Ever-blind Bill Fosdyke came up to him.

'You don't play for the soccer team?' he asked nervously.

'Never played soccer in me life, sir,' said Bunty proudly.

'Fancy a game for the second fifteen?'

'I'll think about it, sir,' said Big Bunty gravely.

I will draw a veil over what Bunty and Roy did to the first fifteen for the rest of the game. Only cunning old Jack fetched Bunty down. Once. By coming in behind him, and grabbing him by one leg. Bunty dragged him ten yards, but he fell in the end.

Bunty and Roy both got a quid out of Apple. They said they were going to the Gibraltar Rock, to spend it on beer.

## 29: Peeping Tom

That was when things began to go wrong. I suppose Emma and I began to take risks. We were as careful as we could be, about where we met; but we hadn't all that much choice. We didn't dare do more than kiss and hug furtively, at Tennyson Terrace. We always had to stay fully dressed, in case Mrs Harris suddenly tapped on the door. I mean, she wasn't at all sneaky or spying, or even distrustful. But she sometimes popped up to see us, with some little cakes she'd just been baking; and for a big woman, she was a soft mover in her slippers. The first thing we knew was her tap on the door, and it was hard enough for us to spring apart and get our faces straight before Emma had to call, 'Come in.'

And the weather was bad, that March. Rain, rain, rain. The only thing we had left was the car, and that was ailing. It often had our hearts in our mouths, when it was reluctant to start, after a couple of hours out in the rain. So there was no hope of driving out to get lost in the country lanes. Emma's only excuse for getting out at all was going to the cinema, or going to see a friend. So we had to park the car in the town itself. We used to explore the back streets for ages, looking for a place where no one would ever come. The place we finally found was awful. The guano factory, the stinking guano factory, left its yard gates open at night, and there was no night-watchman. Who would want to steal stinking guano? And we could drive right round the back and park between the ten-foot high blank wall, and the darkened dead factory. Stinking but safe, with only a pile of half-smashed-up crates for company and, for some reason, an uprooted rusting petrol pump.

We often laughed at the place; said it should have been the graveyard of romance. How different from the hilltop above Vindobala . . .

But beggars can't be choosers, and we were desperate. Once you start doing what we were doing, it gets addictive, like a drug. If we didn't do it, we got very bad-tempered with each other, and began to have stupid quarrels over nothing.

Of course, lying back in each other's arms, inside the safely fugged-up windows, we still talked in between. In our tiny dark safe heaven.

'Got my letter from university today. I'm in. Leeds. They only want three Bs.'

'Oh, *marvellous*.' Long lingering kiss. 'I can come and see you. We could go out to places at Leeds. Nobody would know us.'

'If I can get a room in a students' house – no nosy landlady – we could – in peace and quiet, I mean. Not like this.'

'Oh, you are *awful*. Is it all you think about?'

'No. I still think about beating Newcastle Collegiate. About once a week. But my game's going off. In the scrum, when I shove my arms round the second-rows' bums, even *that* reminds me of you.'

A gurgle of delight. Then, more solemn, still the schoolmistress, she said, 'You will revise for A-level,

257

won't you? Read your set books?'

'For you, anything. I shall lay three distinctions at your feet as trophies. Even Latin.'

'See you do! Mmmmm, *that's* nice.'

Once, I even told her about where I'd first seen her. In the playground at Spring Gardens.

'You sexy little object. At that age! I didn't even *notice* you. I was young and innocent then – only a few years older than you are now.'

'I don't think I've ever been *really* innocent.'

'You? Sometimes I think you're the biggest innocent I ever met. And sometimes you seem like the devil incarnate. What a mixture! I suppose that's what I like about you.'

'It's not the only thing you like about me . . .'

'Hush. Be good.'

'Be *good*? Here? What a waste of time!'

'Beast!'

But then came the night when she suddenly went tense, and grabbed for my hand.

'What's up?'

'Robbie – I think there's somebody watching us!'

'For God's sake . . . where?' The windows were not fully misted up. It was a windy night, and draughts, creeping in through cracks round the doors and windscreen, left little fan-shapes of clear glass.

'Behind that pile of crates. I saw somebody's face peer round the edge of them. White, with dark marks for eyes.'

'Oh, go on. It's a bit of paper caught on a nail, blowing in the wind. There's nothing there now.'

'Wait. Be patient.'

But I was already getting my clothes in order. If I was going to face anything, I would face it fully clad. I had just got my second shoe on, when she whispered, 'There it is.'

And in a stray patch of yellow light, from a distant street lamp, I saw it rising up. I wanted to believe it was a piece of paper, and her imagination. But no, it had a pair of staring eyes, and an open mouth, and a nose, and I even saw its hair stir in the wind.

I just went mad with rage. I never thought he might be a bigger bloke than me; a slum bloke, a nasty fighter, with maybe even a knife or a razor. I just slammed that car door open and launched myself, as if I was coming round the scrum after the scrum half.

He didn't stay to have it out. He took to his heels. He must know I wanted to beat him to a pulp, bang his head against the cobbles, murder him.

He was a good runner. Slim and lightly built; I could see that much now, in the dim light. A shock of dark curly hair. I was within three yards of him by now; gaining. I'd have him before he reached the gate.

And then I trod on a loose plank, that someone must have left lying around. A plank with a big nail in it, sticking upwards. I felt it, I can tell you, as it pushed up through the sole of my shoe. But, worse, it clung to that shoe, and swung across my other ankle, and the next second I was plunging headlong, trying to keep my balance, but knowing I was going to fall. I hit the cobbles with a bang that knocked the breath clean out of my body.

But my head was still up, watching. So I saw him reach the gate and turn left; and in the dim lamplight of the street, I had a sudden niggling suspicion it was somebody I knew. Somebody from school . . . By the time I got myself up, he was long gone.

I tried to console myself all the way back to the car. It mightn't be somebody from school, just somebody of school age, young and thin. Good God, there were three other, secondary modern, schools in the town. It was far more likely a kid from one of them who would be lurking round the guano factory. Looking for something to nick. It wasn't something any of our lot would be interested in. None of them lived anywhere near here. This was slumland, where poor people lived.

And even if it had been one of our lot, he couldn't have seen our faces in the dark. He wouldn't know who we were. He would just have been watching any old pair of lovers. Peeping Toms aren't fussy.

Emma was fully dressed when I got back, in the driving seat with the engine running.

'He got away. I tripped over a plank. He was just some young kid. He won't be back. I gave him the fright of his life.'

She shuddered. 'This is a *horrible* place. Why did we ever come here?' Then, 'Watching us . . . all that time . . . I feel *filthy*.'

'It was dark. He wouldn't have seen much.'

'*Anything* is too much. He could have crept right up to the windows, while we were . . .'

'I'm sure he didn't. He was too timid. I reckon he stayed behind those crates, till you saw him. Where are we going?'

'I'm going *home*. But I'll run you home first.'

'We're supposed to both be at the pictures! The Carlton doesn't come out till ten. Nobody walks out halfway through a picture. Let's drive down to the seafront and just sit and watch the sea. And hold hands and talk.'

'Oh,' she said wearily. 'All right. I could do with seeing the sea. It might make me feel clean.'

We only saw one person we knew on the drive to the seafront. The streets were deserted. Everybody who was out that night was in the cinemas or the pubs or at their grandmas for supper. It wasn't a night to be out, unless you were an unlucky twerp with a dog that needed walking.

The one person we saw was William Wilson, on his way home, head down, only a few hundred yards from his front door. I couldn't help wondering where he'd been. He wasn't wearing shorts, so he couldn't have been to Boy Scouts.

The sit by the sea wasn't a big success. She was nervous, jumpy. She was even jumpy about men with dogs and our fellow luckless courting couples, walking round in circles in the cold because they couldn't afford the price of the pictures. She drove me home, bang on the dot of ten. I had to walk round for half an hour, before I went in for supper.

I wasn't left in ignorance long. Two days later, William Wilson came up to me, while I was on playground duty. He was grinning, in a cocky, not very nice sort of way.

'I need to talk to you,' he said, and his voice carried a weird overtone of authority.

'Run along, little boy,' I said nastily. 'I'm too busy.'

'You won't be too busy once you hear what I've got to say. You won't be too busy ever again.'

With a suddenly sinking heart, I let him lead me up the playing field. He had a kind of new *possessiveness* about him, like he owned me lock, stock and barrel.

'Well, what? C'mon, I've got things to do.'

He looked at me, head on one side, half grinning and triumphant, half scared and trembling. He kept his hands in front of him, strangely, as if to be ready to ward off a blow.

'You had a bit of bother in the guano-works yard two nights ago, I hear.'

'Who told you that?'

'A little bird told me.'

'Your little bird must be bloody blind. I was at the Carlton seeing *For Whom the Bell Tolls*. Ingrid Bergman, Gary Cooper. Good movie.'

'You were in the guano-works yard. With Ma Harris.'

'Ma *Harris*? You must be out of your mind! I was with Joyce Adamson. At the Carlton. Ask her.' I thought my show of indignation was quite good; considering.

'Oh,' he said, with a show of being offhand, though his hands were shaking a bit more. 'I'm quite sure Joyce Adamson would tell lies for you. Till she heard what you'd been doing with Ma Harris . . .'

I just glared at him. I wanted to punch a hole right through his sneery face. What a useless worthless creature he was. The world would be much better off without him. It was lucky for him we weren't still in the yard at the guano works . . . I wondered if I just might have done him in there.

'It's no good, you know,' he said at last. 'I was there. I saw. You chased me. You fell down and said, "Oh, hell."'

I knew it was all up. But I still didn't panic. If he hadn't told anyone else . . .

'Who've you told?'

'Nobody. Haven't breathed a word. I'm a good friend of yours. I was just walking down for the second performance at the Odeon when the car passed and I saw you and Ma Harris in it. Then you turned in at the guano-works gate, and I just couldn't resist finding out . . . How'd you get her to . . . ?'

'Say any more and I *will* bloody kill you. I swear it.'

'Stop shouting. D'you want the whole school to know? You play your cards right, and nobody will be any the wiser.'

'What do you want? Money?'

He laughed. 'Reckon *I'm* getting more pocket money than you. You're hardly Tony Apple.'

'What, then?'

'I want to be your friend.'

It was so ludicrous. '*Friend?*'

'I want to go around with you. I'm tired of being nobody, being beaten up. Boot's on the other foot now, isn't it?'

'You're mad. What have *we* got in common? If we start going round together, they'll say we're a couple of poofters.'

He flinched; went pale. With rage, I think. I was suddenly afraid I'd pushed him too far. His face was all pinched.

But all he said was, 'Well, you'd better think up some good reasons why we should be friends. You're good at things like that. It's that or . . .'

I suddenly thought of Emma, and was terribly afraid. But all I said was, 'You wouldn't *dare*! The head would expel you.'

'Oh,' he said slyly, 'I wouldn't come out with it all just like that. Just a bit of gossip here, a bit there. You know what people are like. No smoke without fire.'

He was right, of course. And we both knew it. I didn't

know what to say.

He smiled at me, almost kindly. 'I've got nothing against you personally, Akker. In fact, you're lucky I like you. You play fair by me, I'll look after you. In July, we all part the best of friends.'

I nearly threw up on the spot.

He actually looked at his watch, as if he were some sort of busy businessman, with another appointment to go to.

'I'll leave you to think it over. I'm sorry you've had a shock. I'm sure we can work something out.'

Then he just walked away and left me.

Until the Tuesday night, I tormented myself. Should I tell Emma, or should I not? But you can't keep that sort of thing secret; it poisons your every look and every word. She soon had it out of me.

She just sat, stunned, unmoving.

'I think I can keep him happy,' I said at last. But she took no notice.

'What am I going to do?' she said, to herself. 'How am I going to manage? When this comes out, I won't be able to get a job at *Woolworths*. I'll have to leave town. It will *kill* my mother – she's got a weak heart. We won't have a friend left. And I'll never get another job teaching. What am I going to do with the rest of my life? All my father's old friends, what will they think of us?'

I mean, she couldn't think at all. I'd thought she would know what to do, that we could work out some plan but . . . she was just a helpless shaking heap.

Then she looked at me, and said, 'I wish to God I'd never met you,' and burst into tears. And even when I cuddled her, those tears were a very long time drying up.

Then all she could find to say was, 'The head will sack me on the spot. Without a reference.' And, 'What will all my mother's friends say!'

I knew he would sack her. The head had sacked the civics master, Mr Thursgood, and he had only been done in the civil courts, by a woman he'd been going round with and then chucked, for breach of promise.

'Look,' I said gently at last. 'I have got a plan.'

She looked at me, her huge eyes like a doomed animal's, without hope.

'First,' I said very slowly and firmly, 'we must stop seeing each other.' It was like tearing my heart out, but it had to be done. I had to get this terrified creature back on her feet, or we were both done for. And I refused to be done for, by someone as contemptible as William Wilson.

But she only said, 'It's too late for that, now,' her eyes inward on some dreadful inner landscape that had drained all the colour from her face, brought beads of sweat to her rounded brow, and made her look older than I'd ever known her.

I shook her gently. 'Listen, secondly, how keen is old Fred on you? You haven't packed him in for good, have you?'

She gave a flicker of a tiny dreary smile. 'He still asks me to go to the pictures.'

'Then go. Go with him all you can. Get seen in public. People won't be so ready to believe Wilson then.'

Again that dreadful remote little smile. 'I never thought to hear you say that.'

'Thirdly.' I was warming to my task now, getting carried away like I always do, once I've got a plan. 'Thirdly, I suppose you couldn't fetch him on a bit? Get him to propose?'

265

'Robbie!' She eyed me with real amazement.

'Well, *could* you? I mean, who's going to believe Wilson if the girls see you walking around with a ring on your finger? They'd just think he was being the spiteful mucky-minded little twerp he is!'

More of a smile now. Though it was like a glint of winter sunlight.

'He's already proposed to me twice. Once, ages ago. Once just recently.'

'That time I saw you laughing by the radiator?'

'Well, not then. Just after that.'

'What did you say to him?'

'He wouldn't shut up till I promised to think about it. Then you drove him clean out of my mind.'

'So you could still say yes?'

'The poor booby's actually carrying a ring round in his pocket. He didn't buy it specially – it was his grandmother's. But it's a very nice one, a ruby.'

'Well then . . .'

'Oh, Robbie, I can't just *use* him – to get a ring on my finger. It wouldn't be fair.' But there was a hesitation in her voice that made me push on with all my strength.

'Look, Emma, it's a matter of *survival*. You're much too valuable to lose your job. Think of all the kids who like you – the ones who will fail their exams if you go. Your exam results are twice as good as Fred's.'

'People would say I'm not *fit* to teach them, after what I've done.'

'But what do *you* say? Has your work gone off since you've known me?'

She said shakily, 'I think I'm better. I think I understand the kids more.'

'There you are, then!'

266

'It's not as simple as that. What about Fred's feelings?'

'Oh, you know what he's like. He'll give you the ring, then he'll start to get cold feet . . . keep on putting off the wedding. It could come to nothing in the end. He'd quite like having a fiancée . . . but can you actually imagine him being a husband and father?' Again she smiled, wryly, briefly.

'I'd have to go through with it, if he wanted to. I'd have to give him the chance . . .'

I felt like screaming then. But I just kept my face straight and said, 'All right, all right. That's a chance we'll have to take.'

'We? You're being very altruistic all of a sudden! Do you want shot of me?'

I looked at her face, at the life returning to it, slowly, the despair going.

'I want you to be *safe*. I couldn't bear it if . . . I'm against misery. I'm against . . . you being *crucified*. By that lot.'

'I don't know.' All her doubts returned, like a load of coal being dumped outside your house. It was all to do again.

But I did it, again. And again. Arguing, bullying, painting a dreadful future.

In the end she said, 'All right. I'll think about it. You may be right. You'd better go now. It's getting late.'

I stood up. She stood up. I have never loved her so much as then, when she looked little and old and weary and nearly beaten. She raised those magnificent brown eyes.

'Whatever happens to us . . . never forget that I think you are the nicest man I ever met.'

It was that last hug I will never forget.

# Part Five

## 30: Keeping People Happy

For some reason, it didn't hurt, the next few days. I don't think it sank in. It was like saying goodbye to someone on a train, before the train pulls out and it's all last kisses through the open window, and then grins and winks and raised eyebrows through the glass.

It was nothing like the empty station with the blowing newspapers and darkness, after the train has gone.

The game was still alive and running. I had something to win, still. I was even decent to William Wilson, the first time he approached me, on the school field. I had decided I would genuinely try to like him. I told myself it couldn't be a lot of fun, being William Wilson, always being snubbed and laughed at, and told to sod off. It couldn't be a lot of fun, being mediocre, when you wanted to be one of the boys.

We walked on the field all the lunch-hour, and I told him about things that interested me, and let him tell me about things that interested him. He seemed to quite enjoy it; especially when kids noticed us walking up and down together. Everyone seemed to want to say hallo to me; I was popular, then; talk had got around about our team's victories. I was one of the glory-boys. They'd be asking for my autograph next . . .

Wilson basked in the reflected glory for an hour.

But, sadly, he was greedy. Just before we parted, he said, 'You're not getting away this lightly, Akker! Keeping me up the field, away from all your wonderful mates. Tomorrow, we join the gang. Right?'

'Tomorrow', I said, 'is the rugger practice. We're picking the side against Newcastle Collegiate. Want a game?' I let the hate underneath flicker into my voice; and he heard it.

'*Careful*, Akker,' he said. 'Think of Ma Harris.' Then he grinned like a fiend, and added, 'I'll come and watch the practice. Keep an eye on you. It should be quite amusing.'

'Aye,' said Big Bunty. 'Us'll play against Collegiate. Us'll help you beat them. But only if you *pay* us. Us are *professionals*, in Rugby League.' He grinned ear to ear. Their Roy grinned too, ear to ear. They were putting on their Yorkshire tykes act, their accents particularly broad.

'For hell's sake.' Jack's voice shot up in volume. 'D'you think we're made of money?'

Big Bunty grinned at Tony Apple. '*He* is. You English gentlemen'll have to *pay* for your pleasures. Us working men need money for beer. And the pictures. And big cigars.'

Brother Roy nodded. They were serious, not just taking the mickey. But taking the mickey as well.

'How much?' asked Jack.

'We'll be fair,' said Big Bunty. 'Two quid each. And two quid bonus, if we win.'

'*When* we win,' said Roy greedily.

'You're a pair of cocky sods,' said Jack, but with a slight hint of glee in his voice. 'What do you say, Apple?

Have you got the dibs, in the old family coffers?'

Tony Apple went a bit pale. 'I could raise it but . . .' He looked at us nastily. 'Why just me?'

'I'll give you ten bob,' I said.

'So will I,' said good old Teddy.

Poor Wilf looked really worried. 'Five,' he said, after great thought.

'And ten from me,' said Jack. 'You're getting off lightly, Apple. Unless we win . . .'

'*One* quid each,' said Apple. 'Three quid bonus, if we win.'

Bunty looked at Roy. 'Mean sods, as usual. Capitalists. Grinding the faces of the workers. We'll just have to make sure we win, Roy.'

'We'll break a few Collegiate legs,' said Roy, evilly. 'See how they like playing thirteen a side.'

'See you at the practice,' said Bunty.

And they went off laughing.

I felt like killing them.

'Hey, Atkinson,' muttered Jeff Cullom as he fell in alongside me, on the way to get changed for the practice, 'you paying them blokes money, if they win?'

'Who the hell told you that?'

'They did.'

I cursed them for rotten Yorkshire swine. I'd get even with them, if it was the last thing I did.

'What about paying me an' all, then?'

'They say they're Rugby League, professionals. They won't play, otherwise.'

'Well, I'm a soccer professional. You can pay me too.'

'Where would I find the money?'

'Try selling something.' He sniggered. 'Or nicking something.'

'Get lost.'

'Don't you tell me to get lost. I'm going to complain. To the authorities.'

Suddenly, I was hating a lot of people. But I said, 'Look. I'll give you a quid. If we win. But it'll have to be five bob a week.'

'Right,' he said. 'I'll be round to collect.'

Before the practice, I began arranging my perfect scrum. The usual school front row; then Bunty and Roy in the second, with me pushing behind them, and Jeff Cullom on my right and George Cutter, good old reliable, on my left.

'What're you doing, Atkinson?' Oh God, here was Bill Fosdyke in his Old Buggerallians strip, whistle on a yellow braid round his neck, ball under his arm. Not wearing his glasses as usual, so eager to join in the game. His face looked vague and stupid, without his spectacles. It looked pretty vague and stupid with them.

'Picking the scrum for Saturday, sir.'

'And who gave you the authority to pick the team? That happens to be *my* job. You can't suddenly chuck good lads off, who've been playing well and faithfully, all the season! Myers and Greenhalgh and Walsh deserve their places!'

Actually, I'd fixed Myers and Greenhalgh and Walsh beforehand. They were on my side; they knew the score. They said they'd rather watch while we thumped Collegiate, than play and be thumped by Collegiate. They were good kids . . . understanding. But then it was the second-last match of the season, and they'd play the

271

following week, in a last walkover against poor old Howdon Grammar.

The trouble was, I hadn't fixed Bill Fosdyke.

Mind you, the rest of the blokes were very loyal. They gathered round and glared at Fosdyke, in a circle.

'We gotta field the best team, sir!'

'Otherwise, we won't stand a chance!'

But it was no good. Fosdyke had the bit between his teeth. He was screeching, by this time. 'You boys will do what you're told. I shall pick the team. Of boys who have earned their place through loyalty. We don't play rugby football to *win* – we play for the joy of playing.'

'Tell that to Collegiate,' muttered Jack. 'Those bastards haven't lost a game for three seasons.'

'Now let's get on with the practice!' shouted Fosdyke.

As we lined up for kick-off, Cullom sidled up to me. I don't think he was just worried about losing that quid; I think he genuinely wanted to take Collegiate down a peg, like the rest of us.

'Shall I fix him, Akker?' he muttered, nodding to where Bill Fosdyke was poised, whistle in mouth.

'I wish you could,' I said bitterly. Not thinking anything of it. It was just a thing to say, to let out the bitterness.

It was about ten minutes before it happened, and I was tying up a loose bootlace, so I never saw it. But the rest said afterwards that Fosdyke was running with the ball, and shouting at the winger to get in position for a pass. He had been a county player in his day, and he was still quite fast, for a middle-aged bloke.

They said Cullom came up behind him, and just tapped Fosdyke's heels together as they passed each other. Fosdyke went headlong, and there was a nasty

272

noise, a bit like a rope snapping. We all heard it. Next minute, everybody was standing round Fosdyke, who was lying on the ground, with both hands on his right knee, and his face white and twisted up in pain. When we tried to get him up on his feet, he screamed out loud. They had to send for the stretcher from the gym, to get him off the field. The gym master came out of the staff room and looked at him, and poked at the knee, making him yell again. The gym master said something about ligaments being snapped, and cartileges coming out. We could all see the knee was swelling up like a pudding.

I gazed across at Cullom with a mixture of awe and growing unease. He gave me an ill-concealed wink. The gym master went back to the school office, to ring for an ambulance.

The ambulance came and departed, and we all just drifted back to the changing-rooms.

'Well,' said Apple, 'that was unlucky, or do I mean lucky? We can pick the team we want, now.'

'Not on your nelly,' said Jack. 'The first thing that bastard will do, in hospital, is to get a sheet of writing paper and send the head the team for Saturday. I *know* him, the sod.'

'What do we do then?' asked Apple.

'Some of our lads are going to have to miss the bus,' said Jack.

How right he was. The team appeared at the same old time on the notice board outside the prefects' room, on the Friday morning. Myers, Greenhalgh and Walsh were duly in position. And there was a list of harmless kids down as reserves, as long as your arm. No mention of Bunty, Roy and Cullom.

'An awful lot of people are going to have to miss that bus,' said Jack. 'But they'd better turn up on the next one, to make it look right. After the game's started, of course.'

'We could do with a few away supporters, for a change,' said good old Wilf.

'Who's the master in charge?'

'Puggy Winterbottom.'

'He's all right. Doesn't know one end of a rugby ball from the other.'

He was a nice harmless little man, Pug. We were all very fond of him.

'Where were you at lunchtime?' asked Wilson. 'I *told* you I wanted to go and meet your gang.'

'Wilf asked me to go and clear the top floor,' I said. 'Milne's absent.' Actually, I'd volunteered to fill in for Milne on top-floor duty. Which is horrible, because the art rooms are on the top floor, and the kids try to creep up and paint each other blue, if you don't keep your eyes peeled. And so are the labs, where the kids try and creep in and pour hydrochloric acid down each other's necks. I don't know why the staff don't just lock the rooms up, except there's always some sixth-former trying to finish the best masterpiece since Van Gogh, or some female sixth-former is still scraping the frogspawn out of a dissected female frog.

'Well, we'll go and meet your gang now,' said Wilson. 'There's still ten minutes till the end of break.' Why couldn't they paint *him* blue, or pour hydrochrolic down his neck?

The gang were standing on the back tennis court, watching Julie Makepeace and Anthea Warner playing tennis. We don't really start tennis until the summer term, but the groundsman had put the net up early, and Julie and Anthea were tennis-mad and hoping for a first-team place this year. And they don't half fling themselves about, and they both have nice legs, and the lads were enjoying the occasional flash of thigh, God bless their innocence.

We drifted casually up to them, but Teddy immediately said, 'Sod off, Wilson!' The coke-chute incident hadn't made him love poor William any more.

'Sod off, I said!'

William wriggled and shrugged, and said, with a lot of bravado and a little nervousness, 'I'm with him!' He jerked his head in my direction.

'What do you mean, you're with him?'

Jack and Apple were now all ears. So was everybody else.

'Sod off or I'll give you a horse bite,' said Teddy menacingly.

Wilson just stood, wriggling and grinning uneasily. 'Akker's my friend.'

'What do you mean, he's your friend?' asked Jack, dangerously. 'You haven't got any friends. Give him a horse bite, Teddy. A big one.'

Teddy reached out, menacingly.

'Akker . . . ?' There was an appeal in Wilson's voice; there was also quite a lot of threat.

'Lay off him,' I blurted. 'He's not doing any harm.'

'Any harm?' asked Jack incredulously. 'He's polluting the air we breathe. Go on, Teddy. Give him a horse bite.'

Teddy reached out.

I grabbed his arm.

It turned into a hand-wrestling contest. He was a strong lad, Teddy. But in the end, I proved a bit stronger; I was bigger. Teddy fell down, as a result of his efforts. The yard was a bit damp; he got his trousers muddy.

'For hell's sake, Akker! These are my best trousers.'

Jack turned to me. 'You Wilson's bodyguard or something? How much is he paying you?' He was genuinely baffled, and, in a slightly sinister way, becoming interested.

'Perhaps he's fallen in love with him,' suggested Apple with a snigger.

'Impossible,' said Jack. 'Akker's only in love with himself.' He aimed a lazy kick at William. 'Sod off, Wilson.' He aimed a second kick, and a third. They were graceful idle elegant kicks; everything Jack did was elegant, economical. But one was going to land sooner or later, and it was going to hurt. William began to back away, his face full of growing rage and spite.

He hovered, about five yards off, shouting, 'I *warned* you, Akker!'

'What's he got on you, Akker?' asked Jack. 'He blackmailing you or something? Or is it some *deep* joke?'

There was just no answer to that. I stalked off, gathering up William on the way. 'I *told* you it was bloody useless!' I muttered under my breath.

'You needn't think you're getting away with *that*!' William was beside himself with fury. His mouth was quivering. 'You better do better than that on Monday, Akker. Or you can kiss your so-called girlfriend goodbye.' I could see from the look in his eyes that he meant it, too.

'Look,' I said, 'Give me the weekend to think it out. I'll work out something.'

'You'd *better*. I mean it, you know!'

'Something will turn up.'

But I knew in my heart of hearts it wouldn't. Like so many little people before him, William just wanted the impossible.

I went to last lesson wondering if it was the last lesson I would ever have in that school, and the last lesson that Emma would ever teach. It gave even Katie Merry's Latin a poignancy it never normally had.

# 31: The Last Battle

Newcastle Collegiate had the greenest grass and the tallest goalposts in Northumberland, even if you counted the county ground at Gosforth. The turf of the pitch was shaved like a billiard table, and even this late in the season there was no sign of what we forwards loved; mud patches, skid marks, tufts; anything to make the ball fly wild. The touchlines had been marked in freshly by their full-time groundsman, clean and straight as Wimbledon. And it was a big, big pitch, as big as Union rules allowed. A ball-handlers' pitch, and many a good team had died there, run off their feet. I swear the posts that marked the corners, with their little green and white pennants, were fresh-new that morning. Ours at home were little more than mouldy rags.

There was only one thing in our favour; a light drizzle was falling, which would make the ball greasy. Their backs would be wearing their little woolly fingerless mittens, which gave them a better grip. And they would play with an old ball. New balls were narrow and heavy and, when passed, flew like torpedoes; but they were sods when wet. As balls got older, they stretched and grew fatter, lighter and easier to catch. Some of the oldest ones were nearly spheres, like a soccer ball. That would suit us forwards, for dribbling.

It would suit John Bowes, too.

We were greeted at the school gates by two gorgeous creatures in green blazers with thin white stripes. Their head boy and captain of rugger. They shook hands with little Puggy, towering over him in a lordly way, and giving him the same kind of respect that Jeeves gave Bertie Wooster. He was obviously half-terrified of them, poor little man, as they discoursed knowledgeably about the last England–Ireland international, and he tried desperately to think of something to say.

I gazed at the smooth clean backs of their necks and newly washed hair, and hated them.

The changing-room leaned its weight on us too. The shiny fat chrome of the shower fittings, the spotless white tiles as high as the ceiling. The green lockers, one for each of us with its own key; unkicked, unscratched and not a whiff of sweaty feet inside.

Puggy walked up and down among us as we changed. I think he would have liked to have given us some sound advice, if he could. But he had none to give. So instead he gave us little uneasy smiles, winks, raised eyebrows. Nice little man.

I got changed, and then went up to him.

'Myers and Greenhalgh and Walsh are still missing, sir. They must have slept in and missed the bus.'

'Oh hell.' For a moment he looked like it was the end of the world. Then he remembered the question he should ask.

'Haven't we got any reserves?'

'Oh yes, sir. Roy and Bunty Wilson. And Jeff Cullom. Good players.'

'Right, right, get them changed.'

I gave Bunty the wave. It was that easy.

\* \* \*

Both sides ran out, kicked the ball about a bit, and weighed each other up. Why were they born so beautiful, why were they born at all, as the old rugger song goes? Tall and lean and very fit, all of them. Full of the fresh eggs and steaks their daddies got for them somehow in spite of austerity. Still carrying the tan of some holiday in France, no doubt. Every green and white hooped shirt was neatly tucked into white shorts; every hooped stocking was pulled right up to the knee. And they kicked and passed and caught the ball with the precision of the Guards on parade.

By comparison, we were a shambles. Apple, for instance, had legs of such peculiar shape that his stockings were already down round his ankles. Like most of us, he wore his strip outside his shorts, so he wouldn't lose his shorts in a tackle. Only about an inch of his shorts were visible, so he looked almost obscene. Our socks and shorts were any old colour we could scrounge; and of course, Bunty and Roy wore their old Rugby League strips, because nothing could be found that would stretch over their barrel-size chests.

And, on my orders, we were moving the practice balls around just as slovenly. Wild kicks, dropped catches; shouting insults at each other. You could really see Collegiate lips starting to curl in contempt. They were already bored with the match they knew they were going to win 40–0. For that was the worst thing about them; they were not allowed by their masters to score more than forty points against us; more would be bad sportsmanship. They always reached that total early in the second half; for the rest of the match they fooled around with us, just passing the ball again and again, running in circles, beating the same men over and over again, while we wearily and hopelessly pounded after them. It would be kinder if they beat us 100–0; less humiliating.

I had to tell our lot to stop fooling around *too* much; drop too many catches, it gets to be a habit. Collegiate were openly laughing at us; and we were secretly laughing at them.

We won the toss, and Apple kicked off. He dropped the ball beautifully among them, just the right length, so our pack could reach it as it came down. Collegiate moved like a well-oiled machine, one man calling 'mine' clearly, and two or three more drifting in front of him to protect him from us; accidentally on purpose . . .

Big Bunty went through the protectors like a charging bull and hit the kid as he caught it. I heard his breath go 'ooof' as fifteen stones landed on top of him. Then an avalanche of faded white and cream bodies leapt on top of them. I saw the ball coming back past my feet; I saw Stevie Prentice's safe red hands pick it up from behind my heels; I heard the thump of boot on ball, and knew from the sound it was a drop kick, which sounds quite different from a punt. By the time I'd pulled my head out of the scrum, the ball was a dwindling dot between the Collegiate goal posts, and Newcastle Collegiate werc four points down. Somebody said afterwards it took less than ninety seconds from kick-off. John Bowes walked back up the field with a little contented smile on his face.

By God, were they *rattled*. They kicked off, and kicked short. It hardly crossed the halfway line; their charging forwards had to double back on themselves. But they were too late. Big Bunty had it. The big kangaroo was in full hop, a fearful sight. We all piled after him, saw his first hand-off, the first Collegiate bum hit the ground. Twenty yards to go. There was one of them hanging on round his neck. Bunty carried him as easily as I would carry a rucksack. Then there were two of them hanging round his neck, and one on to one of his legs. He looked around as he ground to a halt; and brother Roy was there to take the little tiny pass. Already going full out, knees up to his chest. The Collegiate fullback flung himself in, but Roy was already starting his dive. He skidded two yards on his belly before banging the ball down with both hands, right under the posts.

Nine—nil, with John Bowes's easy conversion. Panic among Collegiate; they began to shout at each other; always a bad sign, when a team starts shouting at each other.

In their panic, they tried something tricky. Lined up their forwards on the left, then kicked to the right. There was a race between the two sets of backs, to get to it first. The bounce went against them, as bounces will, and it was a situation when the man who gets the ball scores. Wilf beat their man to it, and nobody catches Wilf when he gets a five-yard start. He had to run seventy yards, though, and collapsed over the safely grounded ball, almost heaving his guts out.

Fourteen—nil. Unbelievable. Our small crowd of supporters were leaping up and down with glee. Among them, Myers and Greenhalgh and Walsh, who had correctly caught the next bus. Greenhalgh held up the fingers of both hands. Ten minutes had passed, since kick-off.

Of course, it couldn't last. They were by far the best side in the county; and they had discipline. They began showing brief flashes of machine-like excellence, and scored one try far out. Eventually they scored another, and converted. Fourteen—eight. But John Bowes was playing a blinder. Time and again his safe hands caught the ball, and his enormous kicks drove them back into their own half. And our scrum, with all the driving force of Bunty and Roy, with me pushing so hard on their bums that I nearly killed myself, shoved their scrum to hell and gone. And every time we got the ball, in their half, John Bowes took a long-range pot at goal.

Two out of five attempts went over. Twenty-two—eight. But they were ferocious tacklers. They learnt the trick of knocking Big Bunty down eventually; first it took three of them, then it only took two. Bunty began to look a bit battered and winded; those cigars were taking their toll.

Then . . . tragedy. They caught a failed drop attempt by John, in their own goal area, and passing from one to the other, first to the left, and then to the right, scored a try. We never got near them. The big Collegiate machine was working at last. The old evil past loomed back over us. When Collegiate always won.

Twenty-two—thirteen.

And then they did it again. Twenty-two—eighteen.

And then the whistle blew for half-time.

'Well,' said Jack philosophically. 'It was good while it lasted.' It was the old days talking.

'We're not damned finished yet,' said John Bowes. I'd never heard him swear before. It was the new days talking. I could have hugged him.

The first scrum of the second half, they heeled the ball. But Bunty and Roy put the big push on, and they heeled it slow. They heeled it so slow we pushed them back thirty yards. And when, head-down, I saw the ball finally trickling out their side, I upped and ran round the scrum like a madman. And caught their scrum half with the ball at last. He was still trying to haul it out past a forward's foot when I came down on him from a great height. He cried out in pain, and the ball bounced loose from his hands.

Jeff Cullom was on to it. That kid could control a ball with his feet! He went through them like Stanley Matthews indeed. They just couldn't understand this wizard of dribble, who was playing soccer, not rugger.

He was five yards from their line before their fullback fell on it. Big Bunty picked the fullback up bodily, Roy picked up the ball, and was over with six men on top of him.

'Try,' said the referee. Then he turned to me and said, 'I want a word with you,' and we walked up the field together.

Their scrum half was still lying there, writhing, with two masters bending over him.

'You see that?' said the referee, pointing at him.

'He'll live,' I said. It's never the writhers I worry about; if you can writhe, there's not much wrong with you. It's those who lie dead still that I worry about. 'He's putting it on to get sympathy.'

'What kind of person *are* you?' asked the ref coldly.

Ah, ref, if only I could answer that question, how happy I would be! Can *you* answer that question, ref, you well-spoken, Gosforth-dwelling middle-class snob?

And just at that point the scrum half got up and began to walk up and down, grimacing delicately, to prove my point. He'd go on playing. But he wouldn't ever forget I was there waiting for him. Waiting to do it again.

'If I see one more example of your rough play,' said the ref, 'I'll send you off. I've been keeping my eye on you, the whole match.' I looked at him; he had a long red nose, and a grey cold eye.

. At that point, I saw that poor old Roy was still lying there, with Puggy bending over him anxiously, in their goal area. Roy was lying quite still . . .

'*Our* bloke's not got up yet,' I said. 'How's that for rough play? Six on to one!'

I thought he was going to send me off then. But he just said, 'I'm sorry for those who have to teach you,' and walked away, to see to Roy.

'And I'm sorry for those you teach, ref!' But I muttered it under my breath.

Twenty-seven—eighteen.

But after that, it was a siege of our goal line. A siege with just John Bowes kicking out of it, like a great gun. How we kept them out, I will never know. Except their scrum half was slower now, always watching over his shoulder for me. They scored two tries, but they were right on the corner flag, so that their kicks failed. Serve them right for having that great big pitch.

Twenty-seven—twenty-four. With five minutes to go. That's the agony time, when you've got to keep screaming at your leg muscles to make them work at all. When your chest feels like you've been having a drag on a painter's blowlamp. When your hands turn sweaty and bloated as a bunch of sausages. Thank heavens they were knackered too; still trembling with shock and rage, and half kicked to bits. Their pale, set, posh faces, like all the gallant war heroes out of good British war movies. But it was our finest hour, too. People did things they'd never done before; that you could never dream of expecting them to do. Tony Apple's suicidal tackle, full length on his face to catch the ankle of their flying thirteen-stone winger. Jeff Cullom, all of nine stone something, falling on the ball at the feet of three of their twelve-stone forwards. Coming up with a split lip and smearing the bright blood across his face and grinning, making the split gape wide and spout fresh bright red beads that fell down his strip. Suddenly, unreservedly, I loved them all. I noticed our team were touching each other a lot, helping each other up, slapping each other in the chest. Love.

The end came quickly. There was suddenly a gap in our defence, twenty yards out, and that thirteen-stone winger was flying through, full out, towards our posts, and only John Bowes racing across to try to stop him. It was crazy; I wouldn't have gone *near* that winger, insane as he was for the honour of his school. But John Bowes ... the incomparable John Bowes ... dear, honest, faithful John Bowes, loyal to the end.

They hit head on; they said later you could hear the clash of bone on bone on the far touchline, a dreadful sound. The ball shot up in the air.

Wilf caught it, and ran. Ran with everything he had left. And all of us streaming behind, while the Collegiate stood open-mouthed at the loss of their certain victory. I was just behind Wilf. He was so tired that he was not able to outpace me any more. He was weaving from left to right, as if there were still men in front of him to beat; weaving because his brain could not control his dead-beat legs. But two of us came up on him, and wrapped our weary arms round him and still ran for the line. I think we carried him the last five yards, and you could hear our supporters cheering far away.

We were still standing there, heaving and coughing like old gaffers, when the welcome sound of that last long whistle went. The short whistle for the try sort of went on to become the long whistle of full-time. Our whole team seemed to be around us, punching us, slapping us, shouting phrases of total gibberish.

All but John Bowes.

Both he and the winger were still lying where they'd fallen. The winger was lying on his side holding his knee. But John Bowes lay on his back, and quite still, with three blokes in raincoats bending over him.

Then some people came hurrying across with a stretcher . . .

# 32: *Summoned*

I dragged myself to school that Monday morning. It was spitting on to rain, under a sky of lead. I ached all over, but especially my right knee was giving me hell, where some dear little Collegiate had trodden on it, in the scrum. I was limping worse than Jack after he'd done something stupid on the field.

The one thing I had to look forward to, amidst the worries that had kept me sleepless all the weekend, was the announcement in assembly of our victory, our great and glorious victory.

But after we'd sung, without much conviction, four verses of 'New Every Morning Is the Love' and prayed for the King, all his ministers and the Commonwealth beyond the seas, and the head came to the announcements, there was no mention of our great victory, though every kid in the school was buzzing with it. Between the news that the girls had drawn two all against Whitley Bay at hockey, and the news that our second fifteen had beaten Wallsend seconds 30–7, there was a great and significant gap. We all exchanged puzzled glances . . .

The final announcement was that the head would like to see Atkinson in his study, immediately after assembly.

Jack whistled softly, and gave me a look that was

almost sympathetic, and at the same time distinctly worried. Apple gave a great guffaw that made the head stare up at us angrily as we sat at the back. I'd never seen such a look on his face.

I let the whole assembly clear, and then ran down the wooden steps. My leaden heart felt it was dragging me down. This was it, the jump off the edge of the world. My mind was empty and exploding at the same time.

I hung around quite a while, outside the head's closed door. Then it opened, but he merely shouldered past me, into the school office. Without looking at me at all. Five minutes later, he shouldered me aside again. Like I was nothing; less than a patch of dog dirt in the school gateway. At least people are aware of dog dirt. They ignore it at their peril. I began to get a bit angry at such treatment; which helped.

Finally, he shouted, 'Come,' through the oak panels. I went in and closed the door softly behind me. He was signing reports for the end of term. Sort of *eating* each report, with his eyes moving down it at a great rate, then he signed the bottom as if he was cutting somebody's throat. I watched him do five, six, seven, eight, feeling more and more a spare part. Then I realised he was having a game with me, like the Black Fan used to play. Demoralising me. That meant he didn't know everything he wanted to know. I decided that silence would be the answer. Tell the sod nothing; let him guess. If you started making excuses, he'd just tie you into bigger and bigger knots.

How strange then, that I immediately said, my voice amazingly low and calm to my own ears, 'I can come back later, sir, if you're busy.'

Hell, I wish I hadn't. When he looked up . . . I've

never seen a human being so angry. It made me give up hope. Which was good in a way, because hope weakens you.

'Wait,' he spat. And signed four more reports. Then he couldn't bear to sign any more, and threw down his expensive pen.

'I've had a complaint about you, from Newcastle Collegiate. Dangerous play. I gather it was a miracle you weren't sent off the field. We have never had a boy sent off, in all my time as head.'

I almost said, 'It was a rough old game.' But that would have been my first excuse; his first opening. So I said nothing. I knew there was more to come. I knew it would get worse and worse. That was his way.

'And Collegiate are asking if two of our players have ever played Rugby League. One of their masters recognised their strips.'

Again I was tempted. To say, 'They're not very good losers, are they?' But I held my peace.

'And there are rumours going round the school that those two boys were actually *paid* to play in that match.' I mean, he couldn't have sounded more dreadful if I'd been caught peeing in a church.

'Of course, none of this would have happened, if Mr *Fosdyke* had been in charge. You took advantage of Mr Winterbottom's ignorance.'

Oh, so poor old Puggy had already copped it, during registration period. I was genuinely sorry about that. But Puggy'd survive . . .

'Which brings us to the matter of Mr Fosdyke's unfortunate injury. Perhaps you'll be interested to know that he will be off school for the rest of this term.'

My heart sank utterly into my boots, but the next

blow was already descending.

'I have spoken to Cullom. He has been expelled. He is no longer a member of my school.'

Yet even in my despair, I sensed that Cullom had told him nothing, admitted nothing.

'It was not difficult to expel Cullom. He was only entered for three O-levels, and without doubt he would have failed those. But you . . .'

This was the moment when I was supposed to break down, to weep, to plead.

I wouldn't give him the satisfaction. As I saw him hesitate, grope for his pen, I realised that total silence is no bad weapon.

'Well, what have you got to say, by way of explanation?' He seemed actually a little hurt that I wasn't playing by the rules. I just stared at the school timetable, which hung above his head. Emma was teaching the upper-sixth girls civics at this very moment.

I was certain the worst was yet to come. I was certain that Wilson had blabbed to his parents or something, over the weekend.

But the head pulled a document towards him. Reading upside down, I realised it was my report.

'But if I were to expel *you*,' the head paused, 'I would be accused of blighting the career of a *brilliant* student – perhaps the best of his year. And a prefect to boot. There would be . . . a great fuss. No doubt your father knows some councillor who is on the Education Committee.'

I couldn't resist that. 'Councillor Widdows, sir. He's mayor this year. Socialist.'

It was a bitter truth for the head to swallow. He said, 'I would be accused of ruining a brilliant career, for some little fuss about rugby football.'

God, didn't he *know* about me and Emma? *Was* she still safe?

'Therefore, I am offering you the chance to leave voluntarily.'

'What about my A-levels?'

'You can come in and sit your A-levels. Providing you do not wear school uniform. In fact, with your powers of deceit, which we are both well aware of, perhaps your parents need not know you have left at all. There are only six days left of this term, and I'm sure you could turn that limp of yours into something a bit more serious. And then, next term . . . well, Easter's late this year. We shall be into the exam period almost immediately, and lots of people take time off at home to revise. Do I make myself clear?'

The conniving old sod! And yet, my heart leapt. If he'd heard a *whisper* about me and Emma, I would have been expelled publicly for sure.

'Do you agree?'

I nodded mutely. I could not trust myself to speak.

He held out a hand. 'Your prefect's badge, please.'

I hesitated. I'd earned that badge, in many a weary lunchtime, battling faithfully against the evil fifth form.

But it was a small price to pay, for Emma's safety.

## 33: Saved

I staggered out of the head's study; I had a terrible job turning the handle to get the door to shut, and in the end I just left it. I managed to get across to the radiator where the naughty boys always lurked, while they were waiting to be caned. Or after.

My first feeling was one of total mind-blowing relief. I was off the hook with Wilson. He couldn't make any more demands on me. And I didn't think he'd tell on Emma out of sheer spite, once there was nothing to be gained. He'd be scared of getting into trouble for nothing. And if he turned up at our house, wanting to be friends, I supposed I could put up with him. He'd soon get bored. It wasn't me he wanted. He just wanted to be famous. Anyway, he knew I'd beat him to a pulp, if he split on Emma . . .

And then I heard someone say, 'Hello! You look like you've lost a shilling and found sixpence!'

Joyce, in her school blazer, every inch the prefect, but smiling at me with warm blue eyes.

'And you look like you've lost sixpence and found a shilling,' I said.

'Shall I tell you a secret?' she asked, still grinning. 'We've just had a lesson with Miss Harris, and *she's wearing a ring*!'

'Well, staff are allowed to. It's just girls that can't . . .'

'It's on the third finger of her left hand, stupid! Sophie Lewis saw it first. She sort of gave a *squeal* and Miss Harris told her to behave, but Sophie said, "Miss, you're engaged." And then we were all squealing, I can tell you. She couldn't go on teaching. We all had to have a look at it. It's a lovely ring – a big ruby.'

'Big deal,' I said. I didn't have to put on the sourness, now it had happened. Even though it was my idea.

'Don't bother asking who to!' said Joyce indignantly.

'Who to?' I said immediately.

'Mr Wrigley, of course. She told us it was his grandmother's ring. Isn't that romantic? Of course he's going to buy her an official one, later on. This is just a stopgap.'

So, Emma, you did it. Just as I told you to. It still hurt like nothing I'd ever known before.

'Why're you looking so bloody miserable?' Her blue eyes were too sharp, she knew me too well.

'I've just been sacked. But it's a secret.'

'But *why*?' Horror-filled eyes like saucers.

'It's a long story,' I said. 'I can't tell you *here*.'

'It's almost break. Let's go up the field.'

Nobody was allowed up the field when the grass was wet. We had it to ourselves. It had stopped raining, and the weak sun was glimmering. But I hardly noticed.

I told her the lot; about the rugby.

She said, 'It's so stupid, all this fuss about rugby – kicking a silly old ball about. Have you heard about John Bowes? He's in hospital – in traction. He broke his leg in three places. They don't think he'll be well enough to sit his O-levels. And they don't think his leg will ever heal well enough for him to join the police force. Which is all he's ever wanted, since he was little. Oh, I *hate* men and their rugby . . .'

I didn't say anything. I had John Bowes on my conscience now, as well. Finally I said, 'It wasn't rugger, it was Newcastle Collegiate – stuck-up buggers with rich daddies. Why should they win every match? Just because they can afford big pitches, and Cambridge Blues to coach them?'

She said, abruptly, 'Some people think I'm a stuck-up bugger with a rich daddy.'

'But *you* don't put on airs.'

She couldn't think of any answer to that. We reached the top of the field, and turned back. The sun was really coming out now, glowing on the red and yellow brick of the distant school, on all its funny little roofs and pinnacles. It looked like a dream of paradise. Just how it had looked to me all those years ago, when I was a fat slug in a brand-new uniform, the wondrous scholarship boy with everything to hope for.

'God,' I said. 'It's all *gone*.' And I suddenly felt so lonely.

'Oh, Robbie, don't be silly. It's not all gone.' She grabbed me by the shoulders. 'You've got your O-levels, and you can still get your A-levels, and you've got your place at university. They can't take those away from you.'

But I still kept my head down.

'And you've still got me,' she said. 'If you want me.'

I looked at her honest, concerned face. At the most faithful pair of blue eyes I'd ever seen in my life. Full of caring about *me*. She wasn't exciting like Emma. Emma was like a dark wine that made you drunk, mad. Joyce was like a clear cold drink of fresh water. But water is what keeps us alive.

'Oh, Joyce,' I said. And then somehow we wrapped our arms around each other, out there on the pitch. And kissed, and there seemed no one else in the world.

Until we heard the faint sound of cheering from the school yard, and turned and . . .

Half the school, still on break, was watching us. Waving their arms in the air in approval.

And I thought, after this, who's going to believe Wilson now? It all fitted together, somehow. Leaving only one tiny problem, so tiny it seemed laughable.

'I don't know how I'm going to get all my stuff home, from my locker.'

'I'll give you a hand,' she said. 'I've got two free periods after break.'

Just then, who should emerge from the crowd in the yard, but the tall forbidding figure of Katie Merry, MA (Cantab). The bell for the end of break went; but people were lingering, to see what was going to happen.

So Katie Merry walked up the field, her black gown fluttering in the brisk breeze, and we walked straight to meet her. What else was there to do?

But it was no contest. Before she could open her mouth, Joyce was at her.

'Atkinson is very upset,' she said, with great firmness. 'And I am going to help him with his stuff, and see him home. I have two free periods. I shall see him settled, and then I shall return for the beginning of afternoon school.'

Katie Merry bridled. But whether she was outfaced by such schoolgirl anger, or such schoolgirl love, or whether the top brass had had enough shocks for one day, and couldn't cope with any more news, I shall never know.

She only set her lips in prim disapproval and said, 'Very well. See you report your return. I shall be at my desk all the lunch-hour.'

Could you ever leave a girl who'd done that for you?

We arrived home with me limping like a wounded war hero. I walked the last few yards leaning heavily on Joyce's sturdy shoulder. But it still put my mother in a fluster.

'I knew you should never have gone to school with that leg,' she said.

'Well, I couldn't have gone without it.'

'Aren't you going to introduce me to the young lady? Is this the one whose father flies the aeroplane?'

They got on like a house afire. Dad, who was on the afternoon shift, actually took Joyce down the greenhouse to show her his tomato seedlings, and she came back with a nice bunch of early daffodils.

While I lay on the couch with my leg up, practising my groans for the expected doctor.

'I don't know why they didn't *drive* you home,' my mother muttered. 'The teachers don't care, these days!'

There's not a lot to add. The rest of them were let off with a good wigging from the head. He told them he was content; he'd dealt with the ringleaders. Oh, how heads do love their ringleaders . . . the real word is 'scapegoat', I think.

I got through the terrible empty burden of that summer without Emma by a mass of swotting. I mean, I reached the stage where I would think to myself, oh, goodie, it's the ablative absolute and the formation of natural lakes tomorrow. I even did my own translation of Vergil's Book Six of the *Aeneid*, and very elegant I think it was. As Joyce kept on saying, when she came to see me, 'Show the beasts just how well you *can* do!' It was a good bullet to bite on, when the loneliness got too bad; when I missed Emma too much. You can't go for long black broody walks, when your mother's going frantic about your leg.

The odd thing was, my other defence against loneliness was poor old Wilson. He turned up quite often, and even brought me some grapes, and had enough sense never to mention Emma again. I became convinced, finally, that he was genuinely fond of me. He married in the end, and had four kids. And became the most successful of us all. Lacking any discernible talent, he went into the jewellery trade, and is now the owner of three jeweller's shops, and never misses the chance to offer the old gang a lift in his latest Jag. Alderman William Wilson, Independent, Priory Ward. Mayor, next year, God help us.

I went down to school with Joyce, the bright sunny August morning the results came out. Everybody was there, clustered, waiting, around the front steps. I kept away from my old mob; none of the rotten sods had even dropped me a line; scared for their own sins, I expect. Joyce held my hand, because I was still uneasy. The exam papers had seemed so simple; that's always a bad sign.

But then Winnie Antrobus came down the front steps; a gale of staff chatter followed her out through the open door, and I realised that they too were all there; only inside, getting a privileged peep at the results while we waited . . .

Winnie's eyes fell on me. Now, after O-levels, we'd discovered we could tell our results from the way the staff reacted to us. Those who'd done badly, the staff wouldn't look at. Whereas those who'd done well, the staff rushed up to them, all laughing and bubbling, and shook their hands; almost embraced them.

And Winnie's eyes did not drop now. A beatific smile crossed her face. Then she removed it; remembering I'd been chucked out, I suppose. But then something seemed to arise within her that would not be suppressed.

She made up her mind and swept across to me, and grabbed my hand and worked it like a pump handle and said, 'You've got four As, Atkinson! Congratulations! Nobody's ever had *four* As before, in the history of the school!' Then she realised that Joyce was there, and added hastily, 'And you've done well too, Joyce!'

And now all the staff were streaming out, and shaking people's hands. And it seemed I was no longer a dreadful criminal; it was as if none of it had ever happened. And then the head came out on top of the steps, and began giving out the little bits of paper.

I should have been the second to get one, after Colin Allen. I mean, that's the alphabetical order. But he was still handing out the bits of paper, when a couple of scruffy-looking characters with dirty open raincoats and loose ties and battered trilby hats pushed their way through the crowd. The one at the back was carrying a well-worn camera with more knobs and buttons and fittings than a radar set.

The *Shields Evening News* had arrived.

'Hey,' said the front one to the head, 'where's this kid who's got four As, then?'

I never enjoyed anything like I enjoyed the look on the head's face. But it was Joyce who pointed to me in the end, and said, 'This is him.'

'Name?' said the front one. 'Address? We'll want a photo. In school uniform. Why aren't you wearing school uniform, like the rest?'

I thought the head was going to blow a gasket. His face was all over the place. I mean, I was a bit worried, but him . . . he couldn't get his face together at all.

Finally he said, 'That can be arranged. You'd better run along home quickly, Atkinson, and get into uniform. These gentlemen want to photograph you.'

It was the sweetest moment of my life. I said, 'I haven't got my prefect's badge, sir!' In a totally innocent tone.

'Oh,' he said, equally innocent. 'I think you left it in my office. I'm sure I can find it.'

Such are the ways of the world. Half the staff were looking like thunder, and the other half were killing themselves laughing. I often wondered how the school governors took it.

It was nearly a month later that I went down to Nana's with a bag of tomatoes. She was pleased to see me.

She said, 'I've got a message for you. Miss Harris would like to see you some time. She'd like to give you her congratulations on getting your exams. She didn't get a chance on the day.'

She looked at me keenly with those bright old eyes. How much did she know? How much did she understand? I knew I would never ask her, never find out.

'I'd call on the way down to Joyce's,' I said. 'Only

Miss Harris might be out with old Fred Wrigley.'

'You've no need to bother about him. She's given him his ring back, second-hand rubbish that it was. He wouldn't even talk about naming the day. He's a hopeless kind of feller.'

Is there such a thing as a soft warm depth charge that can blow your world apart? I mean, I was on my way to see Joyce. We were going to play tennis at Garmouth Park. Carry on the long slow satisfying getting to know each other that had been going on since . . .

I rode up to Emma's house. I was wearing white shorts and socks and plimsolls ready for playing tennis, with just a sports coat over my open-necked white shirt, and the racket fastened by a clip to my handlebars. Joyce would be waiting . . . trusting . . . calm . . . happy . . . keeping on glancing towards their front gate. It was a perfect evening for playing tennis, not too hot, but a balmy breeze blowing on my bare legs. A good hard game, then back to her place for long cool drinks . . .

But it suddenly didn't mean anything. Emma had called to me, and I was all atremble, from head to foot, with some sort of black dark wine running through my veins instead of blood. Because it was all going to start happening again; and that was all that mattered. In vain I thought of Joyce's love for me, her faithfulness when everybody else was against me, how relaxed I felt with her.

It just didn't work. It wasn't in the same world.

I turned into Tennyson Terrace.

It was all just the same, except the flowers were out, and even past their best. Her mother's welcoming face was the same, the dark stair was the same.

I felt doomed and glad, at the same time. The way Heathcliff must have felt, when he was dying and knew he was going to be with Cathy.

But her voice was somehow different, when she called out, 'Come in.' I couldn't place the difference, but it was there.

And when I opened the door, she was not waiting to greet me. She was standing looking out of her window, into the street. She was wearing a formal dark suit. Perhaps, I thought, she'd been to somebody's funeral . . .

She didn't turn round. But she said, 'You've heard I've packed in Fred?'

'Yes.' I didn't sit down either.

'I've decided I can't be doing with second-best. Not when I've known the best.'

It was a compliment, I suppose. But it didn't sound like it. Her voice was so hard; she was like a judge passing sentence.

'I've decided to make teaching my life. I'm afraid love is just too much for me. Too . . . *messy*. I'll never forget you, or what you did to me, as long as I live. It was a lovely sort of . . . madness. But I've made up my mind. *Never* again. You still hurt, every day, but I shall get over it. In time. Or perhaps I will never get over it.

'But I've decided the way forward is *work*. Work till I drop.'

'Emma!' How much agony can you get into two syllables?'

'Be quiet! Hear me out! I've applied for a head of history post in Birmingham. It came up late, in the *Times Ed.* I've been short-listed and there are only three on the short list, because Birmingham's not popular and this school's a bit crummy for a grammar school. I'm told I've got a good chance – and the head will let me go immediately, because of my broken engagement to Fred. He was very sympathetic. I shall never come back here. My mother may come down and join me.'

'EMMA!'

But she drove on, like a kamikaze suicide pilot attacking the American fleet at Okinawa.

'I'm going for a headship eventually. I think I can do it. Headships go to those who want them badly enough. The ones who keep on applying. I shall get it in the end – I think I'll be quite good at it. Anyway, I'm going to try.'

'Emma!' It was almost a squeal. 'Emma, we *are*! You can't destroy us. Just like that, for some rotten old job. Or . . .' The thought had suddenly struck me.

'When I'm at Leeds . . . Leeds isn't that far from Birmingham. Two hours by train . . . we could have whole weekends . . .'

She said, in a whisper, 'Don't be silly. It's over. I just thought you should be the first to know, that's all. About the job. About my life.'

But she was weakening, crumbling. I moved towards her. Her head went down and her shoulders began to shake. I knew I still had her in the palm of my hand . . .

Then she turned to me. A face of such screwed-up agony that I would hardly have recognised her. She looked like a soul in hell.

That was when I realised I wasn't Heathcliff really after all. That sort of agony, I wasn't up to. I grew afraid, watching her face. I suddenly knew I had the power to destroy her. And suddenly I didn't want it, any of it. It was too big for me. I sort of . . . shrank.

'All right, Emma,' I said. 'Go to Birmingham, I won't stop you. But you will write? Let me know how you're getting on. I'll be worried about you.'

'No,' she said. 'Not even a Christmas card.' But her face wasn't crumpling any more. Just pale and ill.

Then I heard her mother's feet on the stair.

'Emma, are you ready? We've got to go.'

'Five minutes, Mother,' she called back, and her voice was quite steady now. Cool, matter-of-fact.

Even then, I was tempted.

But she held out a cool hand.

'Goodbye, Robbie. Have a good life. I shall be hearing of your doings. As, no doubt, you will be hearing of mine.'

She sounded just enormously tired. I wondered where she was going with her mother. Nowhere taxing, I hoped.

I took her hand and said, 'Good luck.' Or tried to, but got a huge lump in my throat I'd never had since I was a kid. Then I just blundered away downstairs for the last time. Her mother never emerged, and I was glad.

I never saw her again. Not till she came back to the town at last. To be head of a big comprehensive in 1970 and I saw her picture in the paper.

And only then did I finally know it was over.